WICKED CURSE

CANDACE OSMOND
REBECCA HAMILTON

D1445635

EVERSCORCH

COPYRIGHT

CHAPTER 1

AFTER A FEW SHORT months at Arcane Academy, I had learned one thing to be painfully true.

Magic really did break more than it fixed.

The way it taunted my willpower, remaining sleepy in my veins and refusing to leave. Rearing its chaotic head when it pleased, just to prove it was in control. I knew so little about my hybrid abilities and worried that I'd yet to see the monstrous iceberg that waded under the depths of my soul, only allowing me to glimpse at the tip that exposed through the surface of my skin.

I knew it was there.

I could *feel* it.

With the midnight moon glowing overhead, my mind wandered with thoughts of uncertainty for the future as my legs dangled over the edge of the cliff that overlooked the chasm near campus. The one I'd nearly fallen into just a few short weeks ago, before Anson saved me from myself. From the same chaotic magic that toyed with my resolve.

As I stared down at the expanse of empty ground, reaching for miles, those thoughts switched to a list of what ifs.

What if I just...pushed a little? Let myself fall to the depths below. I wasn't suicidal by any means, but my mind entertained the possibility.

What if I died? Right here, right now. Leaving behind all the drama and inevitable mess that I was about to plunge into. Which brought me to another what if....

What if I failed the Program, and Nash Crane won? He'd join the ranks of our Dark Faction leaders, and I had no doubt he'd do everything in his power to make my life a living hell.

A hollow echo of wind wafted up from the canyon below, tickling my skin with an early winter chill, and a shiver shook over me as Anson sat by my side.

"Cold?" Anson asked, ripping me from the daze that held my mind in place. He shifted closer and removed his leather jacket to wrap around my shoulders. "We can go back if you want."

"No," I said, my voice practically a whisper in the dark. "I haven't seen you in days. These late nights are the only chance we get to be alone."

"I know, I'm sorry," he said sincerely. "With classes and PA duties, all my free time has gone to practicing for the Courtship Program, trying to get a feel of the full spectrum of my hybrid magic. We're going to need all the help we can get."

I mindlessly swung my leg, kicking free some dirt to fall below. "You should be practicing with Willa and me."

"Can't," he said and handed me an open bottle of white wine we'd swiped from the mess hall as we snuck out. "All teams must practice on their own."

I took a swig, and the sweet elixir burned pleasantly all the way to my empty stomach. "Yeah, but you're not exactly a team, Anson. It's just you. It's not fair that they allowed you to compete."

I handed back the bottle, and he took a big gulp.

"I'll be fine," he said, almost as if assuring himself rather than me. "We just have to make sure we're the last two standing."

The corner of my mouth twitched as I side-eyed him. "No pressure."

He grinned as he let another gulp of wine pour into his mouth. "Definitely not."

A cool breeze rose up from the depths of the chasm, and I hugged myself as my legs retreated from the cliff's edge.

"You're cold," he pointed out. "Let's go back."

I shook my head. "I like it out here. Away from the noise."

He leaned in and playfully bumped my shoulder with his. "To be fair, most of the noise is about you."

I sighed. "Exactly."

His hand slipped into mine and squeezed gently.

I looked into his eyes and immediately felt warm. Safe. At home. "How do you do that?"

His brow pinched. "Do what?"

"You just look at me and make everything go away."

He shrugged. "Magic?"

I playfully shoved at his chest, and he laughed. His other arm wrapped around me and held me tight as the soothing press of his warm lips came to the side of my head. We sat in the silence of the embrace while we both stared out across the canyon.

The other side seemed so far away. Another world. And perhaps it was. I still didn't have a clue where Arcane Academy was hidden or what surrounded it, aside from magical wards to protect us from the mundane world. I often wondered...what protected *them* from *us*? We were a danger to any non-magical being. Well...I was, anyway.

And Anson.

"Hey," I said and peeled myself away from him. "Why aren't you struggling with your powers?"

"What?"

CANDACE OSMOND & REBECCA HAMILTON

"Your magic," I said. "It's just like mine, right? Both light and dark. You've just been hiding it longer than me. Why isn't it all over the place like my magic is?"

Anson's gaze wandered thoughtfully before coming back to mine. "My powers are just as chaotic as yours, Lydia. I just...I haven't let them stretch as far as you've let yours. The outbursts...I've never once gotten to that point. And, after Norah died..." He shook his head. "I stuffed my powers down so deep, only allowing enough to surface when I needed."

I chewed at my lip. "Are you afraid?"

"Of my magic?" His eyes widened. "Or yours?"

"Of all of it," I said. "Our power, the secrets, the danger. Doing this program and risking exposure. I mean, what would our world think of this? We're different. And, just like everything different in our world...we're a *threat*, Anson."

Another shiver ran over me, and he held me again. His face nuzzled my hair, and he whispered calmly in my ear. "You don't have to worry about those things. We're safe. We have each other. And Willa. You'll learn to control it, just like I have. Everyone knows you're more powerful than you should be, but it's expected. You're the first Light Born to be chosen for the dark. That's already something new in itself. And look —you're still here."

"That's not true," I said.

His eyebrows pinched together. "What do you mean?"

"You were chosen before me."

He regarded me thoughtfully. "Yeah, but nobody knows that. My Sorting Ceremony was covered up before I even arrived at the academy. The elders saw to that." He flicked a tiny pebble over the edge and it echoed all the way down. "Makes me think how many more are out there like us. Hiding. Too terrified to speak up or use their magic for fear the Elders will lock them away. Or worse..."

A shiver ran through me and I chewed at my lip as my gaze drifted. "That's a scary thought."

Anson nudged my arm, bringing me out of my daydream. "Doesn't matter, Lydia. There's nothing we can do about it. Let's just get through the next few weeks."

He was right. I put all thoughts of others like us out of my mind and let Anson's words soothe my nerves, but there was one thing he was wrong about. He'd never really had to control his powers because—as he said—he'd never really let them loose. Part of me felt as if I'd tipped over a bottle and was struggling to keep the mess contained.

"Besides, with Winter Solstice approaching, everyone's going to be distracted," he added. "Trust me, Lydia Laveau will be the last thing on their minds."

I rolled my eyes. "Solstice. As if Christmas isn't bad enough."

I felt him grin against the side of my head. "Grinch."

I laughed and tipped my face to look at him. Those gorgeous black voids beamed down at me in the moonlight. "I'm not a Grinch. I just hate all the commotion. All the fuss. Buying gifts and putting up decorations only to take it all down a week later. Seems ridiculous."

"Well, Christmas is a mundane holiday and isn't for another two weeks," he said. "Winter Solstice at Arcane Academy is unlike anything you've ever seen. Trust me." He kissed my lips, once and sweet. "And the Solstice Dance is...something."

My brow raised in mock disbelief. "Mr. Abernathy, I thought you didn't care for trivial things like high school dances."

His face leaned toward mine until there was hardly an inch of space left. His warm breath tickled my face, and his rare smile tempted my heart.

"The Solstice Dance isn't just any dance," he whispered. His lips trailed along the edge of my jaw, and goosebumps raced across my chilled skin. "And we were children in high school. This is real life now, Lydia. The academy. Fighting for our place." His breath hitched as he paused and looked into my eyes, his mouth nearing mine. "Fighting for each other."

I slung my arms around his neck. "I'll always fight for you."

He kissed my waiting lips, slow and deep. His arms tightened, and my body pressed against him. A welcome heat rushed through me, chasing away the chill that hugged my skin, and my heart sped as he grabbed my thighs. I crawled into his lap, our mouths never separating, and I let my legs fall to his sides.

He pulled away briefly, catching his breath as my black hair made a curtain around our faces.

"I love you," he muttered against my lips.

My fingers locked behind his head, holding his face close to mine, and I pressed my forehead to his.

"I love you, too," my words came out in a shaky whisper.

My eyes welled with tears, and I squeezed them shut just as one escaped and ran hot down my cheek. I was thankful that, in the darkness, Anson wouldn't see it. They weren't tears of joy.

Before me was a man who offered his heart, trusted me to keep it safe. But, with what lay ahead, I wasn't sure I could keep anything safe. I had so much at stake—not just my secrets, or the safety of those I love, but everything else, too.

I knew firsthand how hard it was to control the great hybrid power that resided in us both. Anson didn't have a clue how truly frightening it was to let it loose. To harness the unstable and unknown magic that nature decided to bestow upon us. My mind swam with worry over everything. The what ifs and the whys. But only one thought rang hard through it all.

My boyfriend was about to compete in a high-stakes competition of magic and wit, all alone, with no idea how to control the dark magic that lived deep inside of him. Anson professed his love for me, and all I could think about was losing him to that darkness. My heart would be broken, my soul beyond crushed.

And it terrified me.

CHAPTER 2

I WRAPPED my chilly hands around the warm ceramic mug I'd grabbed from the coffee counter in the mess hall. My food sat in front of me, untouched. Thoughts swirled in my brain and removed me from the world on a constant basis. I couldn't help it. I ran over scenarios in my head until I made myself sick. The best to the worst.

Best? Willa and I won the Courtship Program alongside Anson, and all of this went away. I would be ushered into a position where I could make change in our clearly broken world. Help break down the wall that divided the factions.

Worst? We lost, and Nash Crane won. He'd grip that power over me like his life depended on it.

And maybe it did.

I had never hated anyone in my entire life as much as I hated Nash for what he did to me, and for what he attempted to do to Anson. He gained my trust and then used it as a tool to mold me. To use me for whatever dark purpose he and the Midnight Circle had planned.

I sat in the mess hall as Wicked Born busied about, dressing everything for the Solstice festivities. Garland leaves hung from ledges; wreaths of dried branches adorned each archway; the smell of cider and cinnamon wafted through the air.

The world seemed to move around me like some sort of animated movie, but I remained still. Cold. Frozen with worry.

My distracted gaze landed on Nash and Ferris entering the hall to stand in line for lunch. My stomach clenched, and a sudden heat singed through my veins. Hatred. His sly expression scanned the great space and stopped on me. I narrowed my eyes as I pursed my lips, and the corner of his mouth twisted with a grin.

I'm coming for you, Nash Crane.

He moved ahead in line, breaking our eye contact. But Ferris took his place before I tore my gaze away and looked at me with an expression of...pity? No, not for me, anyway. Something else. His eyebrows pinched together as his eyes glistened with...I don't know. Remorse?

I didn't buy it.

"Lydia." Willa's voice broke through the swarm of angry thoughts that fogged my brain. She sat across from me and spooned her oatmeal around in the bowl.

I blinked and rubbed my face, forcing myself to focus. "What? Sorry, I—"

"You've been sorry a lot lately," she replied a little shortly. "You okay? I feel like you're somewhere else. Like, *all* the time."

I let a hefty sigh escape my chest as I sunk back in my chair and took a sip of coffee. "Just thinking about how much I despise Nash."

"I know." Willa side-eyed the front of the mess hall where Nash and Ferris moved down the line for breakfast. "It feels weird. Not sitting with them. Hanging out with them. I mean, two seconds ago we were all friends, and now—"

"We were never friends with them," I said quickly. "Nash had planned all this before he even met me. He's a snake."

Willa opened her mouth, but I continued before she had the chance to speak.

"And so is Ferris."

Willa's shoulders sank. She knew I was right. They were not to be trusted.

"It's more than that, though," she replied. "You're not sleeping. I mean, that is, when you even come back to our room. You're out at all hours of the night. *Every* night."

"It's the only chance I get to spend time with Anson," I said.

She looked me sternly in the eyes. "We should be preparing. The other teams are practicing every day."

I rolled my eyes and pushed at my eggs with my fork. "You and I both know we can win this, Willa. We don't need the same practice as the others."

Willa leaned in, her voice lowering. "You know that's not entirely true. Yes, you're a well-seasoned Light witch. You can easily do any spell using your *light* magic." Her brow lifted in wait, as if I should be reading between the lines. "We still don't know how much control you have over this new hybrid magic. If any at all. What was once a simple spell for you could prove to be difficult. And we can't make that mistake during the program. We *have* to be prepar—"

"Okay, okay," I said and threw down my fork. "I get it. We need to practice more."

She leaned back and crossed her arms as she glanced around the room. "What's Anson doing, anyway? To prepare, I mean."

I shrugged. "No clue. He won't talk to me about the program." But that wasn't entirely true. I knew he worried about tapping into that unknown ancient power that resided in us both.

"You think he's worried?"

"Maybe," I replied. "I don't know. He seems…" My brain ached just trying to figure out the enigma that was my boyfriend. I shook my head. "Forget it. Let's change the topic to something more colorful, shall we?"

Willa chewed at her lip. "My dad called me."

My heart sprang to life for my friend. Her mundane father wasn't too keen on the idea of her attending Arcane Academy and hadn't spoken to her since she'd left home. "Really? What did he say?"

Her cheeks warmed with a soft pink as she smiled. "He wants to talk. When I come home for Christmas."

She appeared happy, but I could sense the unease beneath the surface. I reached across the table and took her hand.

"That's great news, Willa," I said sincerely. Her shoulders relaxed. "I'm happy for you."

She squeezed my hand as her wide, gorgeous eyes glistened. "Thanks." She pulled back and took a mouthful of her oatmeal. "Are you excited to go home?"

I inhaled deeply and let the affirmation wash over me, something I often did after I discovered we'd get to go home for a few days during Solstice. "You have no idea. I *need* this. I need to see my mom."

"I bet," she replied. "She's probably been losing her mind."

I thought of Lace Laveau pacing the marble floors of the giant white house I grew up in.

The dean had finally rigged my phone so I could talk to my mom without the wards interfering. But I still didn't feel comfortable discussing anything remotely outside the realm of classes and casual chit chat. I just couldn't risk it, especially if the dean were monitoring my outside communication. I'd even given up texting Jade, for fear she'd be used as a tool against me if anyone found out she was my best friend. I didn't dare open the door to that possibility. I still wasn't sure if I'd even go visit her during my trip home.

I cleared my throat and willed away the ball of stress that formed in my throat. "Well, everything will be better after

Christmas. We'll go home, recharge, relax, and come back here to resume whatever ridiculous practices you plan for us."

Willa tipped her head. "Not ridiculous. Necessary. We can't afford any surprises during this program. Everyone will be watching and listening. The whole Dark Faction. Lydia," she urged. "This is a fight for leadership. It's a big deal. You need to focus."

My eyebrows pinched together. "I know that. Yes, I'm... stressed...but I'm not worried about our ability to do this. Everything we've tried has been easy. Too easy. Like playing with toys."

"Yeah, but we've only tried a few simple spells from our textbooks," Willa said. "The Game Designers—they'll know you're powerful. I mean, it's no secret now. And they'll assume Anson is, too, being an advanced third year. Then Nash, I'm sure he won't be shy about showing off his powers. He's a contender. A good one."

I scanned her pleading expression. "So? Isn't that the point? The dean picked powerful Wicked Born to compete because the winners will go on to help rule the faction. He couldn't very well just pick anyone. People are aware of that."

"Lydia, the Game Designers will tailor everything to our strengths and weaknesses. They'll measure our abilities and build a fair game that will challenge *all* of us. It's meant to weed out the weak. We have to be in total control of your abilities. We need to make it look easy, but not too easy. Otherwise they'll just keep making it harder, and that's a recipe for disaster. It could cause you to slip and reveal that you're not just powerful, but something else altogether."

I let her words sink in as I sat back in my chair and crossed my arms. "So, what are you saying? We should look for the hardest spells and potions we can find?"

Her face brightened as if a sudden realization had washed over her. "That's exactly what we do," she replied and began packing her things away. "And I know just the place to look."

"Where?" I tossed half an egg in my mouth and stuffed it to the side as I chewed.

Willa glanced around and leaned in. "The other grimoire we stole."

"We gave that back after Nash ratted us out to the dean," I replied incredulously.

She grinned. "I may have made some copies."

I sat back in my chair in disbelief. "But that book is warded against any magic tampering."

"There's nothing magical about a photocopy machine," Willa said. "Say whatever you want, but I just couldn't let all that old magic slip through my fingers."

I let out an impressed guffaw and stared at her admiringly. "You think you can find something good in there?"

Willa leveled me with a serious stare. "We better hope so."

CHAPTER 3

By Wednesday, I'd entered full-on zombie mode. I retreated as far into my mind as one could possibly go. Deep into a pile of thoughts and strategies and worries.

Willa and I spent days studying the grimoire pages she cleverly made copies of and narrowed down our choices to some of the hardest potions, enchantments, and spells. All tasks we're sure to be given during the Courtship Program, and all things I had to master before it was too late.

Willa was right. I was a powerful light witch, but still knew very little of my strange new hybrid powers. What was once simple to me could very well prove to be my undoing in front of the entire Dark Faction. I couldn't afford to slip up.

Gods, I couldn't wait to go home and see my mom. To taste that sense of normalcy, and to be with someone who doesn't have an agenda. I needed that.

Between classes, I paced through the busy halls in a daze, making my way toward the coffee cart before it would be time to meet Willa in Herbology. The heady stares of my fellow students never lessened, only changed, mixing with expressions of excitement at the sight of me.

Those who cared less about where I came from and more about watching me perform in the program seemed to stare the hardest. Whether they loved me or hated me, I was a spectacle in every way here at the academy. A fact I doubt would ever change.

I turned a corner, and something flashed in front of my face. A tiny ember, hovering. The glowing gold fleck danced, carving out letters that singed the air with a message.

The dean requests your presence in his office.

My shoulders slumped under the weight of annoyance. Mr. Blackwood was the last person I wanted to talk to right now. It was his fault I had to deal with all of this in the first place. He'd forced me into the spotlight, and then into the program. And for what? To prove something to the Dark Faction? That Light and Dark can exist together? I'd be on board for that, but part of me still didn't trust the guy. What if he planned to use me as a tool to push his own agenda that I still didn't really understand?

I didn't have a clue what the dean was really up to and, still, I hated him for it.

But he was my elder here at Arcane Academy, and I was nothing more than a first year Wicked Born.

I turned around and made my way back toward the wing that held his office and came to a halt outside the thick, wooden door. I took a deep breath before knocking once and awaited his reply on the other side.

"Come in!" he called.

I pushed at the door and poked my head inside.

"Lydia," Mr. Blackwood said, a smile in his tone. He spun around in his leather chair to face me and stood as he waved me inside, grinning ear to ear. "Do come in, dear. Have a seat."

I hesitantly entered and clutched the strap of my saddle bag tight as I eyed him suspiciously. He was too chipper. Something was wrong.

I sank into the sturdy wing-backed guest chair as he leaned against the edge of his desk. "You wanted to speak with me?"

"That I did," he replied. His steely eyes fixated on me. "How are you doing? How are your classes since the assembly? I trust your peers are a little more accepting of you now?"

As my gut twisted with disgust, I felt my face do the same. "Is *that* why you pushed me to do this program? So, people would *like* me?" I guffawed and relaxed in the chair. "If so, you failed horribly. I'm still a pariah."

He shifted closer, gripping the edge of his desk. His slick silver vest crinkled as he leaned toward me.

"Oh, now, I somehow doubt that," he cooed. "Are you not met with smiles in the hall now? I hear them talking. Your fellow Wicked Born. They're excited to see you compete."

I glared at him. "Only to witness me fail."

"You have such little faith."

"I don't need faith," I said.

He studied my face for a moment before replying. "What is it you *do* need, then, Lydia?"

"Right now?" I crossed my arms. "I need to go home and see my mom."

Mr. Blackwood smiled, one that didn't meet his eyes, and he shoved away from his desk to stroll around to his chair. I swallowed hard against the dry tightness that formed in my throat. Some part of me knew something was wrong.

"What's the matter?" I pressed. "I *am* going home, right?"

He took in a sharp breath of air before sitting down. "Look, Lydia dear—"

"Stop doing that," I snapped. "I don't appreciate being spoken to like a child. Don't dress up bad news with smiles and soft words. Just tell it to me straight."

Mr. Blackwood stared at me; our gazes locked in a silent challenge of some sort. His eyes glistened with a mix of pity and regret. There were moments in my life I wished I could read minds. This was one of them.

"Very well," he finally relented. "I called you here today to discuss your Solstice break."

My lips pursed as I arched an eyebrow. "Was that so hard?"

"No," he said with a sigh. "But I'm afraid what I have to say next will be."

A sudden confirmation swept over me. Cold goosebumps scoured down my body as my brain leaped to the highest conclusion. Somehow, a part of me knew the very words he was about to tell me. I shook my head, refusing to believe them before they were even spoken.

"Lydia, I'm afraid—"

I shot up from the chair, tears swelling in my eyes. "No…"

The dean exhaled, long and deep. "I'm afraid I can't let you go home for Winter Solstice."

"Why?" I asked, my eyes stinging with tears. It was all I could do to keep the wetness from spilling over. A hot ball of anger festered in my belly. "Why not? I have a right to go home. I need to go home. For my sanity. I want to see my mother. I have to speak with her."

He lifted from his chair, and his upturned hands reached out for me in comfort. "Lydia, I—"

"No!" I pointed a finger at him, warning him to stay back. "I want to go home and see my family."

His firm shoulders slumped, and that look of pity filled his gaze again. "You have more family here at the academy than you know."

"Anson and Willa?" I snapped. "*They* get to go home. I'll be all alone."

"It's out of my hands," he said sincerely. "I would love to see you go home to your mother for the holidays, but I simply cannot risk it right now. The Courtship Program—it's never hosted a Wicked Born as young as you, nor as controversial. There are those who…don't wish to see you compete."

All the air pressed from my lungs. I had no words. I wasn't expecting that answer. I wanted to dismiss the idea. Refused to believe that was the reason he wouldn't let me leave. But the more I thought about what he'd said, the more I realized he might be right.

Emotions choked my words, but they squeezed from my throat anyway. "If I win, I'd be the first light Wicked Born to help rule the Dark Faction."

"Precisely," he replied. My evident attempt to stifle my emotions seemed to make him uncomfortable as he cleared his throat and shifted in place, as if he was unable to really look me in the eye. "I'm merely taking precautions for your safety, Lydia. I swear. I care for you, for all my students."

"Yeah right," I spat. "You don't give a shit about me. If you did, you wouldn't have put me in danger like this. Time and time again. I mean, why even make me do the program if you're so worried?"

"There are things in motion that exist far above your head. Ensuring you entered the program was a crucial step forward. For all of us. Both the Light and Dark Factions. We can't continue to exist separately as we do. You're the first light born to attend Arcane Academy East, and I see that as an opportunity."

I wiped at the moisture under my eyes. "But you and I both know that's not true. Is it?"

Realization swept over his expression, but he said nothing in response.

Everyone claimed I was the first to come here. The first light witch chosen for the dark. But Anson had arrived here before me. A fact only a few knew, Mr. Blackwood being one of them. Anson was the only light born in his area to have a Sorting Ceremony that year, and the elders of our factions were swift to cover it up. But the dean *must* have known. Why else would he have pressured Anson and Norah to meddle with advanced magicks?

"You're close with Mr. Abernathy, I take it," he said quietly and fidgeted with a button on his fancy vest.

"Yes, we're...seeing one another." I wrung my hands together. "And *he* gets to go home."

"Mr. Abernathy doesn't have a target on his back. I understand your resentment toward me, Lydia. But I just want what's best for you. For all my students. I want you and I to be in a good place. So," he added with a note of positivity, "as a gesture of good faith, I've made arrangements for your mother to come and visit you here. At the academy."

I couldn't hide the look of surprise if I wanted to.

"She'll be the very first Light Faction leader to step foot on this side of the school," he continued with loose warning. "So there will be rules and precautions, and she'll only be permitted to stay a few days—"

"Can I make a request?" I cut in. "If you truly wish to gain my trust?"

He eyed me, as though studying my every breath. "Go on..."

"I want to stop my special lessons on Fridays. Carol is my rival in this program, and I think it's a conflict of interest to have her preparing me for it."

His eyes widened as if he wasn't expecting me to ask for this. "I can find a suitable replacement for Carol, if that's the issue."

"No, I think I just want to practice on my own. With Willa. I'm more comfortable that way."

He fell silent, his stone-grey eyes never leaving mine. "Very well, then. If it will make you happy. Let it be a step forward for the both of us." He smiled. "Is there anything else?"

"No, this is perfect," I told him, still trying to grasp the idea of my mother being here. "I...I really appreciate it."

"Wonderful," he said. "It's settled then. Your mother will

come for three days during Solstice break, and your Friday lessons will end, effective immediately. You'll resume regular classes with Willa that day. Get her to catch you up on what you've missed."

I nodded. "Thank you."

I turned and made my way toward the door, floating on the new-found joy that sat in my belly. Happy and gloating.

"Oh, one more thing, Lydia," the dean called just as I reached the door. I turned to look at him. "I truly hope one day you'll come to find that I'm not the bad guy in your story."

I pursed my lips, then gave a single nod. "Maybe. One day."

As I entered the empty corridor, I closed the door behind me and stood against the jagged cobblestone wall to let out a deep breath.

I was going to get to see my mom. My useless Friday lessons were finally done. And the dean wanted to gain my trust. It seemed like things were beginning to look up for me.

I just wish I knew why he wanted me to trust him so badly.

CHAPTER 4

LIFE AT ARCANE ACADEMY wasn't anything like I ever imagined it would be.

It was worse.

After a long day of classes, Willa and I entered the sanctuary of our room, and I threw my bag on the floor before collapsing on the bed. I relaxed into the comfort my pillows, blankets, and mattress had to offer.

"I don't know how much more of Hallowell I can handle," I said and slung an arm over my face to block out the light shining down from the ceiling.

I could hear Willa unpacking her bag and placing everything back on her desk. "I know he's a bigot, but you'll have to get used to him. You'll be doubling up on his classes if you're going to be taking his Friday Conjuring class with me. That one's three hours long."

I sat up straight and looked at her. "You don't get it. I shouldn't have to get used to him. *He* should get used to *me*. I mean, he's the adult here. Hallowell hates me based completely on prejudice."

Willa rolled her eyes and tossed her empty bag on the floor next to mine. "Yeah, you're totally right. People hating one

CANDACE OSMOND & REBECCA HAMILTON

another because of who they were born as?" She motioned to her face and raised her brow mockingly. "I wouldn't know a thing about that."

Guilt washed over me, and my stomach churned. "Oh, Gods, I'm such an idiot."

She chuckled and plunked down on her bed across from me. "No, you're not. I know you didn't mean it like that. But I do get it. Hallowell has it out for you, and for no good reason other than his own bias. You should report him to the dean."

"And risk the blow back from those who side with him?" I shook my head. "No way. There are still way too many people in this school who'd love to see me go. Especially now."

I thought of the dean's concern for my safety. *There are those who don't wish to see you compete.*

"What do you mean?"

I looked away. "Nothing. Nevermind. It's dumb." I leaned across my bed and grabbed a pile of notes from my bedside table. "How about we practice some more?" I flipped through the stack of papers with my haphazard scrawl. "Conjuring? We didn't really touch on that one a whole lot. And you think that might be one of the tasks?"

Willa brightened at the mention of practicing magic. Or maybe it was the studying. I could never tell what excited her more.

"Yeah," she replied and scooped up her own notes from the table—a much neater and more well-organized notebook than mine. "I looked up all the past Courtship Programs, and the most common tasks chosen by the Game Designers are potions, enchantments, conjuring, and evocation. So, if we focus on those, we should be fine."

A sudden rapid knock at the door made me gasp, and I went to open it as Willa stuffed our notes under her pillow. I unlatched the lock and swung open the heavy door to find Carol standing there, a disgruntled look on her face as she peered into our room and gawked around with a nosey intention. I wanted to like my former mentor, but she made it increasingly difficult.

"Can I help you?" I asked her.

"Where is he?"

I narrowed the opening at little, keeping her in place. "Where is who?"

"Your boyfriend," she said and stood with her arms crossed.

"Anson? He would have just finished up his last class. Probably back in his room. Why?"

"He's not in his room, I checked," she said as other Wicked Born filled the corridor behind her, busting back to their rooms after a day of classes. "And he blew off his TA duties today. In fact, he's blown it off all week. At least he had the decency to ask me to cover. But today he just left everyone hanging."

My brain ceased as my train of thought came to a screeching halt. Anson hadn't been to his TA classes all week? But…he'd said he was. I'd told him how much I missed him, how I wished we could spend more time together. Not just a couple of hours in the middle of the night. And his excuse was classes and TA duties.

What was my boyfriend doing behind my back?

I quickly squashed down the emotions that bubbled in my gut and attempted to appear casual as I leaned against the doorframe.

"Oh, he's been a little under the weather," I lied. "I'll give him a call to see what's up and let you know when I get a hold of him. I'm sure there's a good reason."

Carol kept her arms crossed and arched an eyebrow. "If I didn't know any better, I'd almost say Anson is trying to get disqualified from the program."

I narrowed my gaze. I was already tired of pretending to be nice to her. "Why would he back out, Carol? He volunteered, for god's sake. Listen, I told you I'd find him.

Now, if you'll excuse me, I was in the middle of something."

I shut and locked the door before spinning around to face Willa in a panic. The look of surprise on her face was expected, but I ignored it and dove for my cell phone on the bed.

"Lydia," she said softly as I hastily scrolled for his number and then put the speaker to my ear.

The call went straight to voicemail. "Damn it!"

I tried again and paced the floor as I waited. But it wouldn't even ring. Instead, the call rolled right to messages, as if his phone wasn't even on. I let out a frustrated growl as I attempted to text him, making typos with almost every word.

Willa stepped closer. "Lydia," she said calmly. "What's going on with Anson?"

"Nothing," I replied, pressing send, and stuffed the phone in my pocket.

I grabbed my leather jacket from the hook on the back of the door and slipped it on. Willa just stood there silently, waiting. Judging by her expression, she was not pleased.

I stopped and took a deep breath, closing my eyes and calming my nerves. It wasn't fair for me to do this to her. We made a promise to one another. No secrets. No lies. We were in this together.

"I'm sorry," I offered. "I'm the worst."

She relaxed her arms and brightened. "No, you're not. Your only friend was a mundane who knew nothing of this life. I get it. You're just so used to doing it alone."

I stared at the floor unblinking as I zipped up my jacket and cleared my throat. "Anson's been…weird. Ever since the caves with Nash."

"What do you mean *weird?*"

"I don't know," I said and looked at her. Willa's eyebrows pinched together, marring her face with obvious signs of worry and confusion. "He's always tired. And he told me he's busy with school. But really, he's been…" I huffed a sigh and slapped my hands at my sides. "I don't know what he's been doing, actually."

"Okay," she replied and glanced around. "So, what are you going to do?"

I shrugged helplessly. "I have to go find him." I plucked my phone out and tried him again. Voicemail. I stuffed the phone back in with a little more force than necessary. "I need a tracking spell, one that's…discreet."

Willa's eyes filled with a distant, calculating stare.

"No, you need a locator spell." She leaped for the rickety bookshelf at the end of her bed and began filling her arms with little pouches and bottles. She placed them on the floor and sat down. "Do you have anything of his?"

One of his notebooks and a piece of broken charcoal sat on my nightstand, left behind from the last time he'd stayed over. I grabbed the coal and handed it to her. Willa bounced on her bottom as she patted the rug next to her. Doing magic always made her happy.

I took a seat by her side. "What's this one? I haven't done a locator spell in a while, but I know there's dozens."

She began sprinkling bits of each item into a stone mortar. "One I saw my mom do a hundred times for our dog who always ran away."

She tossed Anson's charcoal in with the mix of dried herbs and various sands and then stirred it all with a pestle. Hastily, she scooped what she could into a tiny black satchel and closed it with a drawstring before handing it to me.

"Hold this in your hand while saying *ostende mihi unum me quaerere* and close your eyes," she said. "Anson's location will appear in your mind, and the bag will warm to the touch when you're going in the right direction."

I grinned proudly. "What would I do without you?"

She rolled her eyes with a chuckle. "Just go find your boyfriend so we can get back to practicing for the program."

I mock saluted her. "Yes, ma'am."

I stepped into the empty corridor outside our room and gripped the bag as I brought the image of Anson to the forefront of my mind's eye. This had to work. But then an unexpected thought crept in. What if I found something I didn't want to know? What if Anson didn't want to be found and became angry with me?

I glanced at the pouch in my hand and rubbed it between my fingers, mixing the ingredients inside as I contemplated everything. Anson's weird behavior was the last thing I needed on top of everything else I was facing in the coming weeks. But what if he was in trouble?

With a determined sigh, I quietly chanted the words Willa had given me. "*Ostende mihi unum me quaerere.*"

The image of him that I dreamed up seared from my mind's vision, replaced with a clearer picture of Anson in the woods, surrounded by trees and large moss-covered stones. He sat on a rock, his back hunched over, face buried in his hands.

My eyes flew open, and I sped through the school toward the entrance. As the pouch in my hand grew warmer, I increased my pace, bounding off across the vast fields that fronted Arcane Academy and created a divide between the gothic structure and the never-ending forests that kept us hidden from whatever part of the world was out there.

Breathless, I approached the treeline and chanted the words once again, hoping for a hint of which direction to go. The Arcane Forest was vast. Anson could be anywhere in there.

Once again, the image of my boyfriend burned in my mind's eye, and I squeezed the satchel in my palm. I struggled to make out any other details: the sound of water running, which side of the trees the moss grew on. The lush, green growth faced Anson, and I knew then, I had to head north.

My Doc Martens crunched against the damp forest floor, and I zipped my leather jacket up tight around my neck.

Every breath of anticipation turned to fog as I scanned through the dense growth in search of Anson. The pouch in my hand was still warm, so I had to be heading in the right direction.

I heard him before I saw him—an unnatural sound of water splashing the wrong way—and I crept toward the noise. A figure moved in the distance, behind a wall of thin birch trunks. There he was. The back of his grey t-shirt, his muscles tense and moving underneath the fabric as his fists clenched at his sides.

"Anson?" I said quietly, but loud enough to catch his attention.

He froze and spun around, his cheeks pink with frustration. His eyes were glossed over.

"Lydia?" he replied and came toward me. "What are you doing here?"

I stuffed the locator pouch in my jacket pocket as I took in the state of the area. His black jeans were soaked to the knee, the skin on his arms scratched and reddened. Bits of earth lay in crumbled chunks across the forest floor.

"I could ask you the same thing," I told him. Something was off. I squashed down my feelings of betrayal and took careful, concerned steps toward him. "What's going on here? Are you okay?"

He quickly threw on a lighthearted mask, but it didn't fool me. I'd already seen the sheer look of defeat on his face. What was he up to? I glanced at his arms again. Hurting himself?

"People are looking for you," I told him. "You blew off TA classes?"

He didn't answer, didn't even look at me. Just stood there, stewing in his own private misery of being caught red handed in whatever he was doing. I could feel it coming off him in waves.

"Anson, talk to me."

27

His gaze focused on the ground as he toed the dirt with his sneaker. "I've been...practicing."

I dared a step closer. "For the program? Why didn't you just say so? I'm sure the dean would—"

"No." Anson grabbed his hoodie from a rock.

My face twisted in confusion. "No? What do you mean *no*?"

He hastily slipped his head and arms through the black sweatshirt. He ran a hand through his tousled sandy waves and stared at me. "Just no, Lydia. I don't want to tell the dean. I don't want help."

Anger festered in my chest. "Don't do that."

"Do what?"

"Hide behind that façade," I said. "That wall of darkness. Something's going on, I can tell. Don't shut me out."

His deep gaze sparkled with tears as he glowered at me.

"Please?" I pressed.

We stood in tense silence, neither of us relenting in our stubborn ways. What a pair we were. Two hybrid witches with the tenacity of a rock. I wasn't leaving until he talked to me, and he knew it.

Finally, his shoulders relaxed as he let out a grumble. I won.

"I'm practicing with my hybrid magic," he admitted.

I failed to see the issue. "Okay. And it's not working?"

He let a pause fall between us. "No."

"You gotta give me more to work with here, Anson."

"It's new to me," he said, unsure. "It's been a while... I haven't tapped into it since Norah died. I've blocked it out all this time, afraid someone would notice something...different about me. I've been careful to only use my dark magic, thinking I was only stifling my light powers, not realizing that it was so much more than that."

I listened intently and reached for his hand. My fingers eased into his palm, and my heart relaxed when he gripped them. His free hand lifted to my face, and his chilly fingertips brushed my jaw, sending goosebumps scraping down my body.

"I know now, after finding you," he continued, his warm breath tickling my cheeks, "that I'm not light and dark. I'm... I'm something else entirely. And that...terrifies me. I've spent days out here, trying to tap into that power, but it's been dormant for so long. I can't control it. Not like you can."

I guffawed. "If you think I have some sort of control over my magic then you're sorely mistaken. I'm taking it one day at a time."

His thumb rubbed at my bottom lip as he stared at my mouth. "No, you're better than you give yourself credit for. I've seen it. You can wield all four elements. I've known no other witch, not even a light born, to do that."

I shrugged gently. "So? Who cares? This whole hybrid witch thing—it's new to us." I leaned in, placing my mouth close to his. "There may be more of us out there, or maybe we're the only ones. Who knows? But our world isn't ready for us yet, and that's okay, because we're not ready either. We can figure this out. *Together.*"

He didn't reply.

"Anson?"

He gave a slow nod and peered down at me, his expression awash with a mix of emotions backed by thoughts I'd never know. I wished I could read his mind, just for a moment. To see inside that cover he hid behind.

I smiled and stretched on my toes to touch my lips to his. The warmth of Anson's mouth soothed my cold bones, and I melted into his embrace. My tongue slipped out, and I dragged the tip of it across the sharp line of his bottom lip, searching for more.

But instead of returning the kiss, he gripped my upper arms and held me firmly in place as he took a step backward.

"Sorry," he said and blew out a huff of air. "I've been at this all day. I'm just...wiped."

My mind raced for a solution. How could I progress this in a way that wouldn't cause him to retreat again?

"I wanted to figure it out on my own," he added. "Work through this block, this...disconnect."

"Explain it to me," I suggested. "Maybe I can help."

"My powers." He stared down at his hand and cupped his palm in the air. Flickers of blue covered the skin, weaving in and around his fingers. He focused on it intently. "When I tap into my dark magic, everything's fine. It's what I'm used to. But then, when I try and reach down deeper...." His clawed hand tensed and the bits of icy blue turned to static and dissipated. "*That* happens."

My arms tightened across my chest. "Okay, well, clearly you're rusty. Maybe if we—"

"No," Anson snapped. "There's no *we* here. I can't risk affecting you."

My eyebrows cinched together. "Affecting me? Anson, this isn't some disease. You're just out of practice. You've probably been playing it safe for too long. Like you said." I closed the gap between us and stood at his side, unrelenting. "Let me help. Maybe I can...give you a boost?"

That elicited a genuine chuckle from him.

Smiling, I stepped back and held my hands out at my sides as I called to my magic. Past the light, past the dark. I reached deeper inside my gut and felt around for that raw, ancient power. Hybrid magic. I didn't know what else to call it. It wasn't light or dark, but something else entirely: able to filter through either side and morph into something bigger. *Better.* Drawing its source from the universe itself.

I closed my eyes and raised my arms, tapping into the gently rushing water of the creek. I could feel the droplets of moisture in the air leading my senses right to it.

"Now, focus. Reach out," I said to Anson, my eyes shut

tight as I held my stance. "Feel for my magic and adjust yourself to it."

I sensed him wavering. Unsure. But the sudden presence of another source of magic told me he gave in.

I grinned. Anson's power was strong, its force a near perfect match for mine. But I could feel a sort of...*static*... vibrating around his. I waited it out as it lessened. Bit by bit. Until Anson's magic calmed to the same frequency as mine and I could carefully let go.

But something held on.

I felt a tug from somewhere deep in the back of his mind. My vision filled with an inky black and threw me into a cold panic.

With a gasp, I stumbled back as I let go of my hold on the water, my magic severing from it like a snapped band. Breathless, I shot a look at Anson, and he stared back with a wide-eyed look of concern.

"Are you okay?" he asked.

I rubbed a hand over my dry lips. "Yeah, I'm fine. Did you... Didn't you feel that?"

He shook his head. "What do you mean?"

He must have felt that. It came from *him*. That sense of dread and the inky substance that filled my mind. I eyed him suspiciously.

"Nothing," I replied. "I think I'm just tired."

"So am I," he said. "But I think it worked. My powers were too exhausted to hold on for too long, but I felt it. Whatever it is you tried."

"Really?" Part of me didn't believe his sudden turn of confidence.

"Yeah," he replied. "Maybe we can try again tomorrow?"

I nodded and chewed at the inside of my cheek as the slight taste of blood touched my tongue. A sure sign that I was harboring too much stress.

Anson twisted and glanced up at the darkening sky. The

sun went down early these days—which bode well for my powers—but I missed the sun dearly.

"Can I walk you back?" he asked.

I nodded and let him drape his arm over my shoulder as we headed toward the treeline, through the winding birches. Neither of us spoke, and my mind wandered to worries. New ones.

What was that dark presence back there?

Did it come from me?

No, I was certain it didn't. But that left only one other source: Anson.

We walked back toward the school, across the fields and toward all the things I wanted to run from and all the hurdles ahead of me. But, in that moment, none of it mattered. All I could think about was one thing, and one thing only.

Something extremely dark resided in my boyfriend. Either he had absolutely no idea, or...he was lying to me.

The question was, how was I going to find out?

CHAPTER 5

FRIDAY ROLLED AROUND FAST, and I sat at a wide table with Willa at my side as Professor Hallowell paced the front of the room, lecturing the class about the ethics of Conjuring: my new three hour long advanced class that replaced my lessons with Carol. I only listened to bits and pieces of his words as my mind wandered to thoughts of Anson.

I stared out the window—a large stone arch filled with blue-stained glass—until my eyes dried over and I was forced to blink. The warm wetness burned as I glanced around, unsure of what was really happening in class.

"Lydia," Hallowell said impatiently. "Have you been listening?"

"What?" I shifted in my seat. Willa discreetly turned the page of the book I was supposed to be following along with. "Yes, I'm listening."

He arched an eyebrow at me. "I'm only rehashing this earlier content for *your* benefit, Miss Laveau, since you decided to grace us with your presence a third of the way through the year. It would be wise of you not to waste my time, or that of your fellow Wicked Born."

Heads turned my way, all glaring with the same

narrowness that the professor offered. My cheeks went hot and my stomach soured. This was the last place I wanted to be right now. Or any day, for that matter. One class with a professor who hated everything I came from was enough. Fridays had just become my least favorite day of the week.

"Sorry," I muttered and slouched down in my seat as I tucked the book in my lap.

He held onto the moment for a beat before slapping his book shut and tossing it on top of his desk. "Just get Miss Stonerose to catch you up on the ethics material. I won't waste any more time catering to you. We have a lot to cover before the solstice break."

There was so much I wanted to say, but I bit back the words for my own sake. This wasn't high school. This was the academy I'd been preparing my whole life for. Yeah, it was on the wrong side, but still. Hallowell was my elder, and I was required to respect his position. I wouldn't give him material to work with, to use against me and further his unnecessary hate toward my family.

He continued on, moving back to whatever topic the class had been practicing before my arrival. Everyone cleared their desks, Willa included, and I realized then that each surface had the marking of a conjuring board burned into them. Letters and symbols of all kinds covered the wooden slab. I stuffed my book inside my shoulder bag and looked to Willa in anticipation.

"We've been practicing chanting," she told me. "It's imperative you get it perfect when conjuring an entity. Otherwise, you could be calling for the spirit of your dead dog and get a hellhound instead. Pronunciation is everything."

I nodded, my interest piqued.

"This is actually an area I'm not that experienced with," I said with a whisper.

"Really?" she asked, her voice heavily laced with surprise.

I smiled. "Yeah, I mean, I've done it. With my mother.

And I've watched our coven conjure all sorts of things on the plantation." With a shrug, I added, "They didn't know I was there, but I saw how it was done. Pretty intense stuff."

"Speaking of intense." She leaned in, as though aware of everyone within earshot. "I found a few things we can try. To practice for the program."

I brightened. "Seriously? Like what?"

"There's this one incantation I really want to test out. It suspends a living thing in time. Sort of like magical cryogenics. It'll be great for the potions test."

"Perfect," I whispered back. "I doubt anyone will be attempting anything like that. We're sure to win that one."

"We just need a few things. Some supplies. I have a list."

Hallowell eyeballed us, so I pretended to be pointing at something on the conjuring board on our desk.

"Looks like a trip to the apothecary is in order," I muttered under my breath.

Grinning, Willa grabbed my hand, and I felt the slight syphoning sensation of my magic trickling into her as she touched her fingertip to a few letters on the board.

They lit up as if they were freshly burned and spelled out the word *yes*.

I HANDED THE BARISTA—A lovely woman with purple curls neatly tucked back from her face with pins—some money before Willa and I moved to the side to wait for our coffees. The line proceeded after us as another barista prepared our drinks, and I noted how other patrons sat around with their steaming cups and peered at us.

The stares I was getting used to, expected even. But what caught my attention was the mix of giddy smiles aimed our way.

CANDACE OSMOND & REBECCA HAMILTON

"I think we're becoming something of a novelty," I told Willa.

She glanced around. "Yeah, I guess. I mean, look at us. First Years participating in the Courtship Program? We're like rare collectables. They can't wait to see us compete."

I shook my head and remembered the dean's words of caution. "Or see us fail."

"Don't be so pessimistic." She grabbed our two drinks as the barista placed them on the counter and handed one to me. "Come on, let's go."

I kept my head down as we cut through the crowd and bounded for the exit. Just as I reached for the gaudy iron handle, the door swung open and nearly knocked me down. I jumped out of the way and glowered when I saw who was entering.

Nash Crane's smug expression widened as his red-headed sidekick filed in behind him.

"Lydia," Nash purred. "What a pleasant surprise."

I rolled my eyes and reached for the door again.

"Leaving so soon?" he added.

My chest rose with a deep inhale—a lousy attempt to restrain my tongue. "Are you always such an ass?"

Willa tensed and tugged at my sleeve. "Lydia…"

I ignored her. "I can't believe I let you fool me for so long. I'm usually such a good judge of character." I tipped my head to the side. "I guess you just need to have some."

He smoothed back his already slicked hair and chuckled under his breath. "We'll see just how much character I have when the Program starts. Are you excited to compete? I can't wait to stand with you at the end."

I guffawed as he looked to Ferris with a hopeful nudge.

"I'll be at the end," I snapped, "but you won't be standing anywhere near me." I steeled myself against the growing intensity in his gaze. "There's no way I'm letting you win. I'd rather lay down my life than live in a world that *you're* helping to lead."

Ferris sighed and left to get in line. Nash tapped a finger against his lips as he put on a show of seriousness and leaned in so close the smell of his expensive cologne practically choked me.

"Lay down your life?" He clucked his tongue and glowered at me from under his dark brow. "Be careful what you wish for, princess."

He turned on his heel and stalked over to join Ferris. I hated that Nash got the last word, and it took all my willpower not to run after him and tell him off.

Willa tugged at my sleeve again, and I let her lead me out of the coffee shop. "Don't let him get under your skin. That's what he wants. Besides, we've got bigger stuff to deal with."

We strolled down the stone-paved streets toward the village apothecary as the twilight sky continued to darken. Torchlights that lined the way ignited and illuminated everything around us.

"For once I'd like to get under *his* skin," I said and sipped my coffee.

"You will," she said. "*We* will. Together. When we're standing with Anson at the end. Whatever Nash's plans are with the Midnight Circle will be foiled, and you'll be in a position to shut the whole thing down."

I sighed. "One can dream."

She stopped and hauled on the heavy door of the apothecary. Miss Haggy was there, standing in wait as if she expected our arrival.

"Girls," she greeted and struck a long match. Her black silk dress billowed in the breeze as the door closed behind us and she lit a large white candle sitting on the counter in front of her. "What can I do for you?"

Willa rummaged around in her bag and pulled out a list.

"We need some supplies. Hoping you have everything in stock."

Miss Haggy plucked the piece of paper from Willa's fingers and read it over as she adjusted the tiny spectacles that sat on the bridge of her nose. She nodded as she read, a series of hums and haws coming from her chest.

She glanced up with a knowing grin. "Yes, I have everything on your list. What exactly is it you're doing here?"

"Just practicing some things in preparation for the Courtship Program," I said honestly.

"Oh?" She peered at the list a second time, skepticism in her expression. "And what sort of things are you planning on...practicing?"

I pretended to be interested in some dusty bottles on the shelf to my right. "This and that."

Miss Haggy chuckled, a raspy smoker's kind of laugh. "I somehow doubt that the only Light Born to ever compete in our highly coveted event is merely trying her hand at *this and that*."

Willa leaned into the space between me and the shopkeeper. "We're playing around with a few things. Just tweaking some basic potions to put us ahead in the race."

Miss Haggy eyed us for a moment, almost as if she were contemplating even helping us at all. But, to my relief, she gave up prying and turned to her never-ending shelves. Her boney fingers expertly plucked bottles and jars, piling them on the counter with dried goods and a selection of gemstones.

"You know," she said as she portioned up our ingredients into small drawstring satchels, "I have a recipe for an old glamour potion you girls should try. A Morphiem Elixir."

"Yeah?" I replied. "Glamour isn't really that impressive, though. I mean, you learn about it in the first year at the academy. Almost anyone can glamour themselves."

"Yes, but how many can glamour the unknowing?"

Willa and I exchanged curious glances and approached

the rickety wooden table Miss Haggy stood behind. I'd only ever used the simple potion on myself, or seen it used on the caster. Never against someone else. Getting someone unknowing to drink a potion was harder than it sounded.

"Is it easy to learn?" I asked.

She continued to fill little bags with our things. "The potion? Oh, yes. Simple and easy. It's the special ingredient that might be tricky."

"What's the special ingredient?" Willa asked, running her fingers along the counter.

"Anything from the object of your intent," Miss Haggy said. "A hair, piece of skin. Anything directly from the person you wish to glamour."

I thought for a moment. "And one can pick any guise?"

The corner of her mouth twitched. "Yes, essentially. You'll just need something to represent the guise."

I crossed my arms with smugness, happy with the idea of glamouring someone unexpecting. Like Nash. And the perfect time to show off such a potion would be during the Program test. Everyone would see him for what he truly is, not to mention that Willa and I would surely win that round.

"We already have our plan for the potions test," Willa whispered to me. "Remember? The magical cryogenics?"

"Yeah, but we don't know how advanced that might be. What if we can't perfect it in time? We need a back-up," I told her and then raised my eyebrows at Miss Haggy. "Add in the ingredients for the glamour potion." Then a delightful grin spread across my face. "And throw in a jar of snakeskin, too."

Willa gently touched my arm. "Lydia, what are you doing? Is this for Nash?"

I leaned and whispered. "I know you want to practice for the Program, but who says we can't have a little fun on the side?"

She glared a warning at me.

I grinned at the thought of turning Nash into a snake. He

deserved far worse, but I had a sudden desire to watch him slither through the halls of the school. "Come on, I know you want to. It's worth whatever risk there is. What's the worst that could happen?"

Sighing, she crossed her arms. "Better hope you're right."

CHAPTER 6

NOTHING ELSE MATTERS when the one you love is in pain. When you're forced to sit back and watch them suffer in silence, all of life's problems seem to melt away with irrelevance. Well, that's how it seems, anyway. Beating Nash, winning the Program, I knew those things were important, but I couldn't bring myself to care in light of Anson's struggle.

I'd never felt that way before, about anyone. Growing up, my mother never dared show signs of weakness. Never wavered in her stature, her resolve as a leader of our coven and community. She was strong for them, and for me.

But now...

I sat on the edge of Anson's bed as I mindlessly picked at the hem of my plaid skirt while his tall frame bent over the record player in his room. His fingers pinched the arm and placed the needle carefully as the record spun. A gentle layer of Social Distortion filled the room, and I smiled as he turned toward me.

There, in the space dimly lit by candles, I could see the damage of stress on his face. How the shadows caught every wrinkle and hugged the bags under his eyes. His hair nothing but a dishevelled mess of sandy waves. He wasn't sleeping.

Was he worried about the program, his rusty magic...or something else?

He paused from thumbing through the large collection of albums on a shelf to look over at me. "How's practicing going?"

"With Willa?" I asked. "Fine. I guess. I mean, she found us some cool stuff to try. Be better if you were practicing with us, though."

He stood straight and tipped his head my way, those endlessly dark eyes fixed on me. "I want to get a handle on the full scope of my powers before the Program starts."

"I can help with that," I argued lightly. "The other day, in the forest, that was proof. We should be practicing more." He wavered on my words, and I switched to another angle. "Besides, I miss you. We don't have our Fridays anymore, and I hardly see you during the day."

The tiniest hint of a smile touched his lips. "Is that so?"

He sauntered across the room toward me. The denim of his black jeans rubbed against my bare leg, and I craned my neck to peer up at him towering over me. His fingertip crawled along my forehead and tucked a stray lock of hair behind my ear.

"Is there anything else torturing that mind of yours?" he asked, his words nothing but a seductive purr to my ears.

The closeness of him, the smooth and deep tenor of his voice, were always my undoing. I couldn't think straight, let alone control my attraction to him when he came this close.

I sucked in a shaky breath and leaned into his palm as he cupped my cheek. "Just...I constantly think about how this will all play out. We *have* to win, but at the same time, we can't reveal our secret." I hummed in delight as Anson shifted and slipped one of his legs between mine, causing my skirt to ride up. "I'm worried it's going to be hard to hide this new magic, whatever it even is. With all those eyes on us—"

"Stop worrying," he whispered and placed a quick kiss on

my mouth. "Lots of Wicked Born, both light and dark, vary in abilities. Some struggle to get through their five-year pledge while others excel." Another kiss. "It's not unusual that we're both powerful. That's nothing to hide. And I don't even have a supplement, no one's going to be looking at me for displays of power."

He bent over further, dropping both hands to the mattress on either side of me, and leveled his face with mine. My head spun just looking at him. The sharp line that shaped his lips, the blackened gaze that always fell on me with a heavy wanting. The same way I often looked at him. With a hunger, a need to have him.

I blinked away the haze his presence cast over my brain. "But we know so little about our hybrid powers. What if we reveal something telling? Something that shows we're definitely different?"

He didn't answer, only dipped his head to my neck and wrapped his mouth around the flesh there, sending a wave of goosebumps rushing over me. I balled the bottom of his thin t-shirt in my fist and tugged.

"I'm serious." I leaned back and demanded his attention. "These are all things we should be thinking about."

"I do think about them," he replied, his gaze heady and seductive. "I just don't want to think about them *right now*."

I laughed, unable to resist his charm or the tangible desire I felt wafting from his every pore. I realized then, Anson was just as concerned as I was with the whole situation; he just wanted a distraction. I may have had little control over everything that was happening around us, but that much I could give him.

I tugged his shirt again, forcing his face to mine, and planted a hard kiss on his mouth. A deep chuckle erupted from his chest as he leaned forward and I fell back onto the mattress, my legs still dangling off the edge. He nestled between them and hovered over my body like a human cage.

Content in the moment, I reached up and slid my fingers through his hair, holding his head in place so we could look at one another.

"Are you excited to go home for the holidays?" I asked him.

He nodded and turned his head to kiss my palm. "Yes. But I'll miss you. And I kind of wanted to meet your mother."

I guffawed. "Trust me, you're being saved from that whole situation."

He looked at me admiringly. "She can't be that bad if she raised the likes of you."

My skirt shifted farther up my thighs as he lowered himself. I kicked off my Doc Martens, and they fell to the floor at his feet as I wrapped my legs around his waist. He took my mouth in a deep, breathy, all-encompassing kiss so intense it made me wince, and I hugged my arms around his torso, squeezing and urging things forward.

Anson's long body writhed against mine as his expert fingers slid up my thigh and brushed the tender skin in search of my underwear. He slipped them down in one swift movement, barely severing us, and brought his lips back to mine in an instant.

I blindly felt for his belt buckle, but he grabbed my hands and brought them together above my head as he slowly crawled back down my body, unbuttoning my top in the process. My back arched as his warm lips pressed against the skin between my breasts and down my stomach. A gentle cry escaped my throat. I gripped the blanket beneath me as Anson disappeared between my trembling legs, and I gave in to the bliss that washed over me, letting it take me away.

EVEN THOUGH WE shared the secret of being something outside the realm of what our world deemed normal, Anson was the only refuge I had from it all. His presence, his simple touch, was enough to send me reeling away from my worries. If only for a moment. But it was a moment I gladly welcomed. My mind needed the break.

We lay together in his bed. The few candles around the room had long doused, but I was content with the darkness. All that could be heard were the slow lessening of our labored breaths and my rapidly beating heart sitting smug and satisfied in my chest.

I pulled the heavy blanket up around us as his arm cradled my head and played with a stray lock of my hair. His other hand held mine as we mindlessly caressed one another's fingers.

"So," I said, still breathless, "as I was saying."

His chest vibrated with the deep hum of a slight chuckle.

"Are you going home for the entire solstice break?" I asked.

He sighed. "Yeah, my grandparents miss me around the farm. I should probably help out as much as I can while I'm there." His grip around my hand squeezed with assurance. "But I might come back a day early. Wouldn't want you suffering it out here all alone now."

"The only suffering I'll be doing is keeping my mother from taking over the place."

"She's used to being in charge, isn't she?"

"You could say that," I replied. "But I'm hoping to use the time with her to help put my head back on straight. Lace Laveau can navigate her way through any disaster. She'll tell me what to do."

"There's actually someone on this planet who can tell *you* what to do?" he kidded. "Damn, now I'm really bummed I'm going to miss her."

I broke the embrace of our hands to poke him in the chest, and he tittered.

"So, what are your plans?" he asked me.

45

CANDACE OSMOND & REBECCA HAMILTON

"For the Program? We have a few tricks up our sleeves. Willa found this great potion, and if we can perfect it then—"

"No, no," he cut in, "I mean for this weekend."

I rifled through the mess in my brain. What was happening this weekend? Then it hit me, and I groaned. "The dance."

"Yes, the dance," he said. "You never really gave me an answer before. Do you want to go?"

I'd honestly forgotten all about it. "Are you asking if I *want* to go...or if I *will* go?"

"Why do you hate Solstice so much?" he asked, his face pinched with a hint of impatience.

"For someone who claims to be a hermit that hates social gatherings, you sure are persistent about this stupid dance."

He pulled my hand to his mouth and kissed the knuckles. "It's not stupid. It's actually beautiful. Arcane Academy takes Solstice celebrations very seriously. And...since Norah died, I haven't gone with anyone."

My throat ran dry. I was shocked by how easily he spoke about his supplement and best friend. It took a lot of work to pry him open in the beginning but once he did, he made no secret of his feelings. It was a true testament to how much Anson trusted me. How much he cared.

"Fine," I gave in. "Let's go to the Solstice dance. But Willa's coming, too."

I could feel him smiling in the dark. "Of course."

"And I don't hate Solstice," I replied. "I dislike *Christmas*." I let out a slow sigh. "Aside from the super fake convention of it, it was always a time of the year when I was reminded just how incomplete my family was. No father, a workaholic mother with a mountain of responsibilities that often took her away from me. It was usually just me and Meri, my nanny."

His body tensed with laughter. "Nanny?"

"Don't even start with me, Abernathy," I warned lightly. "Meri is family to me."

46

"Well, what about the other stuff? Like all the awesome food and playing in the snow."

"We never got snow where I lived," I said.

"Are you serious?" he balked. "You've never seen snow?"

I shrugged. "I mean, yeah, in movies and stuff. One year I kicked up a fuss that Mom had to leave for coven business, so she took me with her to Tahoe. Took me skiing. But that was it."

"For a rich girl, you're seriously deprived," Anson kidded.

"Shut up!" I laughed and stuck my hand underneath his t-shirt to tickle his stomach.

A stark gasp jumped from my chest at the touch of something there, on his chest. Something…unnerving.

I ripped his shirt up over his torso and my fingers touched the strange, foreign lines I'd never felt on him before. He yanked from my grip and shifted away.

"Anson!" I cried and reached for his shirt again. He moved to get out of bed, but I jumped on top of him and straddled him in place with my thighs. My fingers searched his skin, finding more and more strange protruding veins covering his chest. "What *is* that?"

"I…don't know," he replied, defeated. "They appeared a few days ago. When I began tapping into my dormant magic. They come and go throughout the day."

Hastily, I snapped my fingers and said, "*ignis!*" The candles around the room lit and revealed what my hands felt: a series of blackened veins, almost disguised against the collage of tattoos that adorned the surface of his chest, spreading and fanning out from one source. His heart.

"Jesus Christ, Anson. Why didn't you tell me? You need to get this looked at."

He pulled down his shirt, covering his body, and shifted uncomfortably. His face twisted with confliction.

"No, I don't," he replied, and I rolled off him to sit on the bed by his side. "I'm fine."

My heart beat maniacally. "That doesn't look fine to me. We should tell the dean."

"No!" He flew into a panic and sat up straight. "Promise me you won't say anything."

I didn't reply.

"Lydia! Promise me."

My mouth gaped, and my eyes watered over. "How...how can you ask me that?"

"I swear, I'm perfectly fine," he insisted. "My grandmother will know what to do. She'll fix me right up with one of her crazy potions."

I stared at him skeptically, and my head spun with all the new thoughts of worry for my boyfriend. This issue with his powers was clearly worse than I'd realized. Why was he keeping this from me?

"Just give me time, Lydia," he begged. "I'm alright. My grandmother will have this gone before Solstice break is over, and I'll be back good as new." He swallowed nervously and leaned in. "If you tell the dean, he'll pull me from the Program before it even starts."

My shoulders dropped. "Anson..."

"Please," he said again. "If I'm not better after the break, then I'll go to the dean myself. Just wait, okay? Can you do that? For me?"

I thought for a moment, shuffling through all the possibilities. Plus...I couldn't have him pulled from the Courtship Program. I needed him to win with me. Finally, I sighed and gave him a nod.

"Fine," I said.

Reluctance scorched my gut, and I regretted the affirmation the second it left my lips.

He could go home and get worse. He could die, for all I knew. I mean, how deep did this go? Was this the reason his hybrid magic wouldn't work? Or did his magic do this to him? Or...was it something else altogether?

But I had to put some faith in him. I wanted so desperately to take control of the situation, but I also wanted to trust the man I cared for so much. He said he would get it fixed. I had to believe that.

Or prepare for the worst.

CHAPTER 7

No AMOUNT of magic could stop my brain from exploring every tragic possibility that my immediate future held.

The fate of my boyfriend.

Being left alone for all of Solstice break.

The outcome of each test the Courtship Program threw at us; how we had no choice but to win them all. Whatever it took.

How could I live in a world where Nash Crane won? Watch him be ushered off to special classes and years of prep to mold him into a leader of our community? The thought made me want to vomit.

"So, what should we do for the other tests?" I asked Willa as she sat on the floor of our room and carefully unpacked jars and satchels of ingredients from a small chest we kept them in.

She shook her head. "We should really focus on this one first. The Mors Velox. It's the hardest. Once we have it perfected, we can replicate it during the Program."

I lowered myself to the huge rug that anchored the space between our beds and grabbed the incantation that Willa put together from the photocopies she made of the ancient grimoire. I read it over while unstacking a few ramekin bowls and placed them in the center with the ingredients.

"Well, I know Enchantment is in the bag," I continued and ignored the lustrous sigh from Willa. "I've been enchanting things since I was twelve."

"We should still practice it," she replied. "After we've nailed Potions. I want to go into this test with a hundred percent confidence. This Mors Velox potion is a guaranteed win. I highly doubt anyone else will be trying this old magic. It's too advanced, for one."

I chewed at the inside of my cheek. "And you don't think it's too...risky? Like, if we pull off this ancient, super advanced potion, won't people be suspicious?"

She pursed her lips and looked away for a moment. "Well, it's no secret that we had access to stuff like this. I mean, we willingly handed back the grimoire after the disaster in the caves. And everyone knows that you're a badass. I think..." She nodded to herself as her expression filled with contemplation. "I think people will be awed, not suspicious. Which will bode well for us."

Together, we filled each tiny bowl with the list of ingredients from Willa's recipe while I processed what she had said. Part of me still worried—maybe always would—but I trusted Willa. If she thought going with a Mors Velox was a good idea, then I'd follow her lead.

"It's the Conjuring test I'm not really sure about," I admitted, still going on about the other tests. I knew she wanted to focus, but I just couldn't. "That's the area I've had the least practice with."

"Lydia," Willa said sternly, "none of this will work if you don't concentrate. Potions, Conjuring, none of it. I know you're stressed. We all are." She reached over and patted my leg. "We'll practice for that, too. Conjuring is all about mind control. Casting a circle? Easy. Calling an entity? Also, easy. It's *holding* that entity within the circle that's the hard part."

She tapped her fingertip to her forehead and grinned. "Focus. And now you're taking Hallowell's Friday Conjuring class with me. We're set, Lydia. Don't worry."

I inhaled deeply, willing myself to calm. I reached over to my bedside table and grabbed a flowering cactus plant. "Okay, let's Mors Velox this bitch."

"Are you sure?" she asked.

"Yes, sorry," I replied. "I've just got so much on my mind. It's hard to keep it quiet."

She tipped her head, her eyes tugging together. "How's Anson doing?"

I took in one big breath as I struggled to think of where to start. "He's...I don't know. He swears he's fine and doesn't need any help. But I caught him fighting with his powers in the woods the other day. He looked beaten."

Willa scooted closer to me on the rug. "What do you think is the problem?"

I shook my head. "I have no clue. He claims his hybrid powers are just rusty. He hasn't used them since his supplement died. He just can't seem to properly tap into them. Dark magic is fine. But the second he attempts anything else, it backfires."

"Maybe he should get some help," she suggested. "Get it looked at."

"By who?" I replied.

Willa slumped in defeat. There was no one he could trust to look too closely at him or his magic.

"He said if he's not better after Solstice break then he will figure something out." I chewed at my cheek again; the thing was raw in my mouth. "He doesn't want to get pulled from the program."

Willa raised her chin as if it had all clicked in place. "I get it. The Game Designers only want able witches competing. If they even catch a whiff that any of us are off, they'll pull the plug. They always do. People have been disqualified for far less than a fever. I guess they don't want the blowback if anything goes wrong. I mean, we're dealing with some serious magic here."

"I know," I said quietly and picked at the chipped red nail polish on my thumb.

I contemplated telling Willa about the black veins on Anson's chest but bit my tongue when the words crept up. I'd made a promise. I did my best to show indifference.

"Okay, focusing," I said, redirecting Willa away from the subject of Anson. "Let's try this spell, shall we?" I read over the recipe once more. "You know, *Mors Velox*, that basically translates to *a quick death*."

Willa wagged her finger at me. "Close. More like *death is quick*. I did the research, I swear. The old Latin inscriptions don't really translate well today. I think they mean that the spell could result in a quick death if it goes wrong. But I've read it over a hundred times, played it out in my mind. This should stop a living organism from aging and hold them in suspended time. I'm sure of it."

I moved the planter between us. "Fair enough. Let's do this."

We worked together to mix all the ingredients carefully into one large stone basin, all while chanting the words of the long, three-part incantation. A chant to mix the herbs, another to add the wet ingredients. It turned to a thick, blackened substance. It was one of the most advanced potion spells I'd ever seen, even more than anything I'd tried or witnessed growing up on the Laveau Plantation.

Spells were simple nowadays. With Wicked Born practicing as early as eighteen years old at academies around the world, covens had to work together to simplify our ways. Modernize them. This spell, however, derived from ancient ways, not used for hundreds of years...It was as incredible as it was dangerous.

We worked diligently, quietly and carefully mixing

everything. I could feel my magic creeping through my veins and connecting me to Willa, magnifying and growing with each passing second. It filled me up like a warm liquid, coursing through my limbs and pressing on my heart.

It was almost...too much. But I maintained control, willing my mind and body to be present over the ancient magic that wanted to break free.

Finally, satisfied we'd followed the recipe perfectly, I gently poured some of the potion into a small vial; my fingers vibrated with the heavy dose of power that flowed through them. Willa wrapped her hands around the planter, and I held the little glass tube over the cactus as we both looked at one another in anticipation.

"You ready?" she asked.

I nodded and focused on the plant as I trickled the potion over it and chanted.

O virtus potentia. Ego sum eos.

Apud eundem ictum ac vitae est in me verberat terræ.

Usque ad tempus donec tenere relatorum permiserunt ut iterum fluant.

With every word I spoke, my heart raced, and my lungs protested under the sudden pressure that pushed against my chest.

When I muttered the final word, I let out a breath of relief. We both sat there on the floor in our dimly lit bedroom, and I watched in anticipation as the dark potion crawled over the plant and began to glow. It morphed from a thick, dark goo to a cloudy and iridescent gel. The cactus and the pink flower on top of it were now alive and thriving. Yet, unmoving. As if frozen in place.

My eyes shot to Willa, and her expression reflected the glee and disbelief I felt.

"It...worked?" she said.

"What? Did you expect it to fail?" I asked incredulously and laughed. "You were so sure!"

"I was just trying to be confident!" she replied and stared

at our work with awe. "I can't believe it actually worked on the first try."

Our joy quickly turned sour as the clear substance that held the plant in place began to move again, shifting and rolling over the entirety of the cactus like a living thing. The pink flower shriveled up and crumbled to bits as the plump green body of the plant squeezed itself until there was nothing left but a pile of mush on top of the soil in the planter.

We both gawked in disbelief, eyes watering over with defeat. The disappointment was crippling.

"Shit," I blew out in an exasperated breath and ran my hands through my hair as I leaned back and relaxed. "Good thing we didn't try it on a person, I guess."

"I don't understand." Willa fussed with the papers and her notes. "It should have worked."

"Hey," I said. She ignored me and kept reading. "Willa. It's fine. We have a backup plan. We'll just try the Morphiem Elixir that Haggy gave us."

"I really wanted this to work, though," she replied and tossed the papers on the floor by her side. She threw her back against the side of the mattress behind her. "Damn it."

"I'm spent," I said. "But we can try this one again tomorrow. It's not a big deal. I honestly didn't expect it to work at all. This spell is so old. We could have easily translated something wrong."

She shook her head. "No, it's right."

"Okay, well..." I searched for the correct approach here to ease her dampened ego. "We try again. And we'll try the Morphiem Elixir, too, as a backup. Either way, we'll have a winning potion."

I could see the uncertainty in her eyes, the doubt that toiled in her mind. Willa clearly wasn't the type to fail at anything she tried. She ran her hands over her tired face and looked at me from across the floor.

"Maybe we should practice something else for a while,"

she said. "One of the other possible tests. Maybe Enchantment?"

"Willa, you can't let this get to you. We tried a really hard spell," I said, attempting to sooth her. "And it almost worked. On the *first* try."

She didn't seem convinced.

I let out a gruff sigh and hauled myself to my feet, desperate to reel her back in. Hastily, I darted around the room, plucking things from hooks and hangers. A silk robe, a lace shirt. Some gemstones charging on the windowsill.

"What are you doing?" she asked from the floor.

I tossed everything on my bed and closed my eyes as I called to my familiar white magic and let myself fall into the comfortable safety it provided. My fingers tingled as bits of green crackled around my hands, and I reached out to the very fibers and particles of the objects before me. I felt them reply, reacting to my call, and I worked them all together with an enchantment I learned from my mother.

"Pulchra habitu," I whispered and opened my eyes.

A gorgeous black silk dress with lacy parts, adorned in tiny bits of jagged gemstones, laid across my bed. Willa pulled herself to her feet and came to stand next to me as she peered down at my enchanted masterpiece. I gripped my hips with a smug satisfaction.

"There," I told her. "I can do enchanting with my eyes closed. Literally. And now I have a dress for the dance. Two birds, one stone."

She continued to stare at the garment and crossed her arms. I couldn't tell if she was mad or...something else.

"Willa?"

Finally, she peeled her gaze from the dress and turned to me. A smile crept across her lips. "We're going to win this, aren't we?"

Relief filled my chest, and I nodded. "Yeah. I mean, I hope so."

I thought of Nash and all the horrible things he's done to me and my friends. To those I cared about. And the Midnight Circle, how I couldn't let the seedy underground coven rise up with a leader like Crane.

"We *have* to win," I added. "Because the alternative will turn our already broken world upside down, and there will be no coming back from it."

CHAPTER 8

Mundane Christmas might be an overdone, inflated money racket, but Winter Solstice at Arcane Academy was definitely something to be revered. Anson was right. Wicked Born took this time of year very seriously and squeezed every bit of pleasure out of it to share with everyone.

Growing up in the mundane world, I only ever experienced solstice for a short period of time each year, and it was often from the quiet corner of a room, where I planted myself at whatever lame coven event Mom dragged me to. I was bored, alone, and hated every second of it.

But as I stood in one of the wide entrances to the academy mess hall, I stared around in awe. Willa, at my side, gleamed and inhaled deeply.

"Goddess, can you smell that?" she asked.

"Yeah," I replied with delight and focused on the massive array of food set up around the grand room, buffet style.

Tables were adorned with heaping platters of roasted fowl, every steamed vegetable imaginable, and trays upon trays of baked good and fancy desserts. My mouth filled with saliva, and I followed Willa farther inside where cascades of black and gold linens draped over archways and windows.

Hollies with twisted branches held large candles on the tables.

We loaded up our plates and found a quiet spot near the back to sit. Wicked Born filled the hall, greeting one another with wide smiles and laughter. It was a happy time of year.

"I can't wait for the dance tonight," Willa said between messy bites of her lemon pie. "If this is lunch, then I can't imagine what the Great Hall will look like."

I ignored her statement. The dance held no appeal for me. "When do you head out tomorrow?"

She shrugged as she tore off a bite of a cheesy bun and shoved it to the side of her mouth. "I'm catching a portal early in the morning." She grabbed a handful of roasted nuts from her plate and tossed them in her mouth. "When does your mom get here?"

"The dean told me to meet him in his office after most of the crowd has cleared out," I replied and stirred my butternut squash soup. "I think he wants to eliminate as much exposure of my mother as possible."

"Yeah, a Light Faction leader on the East Side?" Willa said. "I'm not sure it's ever been allowed."

"According to Mr. Blackwood, it hasn't. He's made it very clear that he's *going through great lengths* to get her here." I rolled my eyes, and she laughed.

I made light of the whole thing, but really, deep down, a part of me was worried as hell. Mr. Blackwood seemed to think that my safety was a concern. That there were actually people out there in our world outside the academy that didn't want me to compete in the program.

It made sense. I was a Light Born. But the Sorting Ceremony chose me for the Dark for a reason. I didn't want this, didn't ask for it. I wasn't some spy coming to infiltrate their world and take over. But, if I knew one thing about Wicked Born to be true, it was that they didn't favor change. Our rules and customs had been in place for hundreds of years, and we'd never strayed. Light called to light, even in the darkness. But this time...darkness called to the light.

And I responded.

There was nothing the elders could do to cover it up, either. Not like they did with Anson's Sorting Ceremony, changing his entire life on paper, stating that he was a dark born adopted into a light born family. How ridiculous. To force a man to live a lie like that for the rest of his life just to protect this idea of a world divided by color, by class. It disgusted me how easily they could flip someone's life completely upside down like that. Then, in the back of my mind, a constant thought thrummed in my ears.

How many others were out there? Like me, like *us*.

"Lydia?" Willa said, eyebrows raised high as she leaned in across the table.

I snapped back to reality. "What?"

"You're totally ignoring everything I've said." She motioned over my shoulder. "Ferris is headed this way."

He stopped at the edge of our table. His hands wrought together, but he smiled. It killed me that part of me missed the guy, missed his loveable nature and the warmness he carried around him. He always made me laugh, and it pissed me off that I had to give up that friendship.

It was never a friendship, I reminded myself.

"Ladies," he greeted. "I just wanted to say Happy Solstice."

"Happy Solstice, Ferris," Willa gave in.

I shot her a mock look of betrayal, and she stuffed her mouth with more cheese bun.

An awkward silence held us together. Ferris seemed on the edge of wanting to say something but fidgeted with his red silk scarf instead. Willa spoke to me with her eyes, as if looking for a prompt of some kind. I discreetly shook my head, but she totally missed the intent.

"Uh, are you and Nash heading home for the holidays

tomorrow?" she asked him, and I gently nudged her with my foot under the table.

Ferris brightened and sighed happily. "Yes, we are. We're staying for the dance tonight, though. Are…" He dared throw a glance in my direction. "Are you ladies going?"

I set down my spoon loudly and peered up at him from my chair. "Look, I'm not sure what it is you're trying to do here, Ferris. But it's not going to work. Now leave, before I do or say something I regret."

He stood there, unmoving, his chin held high despite the hurtful look in his shiny green eyes. "You know, I still consider you a friend, Lydia. Both of you. What Nash did in those caves…I had no idea. He completely left me in the dark. For what reason, I'll never know."

I said nothing.

Finally, he accepted this wasn't going to be whatever lighthearted exchange he was hoping for. He turned to leave but then came to a halt after a couple of steps and glanced back at us over his shoulder.

"How…" He pressed his lips together. "How *is* Anson doing, by the way?"

Willa paled, and her gaze shot to mine.

I stood from my chair. "What do you mean?"

Ferris' cheeks softened with a slight pink as he suddenly stumbled over his words. His line of sight flitted from mine to across the mess hall and tensed.

"I have to go," he said quickly and sped off in the direction that caught his attention.

I narrowed my gaze as I stood frozen in place by a familiar anger—a pure hatred for Nash Crane, who'd entered the mess hall—that I found myself unable to let go of now. Something about his presence had stirred Ferris' nerves. Would Nash be mad his supplement was talking to us?

"What the hell was that all about?" Willa asked.

"I don't know." I slowly sat back in my seat, my appetite

61

completely washed away. "But something's fishy. Either they're playing us, or Nash is up to something and Ferris is being left out for some reason." I chewed at my lip in nervous thought. "But one thing's for sure—whatever is wrong with Anson definitely has something to do with what Nash did in those caves."

CHAPTER 9

I PACED our bedroom in a cloud of perfumes and other female products as we got ready for the dance. Willa continued to perfect her makeup while I walked the stone floors a hundred times, my cell phone glued to my hand as I anxiously waited for Anson to get back to me.

"Anything?" Willa asked as she clicked a sparkling jewelled barrette to the side of her head.

I slipped my bare feet into a pair of black strappy shoes and glanced at the screen in my hand again. I'd called and texted Anson a dozen times after our run-in with Ferris earlier.

"No, nothing."

Frustrated, I tossed the phone on my bed as I sat down to fasten the straps on my shoes. I pushed my long black hair in front of one of my shoulders, and it cascaded like a curtain on the side of my face as I bent over.

Willa stood from her desk chair, and her navy lace dress fell to her knees. The garment hugged around her neck and showed off her long, caramel colored arms. I smiled, anchoring myself in the moment as I admired just how gorgeous my friend was.

"You look amazing," I told her. "You know that?"

She twirled around and flipped her thick curls over her shoulder. "I know."

"Where did you get your dress?"

"My mom's a seamstress in the mundane world," she said and began stuffing her things into a tiny sapphire clutch. "She always made most of my clothes."

"Talented *and* a witch," I replied, securing the other shoe in place. I stood and brushed my hands against my thighs as my gown fell and pooled around my feet. The thin and enchanted fabric clung to my body like a glove. "You're lucky. My mother never gave up trying to dress me in pant suits. I think that's why my style is the way it is. Years of teenage spite."

She chuckled. "That's going to be your undoing one day, you know. That spitey anger of yours."

I quirked an eyebrow. "Hey, let me have my spite. It's the only thing keeping me going."

We both laughed as she reached for the door. "Well, let's just head to the Great Hall. Maybe Anson will meet us there?"

She hauled on the handle and swung the door open only to find him waiting on the other side, surprise on his face. The icy tension in my veins melted away. I could finally *breathe*.

"Where the hell have you been?" I asked as he stepped into the room.

Anson looked at me, eyes wide. "Sorry. I forgot my phone in my room. I was in the village." He grinned devilishly. "Shopping."

"Shopping?" I balked, not expecting that answer in the slightest. "For what?"

Anson held out his hands, palms up, and they filled with a blueish smoke as a strange shape formed in each one. Willa and I stared until the smoke cleared and two crisp black roses sat in wait.

"These," he finally replied. "Can't have my dates going without a corsage now, can I?"

A moment ago, I had been filled with anxiety over where my boyfriend was. My growing worry for his declining health would surely be my undoing, not my childish spite. But, as I stood there and stared at him slipping the black rose over Willa's wrist, I couldn't bring myself to be mad. At anything. But also…the ease of which he used his powers surprised me.

He seemed rejuvenated; color touched his cheeks, and his hair shined with a new life instead of looking like the disheveled mess he sported lately. That was when I allowed myself to take a deep breath and really take in the man before me. An all-black suit clung to his tall frame: no tie, collar buttoned tight around his neck. Anson Abernathy was a dream for most girls, but he was my reality.

His dark brow lowered as he sauntered toward me, twirling my rose in his fingers in front of his chest. He motioned to my dress as he blew out a loud puff of air.

"You're a gothic vision, Lydia." His warm breath caressed my face as he leaned in and his lips brushed against my ear. "I can't wait to take that dress off you later."

Hot goosebumps formed on my skin and rushed through my body, tickling somewhere deep in my gut. I leaned into his presence, his taunting and seductive voice, wanting to take his mouth right there. I wanted to let my body respond to my desire for him, but I stifled it away. I gripped his shirt and tugged him closer, our noses touching.

"Don't tempt me, Abernathy," I said. "I'm looking for any reason to ditch this party."

"Are you trying to tell me how handsome I am?" He chuckled and slipped his hand into mine before turning to Willa who waited in the doorway. "Shall we?"

SOUNDS from the Great Hall touched my ears before we even approached it. The deep tempo of cellos, drums, and violins vibrated through the stone walls and created a beautiful, eerie backdrop of music to walk in on. I filled my lungs with a deep breath as the three of us stopped and stood in the grand doorway, Willow and I both with an arm looped through Anson's.

I didn't know what to focus on first. The vast space was a scene of magical gothic fantasy. Hundreds of blackened twigs carried sparkling, candied plums and gold-dipped berries all over the archways of windows and doors and hung from chandeliers that shone down over endless tables of food. Far more luxurious than the feast we'd had earlier. Black and violet silk covered everything in smooth draping.

"Oh, my goddess," Willa exclaimed and pointed upward. "Look at the ceiling."

The three of us craned our necks and peered up to find the ceiling enchanted. It moved like a lifelike movie, shifting effortlessly with a snowy night sky filled with stars. We entered farther into the room, ushered with the crowd of fancily dressed Wicked Born who dispersed all around. The second our feet touched the center of the grand space, the flooring morphed from a dark stone to an enchanted checkered dance floor of white and gold squares.

People filed over and embraced one another as they twirled about. Some wore masks to match their dresses or wiccan crowns of thorns while others sported white skulls of horned animals like a helmet.

"I'm going to get a drink!" Willa exclaimed. "You guys want anything?"

I gripped Anson's arm. "Sure, whatever you're having."

"Still wish you ditched?" Anson said in my ear, his voice barely audible over the music and laughter.

I grinned and pinched his chin between my fingers as I pulled him close for a kiss. "I could stay for a minute."

His firm hand slipped around my waist and held me close. "Then I'd best get in a dance while I can."

He spun me onto the gold and white floor as the tempo of

live music picked up. I was a horrible dancer, but I didn't need to think about it; he was an expert, it seemed. He twirled me around and brought me back to him time and time again, eliciting a loud cackle of laughter from me each time. Anson was dashing on the dance floor and, for a moment, I let everything else wash away. This was the last night I'd get to spend with him before the Solstice break. I should enjoy it.

The song ended and the Great Hall filled with chatter as everyone took a break and dispersed to the food and drinks. Anson spotted something across the room and grabbed my hand as he led me toward it.

"There's someone you should meet," he told me.

We strolled over to a table of fountains that spewed chocolates and cheeses. A young guy, maybe Anson's age or a year older, stood there with a plate and mouth stuffed full of food.

"Tom," Anson greeted, and they shook hands. "This is Lydia. The girl I told you about."

Tom went wide eyed and quickly swallowed the mush of food in his mouth. He wiped his hand on his black and grey plaid shirt—I noted then how severely underdressed he was and immediately envied his comfy attire—and offered it to me.

"Lydia Laveau," he said, remnants of powdered sugar still touching his lips. "It's nice to finally meet you."

Utterly confused, I accepted his handshake with a smile as I sized him up some more. He was cute, in a haphazard way. Blond hair, long and uncombed, barely touched his shoulders. His black and grey plaid shirt lazily slung over a clean pair of black jeans and matching t-shirt said he was either inconsiderate or just truly that unaware of himself.

Or that he didn't care.

"This is Tom Foster," Anson said. "The editor for the school paper."

Realization struck me down, and I shook his hand once

again with vigor. "Oh, yes! Sorry, I haven't actually seen you around before."

He stuffed some more desserts in his mouth. "Yeah, I don't leave the newsroom much. We're all excited to have you on board after the holidays, though."

I hadn't really given it a second thought since Anson told me a few weeks ago that he got me a spot on the paper. Other things kind of took priority in my mind. Guilt sat heavy in my stomach, but I smiled my way through it.

"I'm looking forward to it." The words were true, but I found myself surprised by them. Since I'd arrived at Arcane Academy, I'd faced chaos at every turn. It would be nice to do something for myself for once. Something that I actually loved.

"Hey," Tom said cheerily and motioned to Anson's outfit. "Look at us. Almost twins."

Anson chuckled, a lighthearted reaction I hadn't witnessed him share in a while. "Yeah, you're a little overdressed, don't you think?"

"Well, you know me," Tom replied, "always the showman."

I stood there and found myself enjoying the display of comradery between my boyfriend and this stranger. It was as if they'd known each other for years—and maybe they had. At that thought, I realized how badly I wanted that for Anson. Friends. Normalcy. We both deserved it.

Tom turned his attention back to me. "Are you excited to go home tomorrow, Lydia?"

"Me? Oh, uh, I'm actually staying behind." I pursed my lips and avoided Anson's gaze. It killed me knowing that, by this time tomorrow, I'd be all alone. "You know, lots to do, and all that."

Tom nodded. "Yes, the Program. I can't imagine the prep work you have to do for that." He lobbed off a massive bite of some kind of fancy bun. "I'm staying, too. The New Year's edition of the paper is huge. I'm tragically behind. I'm only popping in here for the food, actually. Then I'm headed back." He pointed at me. "You should stop by the newsroom while you're on break. Get a feel for things."

Before I could answer, Willa appeared out of nowhere, gasping for breath. "Why aren't you guys dancing?"

"Just taking a break," I told her. "This is Tom, the editor from the paper."

"Oh, cool!" she replied absentmindedly as she adjusted her shoe.

Tom regarded her with his mouth gaping, a half-eaten bun still held between his fingers and hovering over his plate.

Willa stood and fanned her face. "I need a drink."

Tom hastily set down his food and grabbed a full glass of water from a tiered tray. "Here."

Willa, seemingly oblivious of how the man seemed utterly taken with her, downed the glass of ice water. "Thanks. Now I need a real one. Anyone care to get drunk and dance till our feet bleed?"

The band eased into a slow tune, a lovely melody that carried softly through the Great Hall. Some took a much-needed seat while others paired up and headed for the center of the room. The ceiling changed to a darker sky, the stars shining brighter as the snow dissipated. Willa quirked a playful eyebrow at us and then to Tom.

"Care to take me for a spin?" she asked. Before the poor guy could even answer, she grabbed him by the hand and led him away.

Nothing stopped that girl. Some people might call me bold, but Willa was fierce.

"She's a real people person, isn't she?" Anson muttered.

I sighed happily as Willa and Tom embraced and slipped right into a comfortable waltz. She was the epitome of wholeness. Too good for most people I knew in this world. I was lucky to call her my friend.

I playfully shoved at Anson's arm. "You're one to talk. I thought you *didn't like people.*"

"I don't," he replied flatly.

"Then what the hell was that?" I jabbed. "You and Tom seem like old chums."

"We…have someone in common." He plucked a piece of chocolate from a tray and nibbled at it. He rolled his eyes when he realized I wasn't going to stop prying. "Tom is… Norah's brother."

"Oh." I uncrossed my arms. "Yeah, I see the resemblance." I thought of the picture Anson had of Norah back in his room. "So, you guys are close?"

He stuffed his hands in his pockets and shrugged. "I suppose. If I were to call anyone in this place a…friend, it'd be Tom." Anson turned toward the crowd and sighed. "He was one of the few people who didn't blame me for Norah's death. Tom's…good."

"Yeah, I can see that." I turned and stood with him, our arms pressed together and our fingers entwined. "I'm excited to start on the paper."

Anson squeezed my hand. "Yeah? Excited enough to dance?"

His eyebrows raised in mock excitement.

I couldn't help but laugh. "Fine. One more dance."

He spun me back onto the dance floor and took me by the waist as a slow lullaby cooed in the air. Our chests pressed against each other, and I held him tight. The feel of his body —lithe and warm—and the smell of his skin soothed my soul. I could get lost in Anson.

His mouth brushed my ear, and a chill tingled my spine. "Did I tell you how absolutely stunning you look tonight?"

I slipped my hands inside his black blazer. "A time or two." My head leaned against his shoulder, and I felt him sigh happily in my arms as we swayed to the music. "I love you."

His heart quickened beneath my ear. "I love you, too."

"Are you...feeling better?"

We swayed quietly for a moment.

"I'm fine," he eventually replied and pulled away. His hands gripped my arms. "Can I take you somewhere?"

"You mean get out of here?" I replied and threw him a coy smirk. "Is it to your room?"

He chortled and pressed his forehead to mine. "Just come with me."

I followed him out of the Great Hall and down a dark corridor. Breathless, we came to a stop. He glanced around. Everyone was at the dance. The halls were empty.

He waved his hand in the air, around and around in a circle until the empty space glimmered like wet glass. A portal appeared, glowing an icy blue, and I saw the dull image of a full moon on the other side.

"Where are we going?" I asked.

He held out his hand. "It's a surprise."

I took his hand, and he pulled me through the portal. We exited on the other side, and I shivered immediately. My tissue-thin dress barely offered a scrap of warmth.

We were outside. On a random rooftop. The tiny terrace must have been only four or five feet wide, but it was enough for us to comfortably stand.

Anson slugged out of his blazer and threw it over my shoulders. I graciously accepted and stuck my arms through the sleeves, relishing in the warmth he left behind. Moonlight poured down over us.

"Thanks." I leaned into him. "So, why are we outside? On the *roof*?"

"I know you're not a fan of this time of year," Anson began, "but it's one of my favorites, so hopefully I can change your opinion."

I shifted in his arms and peered up at him, waiting for him to continue.

"Before my parents died, it was also my mom's favorite

time of year," he explained. "She'd take me out, on this very night, year after year when I was little. She would tell me fantastical stories of the moonlight tonight. How it was so powerful, it could charge all the magic you'll need for the New Year. It was our tradition and, after they died, my grandparents continued it with me."

Awe filled my heart. "I think that's the most you've ever shared with me in one breath."

"Well." He sighed, and a hint of nervousness came through. "You mean a great deal to me, Lydia. I want you to be happy. I want you to be a part of my life."

We collided in one fell swoop, and I planted my mouth on his, dying to get as close as I could to this amazing human being before me. Our connection, whatever dynamic pull of the universe brought us together, was almost painful at times.

My fingers raked through his hair and squeezed at the back of his head as he pressed his lips to mine, warm and hungry. I felt him smile and opened my eyes to meet his pitless gaze.

"And I hope to make a new memory with you on this night," he added.

"Is that so?" I challenged playfully. "What did you have in mind?"

With a grin, Anson held out a hand and snapped his fingers. "To watch the wonder in your eyes."

I felt a change in the air; it tensed, and I held my breath as I waited for something to happen. My heart warmed when a single snowflake fell between us. And then another. And another.

My eyes glossed over. "You didn't."

He nodded calmly. "I did."

I tossed my head back and laughed at the midnight sky as moonlight reflected off every snowflake that fell around us. More and more, they sprinkled down in gentle handfuls, and I delighted in every one of them. They melted on my tongue and piled on my shoulders. It was beautiful.

"Best Christmas ever." I beamed.

Anson took me in his arms and demanded my mouth. I happily succumbed to his influence on my body, and a rush of heat seared through my center. I felt his fingers crawling up my dress, caressing the tender skin of my inner thigh. A gasp escaped my throat, and he kissed me harder.

When he pressed me up against the stone railing, I hiked a leg around his waist, and he leaned into me, his heat burning against my own. And while my body exploded with desire, my mind spun with emotions. I loved this man so much. I needed him like I needed to breathe, and it pained me to even think of ever losing him, after falling so far. It'd crush me.

Which meant I had to do whatever it took to protect him, whether he wanted me to or not.

CHAPTER 10

Loneliness used to be something I lived with. Tolerated, even. But just a few short months at Arcane Academy changed me in ways I never thought would happen. I had people. Willa and Anson. My home away from home. And now they were both leaving for two weeks.

I walked Willa to the grand entrance while I waited for Anson. He wanted the crowd to be cleared out before he left. A quiet exit, he called it.

Willa dragged her rolling suitcase through the winding halls of the school as I walked beside her. Only a few stragglers remained on campus: those who had no families or just simply wished to stay. The dean and a few faculties were tasked with remaining on the grounds, too.

The stone palace echoed with the hum of silence.

"When's Anson leaving?" Willa asked as we entered the front foyer of the school.

We stopped, and she leaned her elbow against her suitcase.

"I'm meeting him here in a few minutes." I stuck my hands in my grey jeans and rocked back on the heels of my sneakers. "I hope you have a nice Christmas."

She threw one arm around me for a quick hug. "Anything you want me to bring back from the mundane world?"

I pulled away. "I would literally kill for some newspapers. Magazines. Anything that will tell me all the juicy things that have happened since I left."

Willa zipped up her poofy navy jacket.

"And a burger. Any kind," I added. "From a drive through. I don't even care if it's cold."

We laughed, and she kicked her suitcase on an angle as she hauled on the extended handle. "See you. Don't do anything stupid."

I feigned offense as she walked away, and I waved before she disappeared outside. I strolled over to the massive picture window that lined the foyer and watched Wicked Born and their luggage vanish through a portal just outside the front steps of the school, all going home to be with their families. Another pang of loneliness crawled through me.

"Miss me already?"

Anson's sudden voice startled me, but the breath of his words warmed my ear. I turned to find him directly behind me, a loaded backpack slung over one shoulder. I shoved at his chest, and he set the bag down.

"Damn, you walk like a cat," I said.

He held me, and I relaxed into his arms where I'd happily stay for the rest of the day. But the magnitude of what awaited me beckoned like a hammer to the head. In just a few minutes, my mother would be arriving via portal in the Dark Dean's office. I had to go.

With a moan, I peeled away from Anson's warm chest and stretched on my toes to give him a kiss. His jaw lowered, and I gloated inside when he took the entirety of my mouth in his. It was an unexpected kiss, full of desperation and the same ache that I felt inside. I didn't want him to go.

He pressed his forehead to mine and sighed heavily against my face. "I'm going to miss you."

"It's only a couple of weeks," I reminded him, trying to play it cool. Really, deep down, I was a wreck.

"I'll try my best to come back early," he promised.

I stepped back, making it easier for him to leave. "Don't worry about me, I'll be fine." My fingers wrung together at my back. "I'm sure it'll take me a week just to find the newsroom," I added jokingly.

He wavered in place, uncertainty on his solemn face.

"Are you…feeling okay?" I asked, my eyebrows raised over widened eyes to insinuate I meant more. His powers. The veins on his chest.

He said nothing but nodded gently.

I inched closer. No one was around, but I couldn't risk the chance of prying ears. "I didn't want to say anything last night. Didn't want to ruin the beautiful evening you planned." I swallowed nervously. "But I think Nash might have something to do with what's wrong with you. I don't think it's your magic."

His purse-lipped response told me it wasn't news to him.

I narrowed my eyes. "You knew?"

His shoulders slumped, and he pinched the bridge of his nose. "No, not exactly. But I…assumed."

"Why didn't you tell me?" I asked quietly. "You let me believe it was nothing, just your rusty powers," I added with spitey air quotations.

"What? And have you storming through the school to break Crane's neck or something?" Anson let his head fall to the side. "Come on, Lydia. You and I both know you wouldn't have dealt with that news well."

My face pinched in offence. "What's that supposed to mean?"

He chortled and slipped a hand around my waist. "Your hybrid powers make you a bit of a hot head. If you haven't noticed."

I crossed my arms in the tight space between us. "Only when it comes to the people I care about."

Anson kissed my forehead. "And that's one of the many things I love about you."

I brightened and tipped my face up to him. "What are some of the others?"

He smirked and tucked my hair behind my ear.

"Don't be greedy, now." He moved to reach down and grab his backpack before kissing me once again. "Leave Crane alone. We'll fix this when I get back. It's probably just residual effects of the magic he hit me with, or some stupid, harmless hex. I doubt he's capable of much else."

We both knew that was a lie. But I said nothing.

"Don't you have to meet your mom?" he said and slung his bag over his shoulder.

I pulled my phone out and checked the time. "Yeah, any minute now." I heaved a sigh. "I'll miss you. I hope you have a nice holiday with your grandparents."

Anson hesitated. I'd give anything to know what was spinning around in that mind of his. But before I could ask, he headed for the door. I stood in place, willing myself not to follow him out of here and to the mundane world I missed so much. As he reached the door, he glanced over his shoulder and mouthed the words 'love you.'

And then he was gone.

Before this morning, I had a world of problems spinning around me in constant orbit: keeping my new powers a secret, preparing for a competition for leadership that I had no right contending in, the health of the man I loved. Among a million other things.

But now I had a new issue that fought its way to the forefront of my brain. I needed to find out what Nash Crane had done to Anson.

A realization swept across my mind. I was all alone, left to my own devices for almost two weeks with the knowledge of where The Midnight Circle secretly gathered. They had all gone home for the holidays, and I bet I could find some answers down in that hidden area.

My phone buzzed with a final reminder to go meet my mom. Super secret covert recon would have to wait. The academy was about to welcome its very first Light Faction leader to the campus East Side, and I was lucky enough to be witnessing it.

Plus…I really missed my mom.

I hurried through the near-empty halls toward the Dark Dean's office and knocked at the door. I expected him to bellow from the other side as he often did but was surprised to have the thick wooden door swing open and a strange, stumpy man in a black suit greet me with an expressionless face.

"Uh, I'm here to…I'm Lydia Laveau." The words almost came out as a question.

He stepped aside and ushered me in. "You're late."

"Lydia, dear," Mr. Blackwood said. He sported his usual slick grey suit, his jacket removed to reveal the pinstripes of his tailored white shirt. "So good of you to finally join us."

The door closed behind me, and I inched farther into the room. Others were there. Hallowell, another faculty member I didn't know, and some woman I didn't recognize. An elder, I assumed. Here to witness history in the making. And a hush hush mother-daughter visit. I felt extremely self-conscious against the way their eyes fell on me as if I were on display. No one, aside from the dean, seemed to welcome my presence.

"Sorry," I replied. "I was saying goodbye to my friends."

"Well, you're here now," the dean said cheerily. Almost… too much. "That's all that matters. Constance was about to open the portal for your mother." He came around to the front of his desk. "Perhaps introductions are in order first," he added and motioned with a hand around the room. "Lydia, this is Professor Hark. He's a fifth-year teacher of Dark Arts.

Elder Constance Matthews, here to assist in opening the private portal. And you know Professor Hallowell."

I nodded and smiled at each of them, even Hallowell, who made no secret of his distaste for me in the way he refused to acknowledge my presence. Constance—an older woman with black curls neatly arranged in an updo to match the professional manner in which she seemed to conduct herself—gave me a smile that didn't quite reach her eyes.

"Right, very good then," she said in a British accent that surprised me. "Stand back, please."

I knew we had Elders all over the world, but I expected someone more…local…for this particular event. How far up did my mother's arrival affect those who controlled our world, to send someone like Constance here to open the portal? Why couldn't the Dark Dean just do it? Was he not allowed? Was he not able?

I leaned against the edge of the dean's desk, just inches from where he stood in wait, both of us staring ahead at Constance who waved her hands in a circular motion. Her eyes closed, and her lips moved with the faintest chant, too low for anyone to hear in the small area.

The air began to hum and morph into a blurry circle, and I felt my ears plug from the sudden pressure around us. Beside me, the dean tensed, and I couldn't help but observe him from the corner of my eye, how his hands gripped the edge of his desk behind him, squeezing hard, his fingers fidgeting.

Was he nervous? What lengths did he go to for this, to get my mother here for me? I hadn't given it much thought until now, but perhaps I owed him more than the disgruntled attitude I threw at him.

The portal shimmered with movement, and a shadowed figure appeared in the distance. Tall, lean, the shape of a crisp pant suit evident. To me, anyway. I'd recognize my mother a mile away. My heart quickened like a giddy child as I watched a leg step through, followed by the rest of her. Lace Laveau in all her glory.

She stepped just inside the portal on this end, and it snapped shut behind her, releasing the pressure in the room and making my ears finally pop.

Silver suitcase in hand and dressed head to toe in white with her blonde hair hanging straight to her waist, Mom grinned as her eyes landed on me.

I leaped for her open arms.

"Mom," I muttered against her chest. I pressed my face to her, relishing in the familiar smell of home.

She held me tightly. "My Goddess, it's good to hold you again."

Someone cleared their throat behind us, and I tore myself away to stand next to her and face them. Constance pulled out a clipboard and read from it.

"Lace Laveau, High Priestess of your coven and a leader of the Light Faction, you've been granted passage to the East Side of Arcane Academy for three days, and three days only. You will be permitted to spend this time with your daughter, Lydia Laveau, who is a student of the Dark Faction. You will not venture outside of the designated areas and shall not be allowed access to our resources or teachings. Do you comply?"

One of Mom's sleek, manicured eyebrows arched. "Yes."

Mr. Blackwood pushed away from his desk and took a step toward us, a hand out as a gesture of good faith. "Lace, it's a pleasure to have you visiting us here on the East Side. I, for one, hope this can be the beginning of something new, something...better for our Wicked Born world."

She didn't shake his hand. "Mr. Blackwood. Firstly, I may not be a standing member of your faction, but I do expect to be addressed with the same respect that my position demands. You'll refer to me as Ms. Laveau during my stay. I am here to see my daughter since you refuse to release her to come home." Her eyes flashed with a glare. "Where she belongs."

The dean held his composure, but I caught the slightest hint of bewilderment on his face as he tucked his hand into the little pocket of his silver vest. "Yes, right. Well, for argument's sake, I'd like to make it clear that Lydia is no prisoner here. I care for her safety, as I do all my students. I was merely taking action to keep her safe."

Mom guffawed and regarded the rest with an unfriendly tone. "Thank you all for being here to ensure my safe arrival. I look forward to spending time with my daughter. It won't go unnoticed. I shall report back in kind to the Light Faction Elders."

"Lace," the dean said but quickly corrected himself when Mom's head snapped in his direction. "Ms. Laveau, we hope you enjoy your time here. Myself and most of the staff will be on the grounds at all times if you need anything, but will leave you alone otherwise."

Hallowell chortled. "A grave mistake, if you ask me."

Mom plastered on a mocking grin. "Well, it's a good thing no one asked you. Isn't it?"

Professor Hallowell crossed his arms in a huff, and part of me was relieved to see him behave that way with someone other than me. Even though it was my mom, his rotten attitude was clearly not generalized toward me as a person. Apparently, his disdain was for *all* of Light Born witches. I didn't know which was worse.

Mom turned her attention back to the dean and raised her chin. "I assume I have my own private quarters?"

He gave a tired smile. "Yes, of course."

Geez, I almost felt bad for the guy. He was a man revered here at the academy, and, while I still didn't trust him, I'd come to find myself sort of liking him. At least, more so than Hallowell. Regardless, no one stood a chance against Lace Laveau's rock solid demeanor. No one. She was like a wall of ice.

"Come on, Mom," I said to cut the tension in the room,

reminding everyone that a student was present. "I'll show you to your quarters."

After we said our goodbyes and emerged into the vastness of the empty campus, Mom glanced around and pushed me aside. Her slender arms wrapped around me, and I secured mine around her waist.

"I just wanted to give you a proper hug," she mumbled against the side of my head. "Away from prying eyes."

I pulled away, tears tickling the back of my eyes. "I missed you so much, Mom. You have no idea. I have so much to tell you—"

She cupped her hand over my mouth. "Not here. Where's my room?"

I led her through the stone halls until I found the guest wing and slipped into Mom's quarters. It was exactly like mine and Willa's, only it had one large bed and a private bathroom.

Mother shut the door behind her, then turned to me with a finger over her lips. I picked up the signal and nodded. She set her bag down and fished around in the pockets of her white blazer to pull out two small vials of a strange purple substance. She handed one to me.

Without question, I followed her lead and downed the whole potion. It burned like salt on a wound all the way down to my empty stomach, and a wave of nausea swept over me. But a familiar taste came to life in my mouth.

"Vesicious?" I asked.

Mom nodded with pride. "You remember."

"Well, kinda hard to forget something I've tasted a hundred times."

She removed her jacket and folded it neatly before draping it over the back of a chair.

"It's necessary. Our words will fall on deaf ears, except our own. Now," she said, gripping my arms and looking me square in the eye, "tell me everything."

CHAPTER 11

I SAT on Mom's bed as she paced the floor in front of me, painfully digesting everything I'd told her so far. What happened after I was taken from the Sorting Ceremony. How Nash and Ferris befriended me, immediately gained my trust, and then betrayed me. How the Dark Dean pushed me into this Courtship Program.

I'd never seen such a variation of expressions cross my mother's face in such a short amount of time. It was a lot. I knew that. But I'd been dying for weeks to tell her, to get her input and stick my head back on straight.

So, why didn't I feel any better?

"Okay, so this Nash Crane," she said as she continued to pace. "He tried to kill you?"

I sighed. "No. Not really. I mean...I'm not sure what he was trying to do, actually." I slid back on the mattress and brought my knees up to my chin. "He needed me, *still* needs me for something. I'm just not sure what. Willa and I have a theory that he just wants to be tied to me. To my name, the attention that constantly surrounds me."

"To gain authority in this Midnight Circle?" she asked.

I shrugged. "Maybe. I honestly don't know. He's so seedy.

So...calculated. It's difficult to know his true motives behind any of his actions. But one thing's for sure, this secret coven he's part of? They're trying to tap into this ancient power from a witch named Talia Blackstone."

"Why would they need you for that?"

"I think...I have reason to believe...that she was special. Utterly insane and evil, but special, nonetheless. She could wield both light and dark magic. Like me."

Mom came to a halt and regarded me with a calculating stare. "How——" She shook her head slowly. "Why would you think such a thing?"

"Mom." I tipped my head to the side. "Come on. Do you honestly think I'm the only one? This hybrid magic, it's new, but at the same time, old. So, so old. I can feel the ancient tie to it, deep down in my gut, every time I tap into it."

Quietly, Mom sat next to me, and the mattress gave with her meager weight. "Tell me more about this hybrid magic."

I rifled through my brain for a way to explain it. It still made zero sense to me. "It's like...a source, deep inside my soul. Something that was awakened during my Sorting Ceremony." I hung my head and picked at a fraying hole in my jeans. "But maybe I felt it before that. The more I think about it, I sensed this coming. Felt there was something different about me for a while now."

"A mixture of your light and dark magic?" she asked.

I gnawed at my lip. "I have my light magic; I can feel it's familiarity. And then my new dark magic. It's simple, easy to harness. Hums under the surface of my skin, ready to use." I inhaled deep and slow. "Then there's..."

Mom turned to me. "The hybrid power."

"It's something else entirely. I can reach deep and tap into it, and it funnels through my light and dark magic, depending on what I feel like using. But I haven't quite figured out how to regulate it. I...sometimes lose control."

"What do you mean?" Mom reached across the bed and held my hand. "Has anyone seen this?"

I thought of the time I ran across the fields, screaming and burning everything in my wake. That was the first time I'd kissed Anson. A smile crept across my lips, but the sudden strain on Mom's face to elicit information from me made me uneasy. Almost as if she already knew this information. Or parts of it, and I was only filling in some holes.

What was she not telling me?

"No," I said curtly and relaxed my knees to lay my legs flat in front of me. "No one saw. No one knows."

Mom's eyebrows pinched together. "Not even your supplement?"

"Willa, Mom," I replied. "Her name is Willa." I'd almost forgotten the tone Light Born used when referring to the half witches. But the discrimination wasn't any different over here. It reminded me just how important it was to protect my secret, and something in the back of my mind told me to keep it that way. A secret. "And, no. She doesn't know I'm a hybrid witch. She just thinks I'm a powerful Dark one."

My stomach soured with every lying word I uttered, but something deep in the very fibers of my being screamed to keep that a secret. During the few short months I'd spent at Arcane East, I'd wanted my mother so desperately. Her stern but wise mind always pointed me in the right direction. Even when I didn't want it to.

But now I saw her in a new light. She seemed...desperate. Anxious. Maybe it was from being submersed in the Dark Faction, or maybe I was just paranoid. But Anson and Willa were the only ones who knew my secret, and I hadn't truly considered how much danger could fall upon them if the wrong people found out they knew. They could be used as tools against me.

It would only be a matter of time before people found out that Anson and I were the same. We'd be thrown in some magical lab somewhere and studied. At best. I couldn't put that attention on them.

Mom stood and began pacing again. "Tell me more about this Courtship Program."

I sighed in relief at the change of subject. "I'd never heard of it before. The Dark Born certainly covet it and protect its secrecy to the highest degree. It's how they elect their leaders. The strongest Wicked Born students are handpicked by the dean, faculty, and elders. They compete in a series of magical tests until there's only one man and woman left standing. Those two are then ushered into special classes for leadership for the remainder of their pledge."

My mother slowly nodded, her gaze distant and deep as she gripped her hips.

I wasn't sure how much more I could share with her, and our hour was running out. "Have you ever heard of anything like this? Does the Light Faction have some kind of program like that?"

She shook her head. "We choose our leaders based on merit and power. This Courtship Program sounds ludicrous and barbaric. Are you expected to...*be* with the male winner?"

My eyes widened. "Oh, no. *No*, not at all. Not romantically, anyway. It's how they keep things fair, so the scales of leadership don't tip too far to one side. The two winners will be groomed together and represent the new generation of Dark Wicked Born. They will make decisions together and stuff, but not actually be together in any way. Not if they don't want to." I paused and thought about Anson. "Willa and I hope to be the last team standing, next to...my boyfriend."

Mom froze, her eyes going wide. "Boyfriend?"

I smiled nervously. "Yeah, Anson. The one I told you about from the cave incident. We've been dating."

"And you were both chosen for the Program?"

"Not exactly," I replied. "The dean chose me. But Anson

volunteered after he saw that Nash would be competing with me. He doesn't have a supplement so it's just him. But he's..." I couldn't tell her his secret. It wasn't mine to share. "Anson's a third year Wicked Born here, and he has a fair chance at winning with me. Even though he's doing it alone, without a supplement."

She took a couple of steps toward the bed and peered down at me with a motherly gaze. One full of worry and...something else. Something she wasn't saying. "But do you want to win?"

"Well, of course I want to win. The alternative isn't so great, if you recall..."

"Let me rephrase," she said and brought her hands together, her back straight as a board. "Do you want to *compete?*"

I cringed. "Well, no. Not really." Words seemed to evade me as I fought with a sudden rush of unexpected feelings toward the whole ordeal. I felt a sense of...protectiveness. But over what, exactly? "I mean, I want to compete and win to ensure that someone like Nash doesn't."

"Yes, but what do *you* want, baby?" Mom repeated with urgency and knelt at my feet. She peered up at me with a look of desperation.

I shook my head helplessly. "I want what I've always wanted. To be normal. To practice magic as I see fit and live a quiet life in the world I grew up in."

The words rang true. I'd thought them over and over for years. But now, saying them out loud, hearing my own voice speak my lifelong feelings...they seemed alien. In just a short amount of time here at the academy, my needs and wants had changed completely. I had people I cared about, people who would do anything for me. A family. People who understood me and could share in the secret world I had to work so hard to hide all my life. I found my people in Anson and Willa.

"Why, Mom?" I asked finally. "What's with all the questions?"

She cupped a hand on each side of my face and searched my eyes with a sense of protection. "I'm going to get you out of this."

"What? The Program?"

"All of it," she replied. "The Courtship Program, the Dark Faction." My heart thumped hard and fast in my chest. "I'm going to take you home."

~

THE WISPY TENDRILS of a dream tugged at me from all around. Still, I carried with me all the torment and stress of my real life. It weighed me down like a bag of rocks, and I dragged it across the blank threshold of my empty dream.

Darkness surrounded me. All except for a tiny spot of light in the distance. A little speck, like a single star in a black sky. It grew larger the closer I got until I stepped through into a sun-filled room. Glass hovered above like an invisible canopy with vines crawling over every nook and cranny.

"Lydia?" Anson spoke, and I whipped around to find him standing there, stunned that I was in this strange place. "What are you doing here?"

I ran to him, across the eerie solarium, and we collided in a painful crash. Anson gasped in my arms, and his face twisted in pain as he looked at me with betrayal in his eyes. Confused, I pulled away and glanced down to where his hand pressed against his chest. Crimson dripped over his fingers.

"Jesus Christ! Anson!" I cried and reached out to him.

He backed away. "Why? Why would you do this, Lydia?"

Fear paralyzed me. "Do *what*? What do you mean?"

From one blink to the next, the handle of a dagger appeared in his hand, the blade buried deep in his chest.

Shaking, I slowly raised my hands and looked at them in horror. They were covered in blood.

Another blink and the dagger was now in my grip, and I shrieked before letting it drop to the floor. Anson leaped toward me and grabbed hold of my arms, shaking me with rage.

"How could you do this to me?" he bellowed. "You knew this would happen, didn't you?"

Dumbfounded, I shook my head as tears froze in my eyes. "I-I have no idea what's happening!"

"Yes, you do," a voice sounded just to our left.

My head turned slowly, despite the panic that coursed through my body, as if the confines of the nightmare struggled to hold me in place. The stranger was a man, tall and slim, dressed all in black. A hat tipped over his face, and he raised his head to reveal himself. Familiarity tickled my mind as I stared at him.

Then it struck me.

"You!" I said accusingly.

The memories of our first and only encounter seeped to the forefront of my mind. The night before my Sorting Ceremony. The man who gave me that potion vial I drank under the tree which led me to completely ruin the big evening Mom had planned.

"Who the hell *are* you?" I asked.

The man disappeared in a puff of smoke and then reappeared right in front of me, where Anson was standing only seconds ago. The only proof my boyfriend was ever there was the pool of blood at my feet.

"You know who I am," he said, his voice now different. Familiar. "You wanted this. All of it."

"No!" I shrieked and backed away, my blood-covered hands shaking. My eyes squeezed shut. "Not this!"

"Open your eyes, Lydia," he said calmly.

I refused. I just wanted this nightmare to end. The threads

that held the dream together began to unravel, and I felt myself drifting. Relief pulsed through my veins; I was waking up! But the man's strong hands gripped my shoulders, holding me down, and he shook me so hard I thought my neck would break.

"Look at me!" he bellowed.

My eyes flew open just as I felt the tangible pull of reality yanking me away and the man's face had changed from the stranger to that of someone I knew.

Mr. Blackwood.

He reached for me as I drifted away, but I couldn't go back now. I let the call of morning take me, and I woke with a start.

I laid still, quietly gasping for breath and taking in my surroundings. Sweat covered my tense body as I glanced around and noted that Mom slept next to me. We crashed in her room during some late hour last night. I rolled over and stretched uncomfortably. I missed my bed.

"Morning," Mom croaked and rubbed her face as she pulled herself upright. "Sleep well?"

"Like the dead." I slung my legs over the side of the mattress. I still carried the trauma of my nightmare on my shoulders. "I'm going to grab a shower. Do you want to get some breakfast afterwards? We can do the mess hall, or there's a few places in the village."

Mom's platinum hair glowed in the sunlight streaming through the windows, and she smiled tiredly. "Best stick to the mess hall. I'm not sure how far my invitation extends."

I nodded. "Right." My feet slipped into my sneakers, and I stood. "I'll meet you in the mess hall in half an hour then? You know where it is?"

"I'm sure I'll manage," she replied and tightened her robe sash as she began making the bed. She paused for a moment and examined me standing there like a zombie. "You okay?"

I blinked away the film that skimmed over my eyes and grabbed my hoodie from a chair.

"Yeah, just tired." I headed for the door. "See you in a bit," I added and then left, my sloppy footsteps the only sound to be heard as I walked the empty halls toward my room.

I couldn't shake the chill that inhabited my body. The cold sweat that came from the nightmare that still poisoned my brain.

What did it all mean? I'd had prophetic dreams before, but nothing like that. Was the stress of everything just weighing too heavy? Things like Anson's degrading health. Or the safety of those I cared for. Or what plan Mom could possibly have that would get me out of my pledge.

Did I even want her to?

I shoved it all aside as I got ready and headed for the mess hall to meet her. But try as I might, I couldn't get the nagging thoughts out of my mind. I expected having Mom here would help clear the clutter and set me on the right path, but I'd only piled more questions on top of the mountain that sat on my conscience.

As I entered the mess hall, I immediately spotted my mother. She waved at me from an empty table, one of many in the sea of long surfaces. Only a few Wicked Born hung around, sipping coffees silently as they read a book or trudged tiredly around in their pajamas. They gave me weak smiles, which was more than I could ever expect, but I caught the leering glances at my mom. I was an outcast misfit, but she truly didn't belong.

I sat across from Mom—two servings of oatmeal and coffee in front of us—and her lips pinched together. "I don't know how you put up with this every day."

I shrugged and grabbed one of the two coffees. "You get used to the weird stares. It's expected. I mean, I'm different." I sipped the warm java and threw her a sarcastic smirk. "And you know how much our world loves different things."

Mom sat rigid and tense as she daintily spooned her oatmeal.

CANDACE OSMOND & REBECCA HAMILTON

I sighed. "It helps to have friends. People to care about you."

"Well, you won't have to deal with it much longer."

I stifled the impulse to say anything at all; I still had to sort through my feelings on that. I could escape all of this. Leave this nightmare behind and get back to Jade, back to my life. But was it my life, really? Things had changed so much in my short time here. Now I had Anson and Willa. And I actually enjoyed my classes. I was becoming my own person.

"Tell me more about this boyfriend and supplement of yours," Mom said cheerily, a weak attempt to change the subject.

"Anson and Willa, Mom," I said and fought back an eye roll. Was she purposely refusing to say their names? "Willa is...I feel like I've known her my whole life. You'd adore her. She's a genius, hard working, doesn't let me get away with my usual crap."

Mom nodded thoughtfully. "And your boyfriend?"

"Anson is..." I smiled as I thought of him. "He's amazing. He's everything I could ever hope for. He's sweet, smart, passionate, and so many other things."

"Handsome?" she asked and drank from her mug.

I laughed. "Oh yeah, you have *no* idea. Sometimes I wonder if he's too pretty for his own good."

"You never showed an interest in boys back home," she replied.

"I guess I never wanted to make those connections, those reasons to stay. It was hard enough leaving Jade."

A ping of sadness stung my chest as I thought of my childhood best friend. Jade stopped replying to my texts a while ago, and I didn't have the heart to keep nagging her. I had nothing to offer our friendship anymore and didn't want to drag her back like that. Waiting for me, when it would be years before I could really see her again. Maybe longer now; I had no idea the roads that leadership could lead me down after the Program was over.

If I won.

Things would be even worse if I didn't.

"But you have Willa now," my mother quickly said as if my melancholy had splashed on my face.

"Yeah." I brightened and shifted forward in my seat, eager to share more about my friend. "She's so powerful, Mom. I've never seen anything like it. And just as smart. I had no idea supplements were like that. It's not as Light Born assume; they're not leeches. They're...an extension of us. She's a catalyst for my magic and, together, we're a force to be reckoned with. Even now, in these fledgling years of our pledge. I can only imagine what we could do in a few years."

"Would she come with you?"

"What?" Her question didn't fit in my mind as I revelled over the idea of me and Willa. But then I realized what she meant. Come with me, away from the academy. Away from the Dark Faction. I masked my mixed emotions with a shrug and lifted my steaming mug to my mouth. "Maybe."

What was happening? A couple of months ago, I would have jumped in my mother's arms at the slightest mention of getting me out of there. But now, after everything I'd been through—with Nash, with Anson, getting closer to Willa—I couldn't bear the thought of leaving.

I had a place here. Responsibilities. Goals. Things to prove. I suddenly questioned everything. Like, where did my true loyalties lie? With the world I grew up in?

Or the one I'd been chosen for?

CHAPTER 12

Mom and I spent most of the day wandering the campus as I showed her all the places I frequented: the solarium, the library, and a few of my classrooms, mostly empty of people.

Maybe a dozen Wicked Born had stayed behind, and a small handful of faculty. And Arcane Academy was a monster of a castle. It needed our presence like we needed to breathe. Without its walls cinched with witches, the stone beast slept in an eerie silence that echoed through the halls.

"So, that's about it," I said and flapped my hands at my side as I turned to face Mom. We stood in the mess hall after making a full circle around campus. "The only thing left to show you is the quarters I share with Willa." I smiled. "My... home, I guess."

Mom peered around the cafeteria, slow and content. My nose told me supper was being made in the kitchen. Something spicy.

"It's lovely, Lydia," she said and glanced at me from the corner of her eye. "Much like the West side, yet...different, still." She turned to me straight on and sighed happily. "Lead the way."

I was silent as we walked to my room. Much like I was for

most of the day. I was stuck in an internal battle with myself over how I truly felt about leaving. Mom seemed so sure she could get me out, but part of me didn't want her to. A large part.

I unlocked the door and gave it a shove as Mom filed in behind me. I grinned at the physical display of mine and Willa's personalities in the side-by-side fashion of our bedroom.

My end was full of belongings haphazardly tossed and an unmade bed, while Willa's side looked as though it were professionally cleaned with everything neatly tucked and smoothed, her many books and witchy possessions carefully lining the shelves almost to Lace Laveau standards.

Mom stifled an eye roll at my side and examined everything to the right with a look of surprise. She glanced over at me with a grin. "I think I quite like her."

I gave an exaggerated moan and plopped on my bed. My nest. I liked it messy. The blankets stayed warm longer and held the aroma of Anson for days. I inhaled deeply, as discreet as I could.

My mother—arms crossed across her white blouse—slowly paced the bedroom, looking at our stuff with a motherly inspection. She nodded approvingly at Willa's book collection. I noted then just how lacking mine was. The same bookshelf sat near the foot of my bed and looked twice as big as Willa's because it was so empty. Only a single stack of texts, a few papers, and a couple of knick knacks could be found. A trip to the bookstore in the village was in order.

But wasn't I leaving?

"Your grandmother's grimoire," Mom said as she picked it from my shelf. Her face softened as her fingers reached for something else. "And your father's athame." She set them back and stole a glance at the suitcase on the floor. Still half full of clothing. "Your shelves are almost empty. It hardly looks like you even live here."

"Yeah, I haven't really had the chance to get settled in and fill the space yet." But I wanted to. The realization swept over me hard. I wanted to collect grimoires and stones and stock every corner of the room, the school, with my presence. So... there was my answer. "Mom, don't do anything stupid...to get me out."

She blinked quickly. "Stupid? Lydia, please. Don't you think I have a plan or two? I'd never do anything to jeopardize you. Getting you out shouldn't be hard. I just have to talk to a couple of people." She swallowed. "If...that's what you want. If you're not happy here."

The conflicting urges toyed with my emotions, leaving me unable to really trust my own will. I had an out. I could pack up my stuff and leave this whole nightmare behind me forever. Everything that had happened to break me down—Nash, the Program, being the scourge of the school—all of it could be erased. If I just let Mom help me.

But that wasn't my life now. Despite all the bad things, I found hope among the chaos. Anson and Willa. They were my family now, a part of who I was becoming as a witch. As a person. I couldn't just abandon my supplement; that bond was for life. And I highly doubted Willa would simply leave the academy, not after she sacrificed her relationship with her father just to get here.

And Anson, my heart. I couldn't bear the thought of leaving him now, struggling with whatever was happening to his magic. He hid in the shadows of the school for years before I came along, terrified to reveal his secret. He needed me now more than ever. Almost as much as I needed him.

I inhaled a long, sharp breath of air through my nose, and my stomach clenched. "What would happen?"

"What do you mean?" Mom replied.

"To me. If I leave. What would happen? I've never heard of a Wicked Born abandoning their pledge before."

She came and sat next to me on the bed, her expression

locked in thought. "Well, you're not prisoners in the school. The pledge is a choice. But, if you were to abandon it, you'd no longer have the support and connection to the Wicked Born world." Her lips pursed. "You'd be a rogue witch, like the Irish Travellers or the Romani."

I chewed at my lip. "You know, I'm not...unhappy." Her hands wrought together in her lap.

"I was at first, completely and utterly miserable. Especially when Nash and Ferris betrayed me. I felt like a fool. But I have Anson and Willa now, and they mean a great deal to me. I'm not sure I can leave them. And the Program...my lessons...I'm learning a lot and I think I can actually win this thing. I could move up and become a leader. Have a real say in how our worlds operate." I picked at my chipping nail polish. "That's what you always wanted for me, wasn't it?"

Mom guffawed and shook her head with an incredulous smile. "Yes. I just always imagined you rising up in the Light Faction. Beside me. Here, I'm absolutely mute to your life. I worry every day."

"I'm okay, Mom," I said and reached for her hand. "I promise. You know, it's funny. This whole time all I wanted was for you to come and save me, to fix everything. Like you always do. But having you here is making me realize that I knew the answers to my problems already. I *can* do this."

She gently held my cheek in her hand. "I know, baby."

I stared into her glossy eyes and found in her gaze a rampant mixture of pride and love. But I could still see a hint of worry there, too. Maybe it was a motherly default, or perhaps it was a sign of things to come. Either way, it didn't matter. I knew what I had to do now.

Stay the course. Truly accept my responsibility and embrace the life of a Dark Wicked Born. Settle in and make a life for myself here.

Mom patted my lap as she shook away the soft emotions. She stood and straightened her crisp white blouse and silk slacks. "Why don't you show me that newsroom you'll be working in?"

"I haven't actually been there myself yet," I told her and fumbled to my feet. "But I was going to pop in there over the holidays. Let's go."

It wasn't as hard as I thought to find the newsroom. I ventured to the corridor where Mr. Blackwood's office was and continued down the stretch of narrow space to where a number of other office-type spaces were.

The newsroom sat at the very end, bright and airy from the full wall of windows on one side, to the half a dozen small desks on the other. Overloaded cork boards and messy stacks of newspapers and magazines adorned most of the surfaces. One large rectangular wooden table anchored the room in the center.

Tom spun around in his chair and pushed out from one of the small desks with a welcome smile.

"Lydia," he said cheerily. "I didn't expect to see you around here yet. Bored already?"

I chuckled. "No, I was just showing my mom around and figured I'd pop in."

Eyes wide as he took in my mom, Tom stood from his chair and wiped a Cheeto stained hand on his ripped jeans before offering it to her. "Mrs. Laveau. It's a pleasure."

To my surprise, Mom graciously accepted his hand and gave it a firm shake. "Pleasure's all mine."

"This is Tom Foster," I told her. "He's the lead editor here at the paper."

"We're all excited to have Lydia on the team," he assured her. "I can't wait to see her contributions to this school year's issues."

Mom peered sideways at me. "Well, I'm sure you won't be disappointed. Lydia's a talented journalist."

Tom flipped his messy blond hair away from his face and adjusted his glasses. "I hope so." He looked at me. "I have a pretty awesome first assignment for you, when you're ready."

My chest rose with excitement. "Really?"

"Yeah." He gathered a heap of papers on his desk and came back to us. "Wanna see?"

I was about to reluctantly decline when Mom placed a hand on my shoulder.

"I've got business with the dean to tend to," she said. "You stay. We'll meet up for supper later, okay?"

"Are you sure?" I asked. "You leave tomorrow."

She nodded. "It's just a short while. I'll see you in a bit."

Mom left, and the click of her thick heels against the stone floors of the corridor faded as I entered farther into the room. Tom pulled out one of the chairs that circled the long table and motioned to the seat next to him.

"Sit," he said kindly and rifled through the stack of papers with excitement. He found whatever it was he had been looking for and handed a sheet of paper to me with a list of questions. "First, I have to ask. How are you doing?"

My face twisted with slight confusion. "Doing? Like, overall, or are we talking specifics here?"

Tom chuckled. "Overall, I guess." He took in a deep breath. "Anson asked me to keep an eye out for you."

I nodded in realization.

"He really didn't want to leave you here all alone," Tom added. "But his grandparents—"

"I know," I cut in, not wanting the emotions I stuffed down about missing Anson to bubble up. "They needed him on the farm." An awkward silence fell between us. "So, why did he ask you to keep an eye on me?"

Tom's cheeks reddened. "Uh, well, actually...I offered. He was on the fence about leaving, and I know his grandparents. They would want him to come home, and it would have caused a problem if he hadn't." He neatened the paper stack in front of him. "He wasn't too keen on feeling like he owed me anything, so I played it off as me really needing your help for the New Year's issue."

"Why does he hate owing you anything?"

"It's a bit of a long story..."

I thought for a moment. Then it clicked in place. "Because of your sister."

Tom's face brightened. "Wow, he really does like you."

I said nothing as he stood and leapt for a mini fridge in the corner. He grabbed two bottles of water and sat back down before sliding one over to me.

"Anson will take the guilt of what happened to his deathbed," he went on. "But it was just an accident. An unfortunate accident. Norah knew what she was getting herself into. And I know she'd want me to hang around and keep an eye out for him. And now, by extension, for you."

I cracked the top on the water bottle and took a long sip. "I wish I had the chance to know her. Your sister."

His gaze fell to his lap. "Yeah, she was...amazing. There was nothing she couldn't do. Her and Anson, their bond solidified immediately, and they became inseparable. It was her idea to join the TA program and train to be teachers here at the academy. Sometimes I wonder...if Anson stuck with it for himself, or for her."

A tinge of sadness filled my heart at the thought of never being able to share that with Anson. That connection he had, and then lost. I wished I knew him back then, back before he threw up all those walls I worked so hard to climb over.

"Well, she sounds like she was pretty awesome," I said finally.

Tom pushed a booklet toward me on the table. "She was. And so is Mr. Blackwood."

I stiffened. "What?"

He smiled. "He's your assignment."

I glanced at the list of phrases in my hand. They were interview style questions. "For?"

"The dean has a lot of attention on him right now, being the host of the current Courtship Program. I'd like to have a big feature in the New Year's issue of an in-depth interview with him, and you're the perfect person for the job."

I shook my head as my mouth gaped with an empty response. I had no words. I couldn't imagine sitting in a room and prying the dean with questions he *had* to answer.

I let the idea roll around in my mind for a moment, and a sudden smile crept over my lips. The stolen grimoires, the loose details around my role here at the school, his true reasoning for pushing me into the program...

Maybe I *did* want to keep him in a room and wrench some answers out of him. Lord knows I wasn't getting them anywhere else.

Tom leaned forward, hid hands fidgeting with his files. "Do you not want it? I can assign it to someone else if you have a problem doing it. I mean, I'd understand—"

"No, no." I grabbed the booklet from the table—the title said something about the history of the program—and stood with a triumphant grin. "I'll gladly take it."

I just hoped Mr. Blackwell would cooperate. Something told me there was more to this assignment than Tom was letting on...

CHAPTER 13

I spent the night raking through my brain of all the things I could ask Mr. Blackwood in the interview. So much so that it carried all the way into my tense dreams, and I fell down a rabbit hole until I slammed back into my body the next morning.

I considered telling my mother about my assignment, but part of me whispered worries in my ear. What if she gave me a reason not to? What would she say about me poking around in the dean's mind after she told me to be weary of his actions? And then my own personal concern: how would *he* react? Would he graciously answer everything? Would his answers be lies? Or would his answers only place me in further danger?

Mom and I spent the morning camped out in the library, under the sunny blanket of the solarium. We enjoyed the simple silence as we each read a book and then grabbed some lunch in the mess hall before Mom excused herself to her room for a while.

I paced mine and Willa's bedroom, tidying things and finally finding places for some of my belongings. My bookshelf —while nowhere near as adorned as Willa's—was now half-filled with some things I'd brought from home: pictures and some of my favorite books. I reminded myself of the promise I made to pay a trip to the little bookstore in the village the first chance I got.

The haunting melodies of The Pretty Reckless filled the room as I stuffed my now empty suitcase under the bed. A knock came at the door, and I dodged for it, knowing it would be Mom. She stood there with a pile of objects in her arms and a wide smile on her face.

I glanced at what she brought: jammies neatly folded, a couple of DVDs, some snacks from the mess hall, and a tiny red box on top.

"Christmas movie night?" she asked.

The suggestion drudged up all the memories of the mundane Christmases we used to share together, back during a time when she happily entertained my love of the human world and all its campy traditions.

Solstice was always a busy time for her, having to travel all over the country for the coven to deal with special events and New Year rituals, but she often made time, one night a year, to spend with me. It'd been years now since we binged movies in our pyjamas and exchanged gifts while gorging on junk food. But I wanted it, right then, in the moment. Amidst the chaos that was my new life in the Dark Faction, I wanted some semblance of a simple existence.

I opened the door farther for her to enter. "That sounds exactly like what I need."

I closed the door behind her and watched as an impressive look cast over her. She turned to me. "You cleaned your room."

I shrugged. "I hadn't realized how much of a disaster it was until I saw the sheer look of disapproval on your face when you first got here."

She set her things on my neatly made bed. "And to think, all those years, I could have saved myself the frustration of lecturing you about it and just given you a stern look."

"I'm sure it would have been a failed effort either way," I replied cheekily as I fished a pair of sweatpants and an old band t-shirt out of my closet.

"Most likely," Mom agreed and snapped her fingers. In an instant, her well-pressed cream jumper turned into a set of white pyjamas with silver polka dots. She tied her platinum hair back and grabbed the tiny red box she'd brought. "Here," she added and handed it to me.

"A present?" I asked.

Mom shook her head, a knowing grin on her face. "Not quite."

I held it in my palm and looked closer, noting the intricate filigree detail that blended almost with the same color as the rest of the box. I knew what this was; I could sense the familiarity, and I turned it over in my fingers as I thought. "Wait, is this a Pandora box?"

"Yes," she replied. "I knew it was the only way to bring everything we needed for tonight."

No way.

I rubbed my thumb over the intricate detail work that covered its six surfaces. I hadn't seen a Pandora box in years. There were only a few floating around in existence, and they could really only be acquired through channels unavailable to most Wicked Born because they had the ability to hold entire worlds inside of them.

No one really knew where they came from or who made them, but ancient Wicked Born scoured the Earth centuries ago and made sure they didn't fall into the hands of the wrong people. The Laveau Family possessed two that I knew of. But I'd never seen Mom actually *use* one. They were more like decorative relics on display in her office.

I set the little trinket down in the middle of the rug that divided the room and stepped back as my mother let out a strange whistle no louder than a hum. It carried through the air with colorful wisps and swirled around the Pandora box. The little cube began to glow red and rattle on the floor until the sides fell open and the top disappeared inside.

The air thickened as a bright white light poured out and distorted the space before us. Mom stepped closer to me, and we watched together as a large triangle shadow formed on the rug, standing tall. It quickly sharpened into a Christmas tree, decked out with all the bells and whistles. Garland shot out from the Pandora box and hung themselves from the window and around the tops of shelves.

Then the box snapped shut, leaving us with a six foot, fully decorated tree and a room stuffed with green garland and red bulbs. Twinkle lights added the final touch, and I turned to Mom with a beaming smile.

"You used one of the most ancient and rare artifacts of our world to sneak a *Christmas tree* in the academy?" I asked in bewilderment.

Her shoulder shrugged once. "I knew how much you loved the mundane holiday." The white lights reflected like diamonds off her crystal blue eyes. "And after everything that's been going on, I thought you could use some…normalcy."

Tears pricked behind my eyes. "That's…that's *exactly* what I needed, Mom."

I couldn't help but stare at this woman in awe—the woman I missed so much, not just since my arrival at the school, but for years now. She'd been so cold and distant, strict and full of expectations. A far cry from the fun, loving mother who was there during my childhood. Now I saw a glimpse of that person, here, in my room. In this intimate moment we shared.

We sat cuddled in my bed, surrounded by endless junk food, with my laptop balanced on a small stack of books as we made our way through the DVDs she brought, which included all of my favorite holiday movies: Elf, Home Alone, and A Nightmare Before Christmas. It was the most content I'd been in weeks and, if I closed my eyes, it almost felt like I was home.

But that wasn't my home anymore.

My stomach clenched as the thought sprang to life in my mind. My home was here now. At Arcane Academy. I would spend the next four years of my adult life learning to be a proper witch in our society, navigating the obstacles of adulthood as I discovered who I really was.

And train for leadership, if I won the Courtship Program.

Part of me had finally accepted the path I'd been thrust down. I could embrace life in the Dark Faction, could make a home for myself and Willa until we ventured back into the mundane world. There was still so much I had to figure out about myself, about life and the things I wanted from it. Questions about my future—and my past—that still needed answers.

I fought against the dryness in my throat. "Mom?"

She shoved some popcorn to the side of her mouth. "Yes?"

"Would you...tell me about...Dad?"

She struggled to swallow what was in her mouth as she turned toward me, eyes wide. "Why? What do you mean?"

"I know it's hard for you to talk about him," I replied. "I mean, at all. You've told me nothing about the man who I'm literally half of. I have no clue what he even looks like or how he truly died." Another thought occurred to me. "I don't even know his name, Mom. You didn't take it."

"We never married," she said curtly, her gaze averted from mine and far away in thought. She blinked a few times and finally looked at me with a sigh. "I guess maybe it's time to talk."

I pushed at the mattress and sat up straight, my heart anxious to hear anything she was willing to give. I'd pried for years as a child, only to be met with shortness and anger. I learned to keep my mouth shut the older I got. But I had a right to know.

"Your father was...brilliant," she said, barely above a whisper. "He radiated this happy energy all the time, and people gravitated toward him. Myself included. He loved fearlessly, always had an answer for everything, could sweet talk his way in and out of any situation. His favorite drink was tea. He would eat chocolate until his stomach hurt." A grin appeared on her lips. "And he was devilishly handsome."

My mother had just divulged more details about my father in one breath than she had my entire life. I let the words sink into my mind, take hold of my heart and root there. Tangible details about my dad, the mysterious man I never got the chance to know. The man whose death broke my mother's heart into so many pieces she didn't have the will to put them back together. It must have been hard for her to say so much in that moment.

I squeezed her hand on top of the quilt and inhaled a bubbly breath.

"We fell in love in high school," she continued. "He...left this world shortly after we graduated, right before my Sorting Ceremony. I didn't know I was pregnant at the time."

We let a warm silence hang between us.

"You miss him," I said.

"Always," Mom replied and gingerly tucked my hair behind my ear. "Hard not to when I look at his face in you every day."

My heart warmed. "Really?"

She nodded. "When you came out with that head of stark black hair, I cried for days." Her finger gently traced along my jaw. "The shape of your face, the bridge of your nose. Your eyes, although not quite the same blue as his, have the same wide almond shape to them."

"Thank you," I said quietly, tears brimming in my eyes.

"For giving me that. I know it's not easy for you to talk about him."

I thought of Anson then. Only a short time had passed since we met, but I felt our hearts entwined. A bond that could never be severed. It was love, and it would break me in half if I ever lost him to death. I just couldn't imagine the world without him in it, and I finally met my mother on the same level.

I could see my life through her eyes: the choices she made and the silence she kept about him. She was protecting her fragile heart and probably didn't want to fill mine with someone else's memory of a man I never met.

She flung the blanket off her and turned her back to me as she wiped her eyes. "I, uh, I almost forgot that I brought you something else."

"More surprises?" I moaned. "Mom, no. I didn't get you anything."

She fished around in her large handbag and pulled out a small gift wrapped in white paper, a thick silver ribbon beautifully tied around it. She handed it to me and crawled back under the quilt.

"You don't have to get me anything, Lydia," she replied disapprovingly. "I'm your mother, and I have everything I could possibly ever want in this world." She motioned to the present. "Open it."

I pulled at the ribbon and realized it was enchanted when it disintegrated into thin air. The paper unwrapped itself in my hands and turned to nothing but a wisp of air, leaving two objects sitting in my palm. A black leather belt and a wide, gold ring with a large emerald cast in its center.

"Oh, wow. Thanks, Mom," I said sincerely.

"The belt is meant to hold your father's athame," she told me. "I...don't know why I didn't tell you the night I gave it to you, but the knife is enchanted to only work for him. For his blood. The same blood that runs in your veins. If anyone else were to wield it with intent to harm, they'd be severely burned."

I admired the fine stitchwork on the thick leather strap.

"And this?" I asked, holding the ring between my fingers.

"I acquired this after we spoke through the Mandela Mirror," she explained. "It's a syphon. Wear it on your dominant hand, and any magic you call upon will filter through it and be easier to control." She placed her hands over the items in my grasp. "Keep these with you at all times."

"I will," I promised and slipped the ring over my middle finger. It was more of a miniature cuff and stopped just before my knuckle.

"Especially during the Courtship Program," she added. "From what you tell me, the tests are going to be hard, and everyone will be watching. It's clearly no secret that you're powerful. I imagine people here accepted that with the knowledge of your background. But you need to keep your hybrid magic in check and away from the prying eyes of this faction. Your life depends on it."

I made a fist, and the metal squeezed against my skin. "I'm going to win this, Mom." I heard her breath hitch, and I stared at her with purpose. "I'm going to win the Program and lead this faction into a better future."

Her bottom lip trembled but she smiled through it, her eyes glossy. "I know. That's what I'm afraid of."

CHAPTER 14

THE THREADS of a nightmare held me in place once again. I could feel the elastic bubble of its confines pressing in on me. I stood alone where Anson and I first kissed, near the cliffside away from the school. A chilly wind whipped around my face and blew my hair into disarray.

Nash appeared at my side, and I narrowed my eyes.

"What are you doing here?" I asked him. My words sounded clear in my mind but came out in a stifled muffle. But he heard them. His answering sneer said as much. "What do you want, Nash?"

He didn't reply, but stepped aside to reveal a shivering Ferris standing behind him. Before I could register what was happening, Nash gave his best friend a gutsy shove and sent him soaring over the edge of the cliff. A scream died in my throat as Ferris' green eyes cried out to me.

Then, he was gone.

With an angry growl, I leaped for Nash and grabbed him by the throat. I let my magic boil to the surface and coil around my arm, strengthening the grip I held around his neck, and I squeezed harder. He clawed at my hand as his face turned from red to purple, his lips greying. I took delight in his pain.

A gentle touch on my other arm pulled my attention, and I looked back to find Willa standing there, a worried expression on her sweet face.

"Lydia, don't," she said in an echoey voice. "Don't give in."

"Give in to what?" I muttered.

She pointed at Nash, and my head whipped around only to discover that the snake in my grip had disappeared, replaced by the man I loved. Anson's pale face cried out for breath as my hand kept its steady hold on his neck.

I let go with a startle, and his limp body crumbled to the ground as a fierce scream gutted me. It pierced the air and sent a wave of light shooting through the air, disintegrating the dreamscape.

I shot up in my bed, as if I fell back into my body like a heavy stone, and the weight of the nightmare pressed on my chest. I heaved for breath, and sweat dripped down my back as I yanked the blankets off me.

Mom was gone. She must have slipped back to her room after I drifted off somewhere in the middle of Elf. I sat on the edge of my bed, feet firmly planted on the cold floor—it felt good on my burning skin—and raked my fingers through my sweaty hair.

"What's *wrong* with me?" I whispered to myself.

I couldn't be alone. Not tonight. Mom was leaving in the morning, and I couldn't possibly get back to sleep after a dream like that. I threw on my black bathrobe that I grabbed from the end of my bed and crept across the sleeping school toward my mother's guest quarters.

The gothic castle creaked and moaned like an old, tired beast. Vacant and lonely. A ping of sadness touched the bottom of my gut at the sudden realization that I missed the walls brimming with life. The sound of the voices that filled its rooms and the bustling feet of all my fellow Wicked Born. I missed Willa by my side each day, and Anson's arms around me each night. Perhaps I was already beginning to settle in here, before Mom came, and being left alone had finally made me realize it. *This* was my home.

I rounded the corner to the mouth of the hallway where Mom's guest quarters were and tip-toed down the narrow space. The sound of jarring voices spilled out from the half-opened door. They whispered, but with barely contained anger, and I carefully approached the sliver of light that cut the darkness in the hallway as I peered in.

"Bottom line, Arthur," Mom said firmly, "is you had no right forcing her into this program, knowing very well she could fail and what that would mean."

"I have every confidence that she certainly won't," the dean rebutted. "Think of what it would mean if she won, Lace. Truly, *think* about it. She could change our whole world, on both sides." He let out a stressful sigh. "Something you used to want, once upon a time. If I recall."

Mom chortled. "That was a long time ago. Before Lydia came along. Before everything…changed. I had a responsibility to the Light Faction to step up and take my place among its leaders."

Mr. Blackwood groaned. "You Light Faction and your precious bloodlines."

"What?" Mom balked. "And a barbaric series of tests is a better way to choose leaders?"

"At least it's fair," he argued. "It gives the Wicked Born more of a choice. The day you accepted that role was the day you gave up everything you stood for. Everything that you ever wanted."

I couldn't see Mom as she stood behind the door, but I heard her sniffle back tears, and it rattled something inside of me. Mom never cried. Especially not in front of her opposing peers.

"We were all children back then, Arthur," she said, a hint of defeat in her voice. "And it was all to protect Lydia."

"Yeah?" he pressed. "And how well did that work? She's here anyway." I could see part of his back, and it stiffened with pride. "And she's going to lead the Dark Faction one day."

"If Lydia dies, it's on you. And just know: I'll avenge my daughter's death with my very last breath," my mother warned.

The dean let out a breathy exhale through his nose. "If Lydia dies in this program, then I'll gladly lay down my life for you to do so."

My heart beat quickly in my chest, and a gasp escaped my throat. I stumbled backward and pressed up against the stone wall of the corridor. A few loose bits of rock released from the grout and sprinkled on the floor at my feet.

They shushed each other, and panic pulsed through my veins. My eyes widened as I heard them whispering about the noise I made.

Mr. Blackwood walked toward the door, and I slunk further into the shadows as I snapped my fingers and cast an invisibility enchantment over me. I struggled to contain my rapid breathing. I didn't dare try and make a run for it; they'd hear my footsteps. The dean poked his head out into the hall and glanced around curiously.

Standing there, frozen, I willed my breathing to calm as his eyes grazed the dark hallway, left and right and then…on me. A lump formed in my throat, and I held my breath; the dean's steely stare fixed on me. But that was impossible. I flexed my magic to check that the cloak was still there. It was. So how could he see me?

I waited in a cloud of fright, expecting him to open the

door all the way and betray my presence to my mother. But his lips pursed as if in thought.

"Is someone there?" Mom asked from inside the room.

Mr. Blackwood's gaze remained fixed on me, as if he were contemplating whether or not to give me up and rat me out for eavesdropping.

Mom would have a fit. As a kid, I would always hang around outside her office door, listening in on secret coven business. I didn't understand half of it, but she flipped out, nonetheless. This particular argument between her and the dean didn't strike me as one she'd like me to hear.

I was just about to let go of the cloaking veil, to beg him not to say anything so I could slink back to my room, when he stepped back and narrowed the opening of the door.

"No," he assured her, his stare unmoving from mine. "Nobody's there."

My body limped with relief as the dean eased the door closed, leaving me standing in complete darkness and a pool of total disbelief.

How could he see me? And why didn't he tell my mother? And beyond that…what sort of things were they hiding from me about my own past?

How well did they know one another, anyway? They seemed more than well-acquainted to me. Yet Mom had never mentioned that she personally knew the dean of the Arcane East.

I raced back to my room with a heavy load of questions in my brain. Would I ever get the resolutions I so desperately wanted? Or would even more questions arise?

Then another thought occurred to me: Everyone I loved or trusted had kept these things from me, surrounded me in these lies.

So, who could I really trust to get me the answers I needed?

CHAPTER 15

IT WAS hard to walk around with a head full of secrets and questions. With my neck beginning to tense from all the stress, I slowly careened it from side to side, releasing a few unsettling cracks, and rolled my shoulders as I strolled through campus with Mom by my side.

We walked quietly, neither of us wanting her visit to really end, but also both eager to get back to our lives. So different they'd become in a few short months. Mom's world remained steady—her duties as high priestess and running the plantation kept her on a straight course in life—while my path had veered so far to the left that it felt like I was going in circles at times.

Still, I was going to miss her.

Having Mom here these last couple of days helped shed some light on myself, my past, and provided more questions about my future that I was eager to find answers to. And now I knew I would never get those from her. Mom's past had jaded her view of everything. I'd had absolutely no idea she once rallied for the same things I now represented.

Change. A bridge between the two factions.

I could see why she did the things she did. If the coven or

the elders of our Light Faction ever found out that Mom's loyalty could possibly waver, it would paint a target on her. It was hard enough having a prodigy daughter chosen for the dark. Although, she had no control over what happened at my Sorting Ceremony; probably the only fact that's kept any suspicion toward her at bay.

But there was one thing I had to know before she left.

I stopped in the corridor after we passed the mess hall and touched her arm. "Mom?"

"Yes?" She set her suitcase down and turned to me.

"I wanted to ask you something before we go into the office. I want to give you the opportunity to tell me the truth, because I don't want to wait until we're inside and ask you in front of everyone."

Her eyebrows pinched together. "Okay."

I inhaled long and deep. "How do you know Mr. Blackwood so well?"

She examined my face, her eyes alight with guilt, and a sudden wave of realization washed over them. "You we're in the hallway last night, weren't you?"

I pursed my lips. "Only for a moment. Nothing of what I heard makes any sense to me, but I could tell you guys have a past."

"No." She quickly shook her head. "Not like you think. Yes, we know one another from years ago. High school, to be exact. We hung around in the same group of friends, but he was a year older and a dark born. After his Sorting Ceremony, he was inevitably chosen for this side, and I haven't spoken to him since. Just like so many of our friends back then."

I dragged my teeth across my bottom lip a few times as I contemplated. I never imagined my mother hanging around a group of Dark Wicked Born kids, but knowing that explained a lot of things about her behavior and the way she raised me. She must have had to distance herself as far as possible from who she was in high school in order to take on the role she now carried so well.

"Is that all?" Mom asked, a hint of forced lightness in her tone. She smiled. "Or are you just trying to delay my departure?"

I stared at her. There were a thousand things I still wanted to know. About her past, my father, myself. But I saw it now: the hard work and things she sacrificed to give me the life I had. The responsibilities she took on every day for the coven. Mom had a right to keep her secrets in the past, just as much as I had a right to protect mine here in the present. Besides, I had other means of getting the answers I so desperately wanted.

I shook my head. "No, that's it." I bent down and grabbed hold of her suitcase with a cheery smile. "Let's get you back home."

The process was short. The dean welcomed us into his office, and I stood by as Constance opened another portal. Mom said her goodbyes, thanked them all for allowing her to visit, and kissed my cheek before stepping through.

The portal closed behind her, leaving an emptiness in the room. I avoided looking at the dean, the man who caught me snooping the night before, and left the office. I had nothing to say to him. At least, not in front of Hallowell and the elders. No, I'd save that for later when I could hide under the guise of a journalist.

With that in mind, I headed back to my room to prepare a list of questions to drill him with now that I knew I'd never get those answers from my mother.

~

LATER THAT AFTERNOON, I approached the dean's office doors with my notebook and pen in hand, ready to get what I needed for the paper while also prying him for answers about what he and Mom had been arguing about. I gave two quick knocks and waited for him to answer on the other side. He called me in, and I closed the door behind me.

He glanced up from his desk and removed his glasses as he leaned back in his chair. "I was wondering when you'd show up."

"I'm actually here on official business for the school paper," I replied.

His eyebrows raised. "Is that so?" He stood and strolled over to a large, dark, wooden hutch filled with glassware and tins. "I forgot you landed a spot on the paper. Have a seat." He snapped his fingers, and a small teapot began to steam in front of him. "Tea?" he added and gestured toward it.

"Uh, sure," I replied and slid into the leather chair across from his.

I waited quietly, mulling over what I was going to say, as he prepared two cups of tea. He set one down on his desk in front of me and then took his seat.

"Now, what can I do to help with this official paper business?" he asked with a grin.

"I'm doing a feature on you," I said. "About the Courtship Program, and I have a lot of questions."

He looked at me with a calculating stare. "Yes, I'm sure you do."

His reply was short, but those few words held a deeper meaning. He must have expected me to come and bombard him with questions about last night. And I would. Just not yet.

I opened my notebook and shuffled the few sheets of notes I had, bringing Tom's required questions to the top.

"How do you feel about being the current host of such a coveted event?" I asked him in my most professional voice. I clicked my pen and waited.

Mr. Blackwood grinned delightfully. "I feel great. I have a

school full of wonderful Wicked Born, whom I'm so very proud of. Our contenders for the Program are strong, talented, and are sure to put up a good fight."

I hastily jotted down his answer. "And are you prepared for the influx of guests that will no doubt arrive in the coming days?"

He sipped his tea. "Yes, of course. The campus has a large wing of guest suites and our faculty are all up to speed on what needs to be done."

My pen scratched across the paper as I wrote, and I could feel his eyes on me. Wanting, waiting. As if he knew these trivial questions were just fluff that was delaying what we both wanted to talk about.

"Given the unease amongst the faction, do you regret nominating me as a candidate?"

He shook his head. "Absolutely not. Change does not happen until those who are comfortable are forced to be uncomfortable. I only wish for the best for you and Willa in this program. I see the potential you both have." He shifted forward in his seat. "It's time for change in our world—a leader with ties to both sides would be ideal right now."

My mouth pinched together as I tapped the back of my pen against my notebook. "Not everyone sees it that way. You said so yourself. Did you ever consider the danger you are putting me in?"

"Is that a question on your list?"

I swallowed loudly, my throat dry. "No."

Mr. Blackwood brought his hands together and leaned forward on his elbows. "I truly apologize for pushing you toward this, Lydia. But please believe me when I say, again, that I wouldn't have done so if I didn't have the utmost confidence that you could win this."

He'd told me as much before. This time…a part of me actually believed him. Mostly because I believed it myself. Willa and I could win in the end. But there was always the chance we would all be wrong, and the consequences were pretty dire if we were.

"Any further questions?" he gently pressed. "I'm open to answer...anything at all." His eyes flashed with a prompting yearn.

He wanted to talk about last night.

I closed my notebook. "How do you know my mother?"

"I would have thought she'd told you that by now."

"She did," I said, my expression staid. "But I want to hear what you have to say about it."

He leaned back and rocked slowly in his big leather chair as he ran a hand over his slicked black hair. "Lace and I attended the same mundane high school. We had the same group of friends, young Wicked Born from all walks of life." He sighed. "But, once we were all sorted into our expected factions, we lost touch."

"Why didn't you give me up last night?" I asked. "In the hallway. You knew I was there, didn't you?"

He wagged a finger in the air and grinned. "Not much happens in my school without me knowing. You think that's the first time a student has tried to sneak around unnoticed? I can sense an invisibility cloak a mile away." He took his mug and held it with both hands to his chest. "But I didn't say anything about your presence because you're an adult now, Lydia. Not a child to be blinded from things, especially if those things pertain to you."

No one has ever said that to me before. I'd always been left in the dark, shielded from information, lied to and expected to keep secrets all at the same time. But not with him.

A thought suddenly occurred to me: I could probably ask the dean anything at all in that moment and he'd tell me what I wanted to know.

"You say you and Mom had the same group of friends in high school."

He nodded once and sipped his warm beverage.

"Did you…know my father, then?"

Mr. Blackwood set his mug down on the desk with a perplexed expression. "I…did."

"Well?" I added.

He wavered. "One would say." He adjusted his silken grey suit vest. "How much do you know about the man?"

My shoulders hunched. "I only ever knew two things. That he existed, and he died. Mom…" I dropped my gaze to my lap and picked at what was left of my purple nail polish. "She was too heartbroken to ever talk about him. I learned pretty early to stop asking."

The dean blew out a long, exasperated breath. "That's very unfortunate. I knew him well, indeed. He was…He would have been a wonderful father to you, Lydia. He… would have loved you fiercely."

A hot lump formed in my throat, and I smothered the sudden urge to cry. I struggled to keep the tears at bay, and he gave me the space to fight it, waiting patiently as he sipped his tea. Finally, I won, and kept the emotions away.

"Do you, uh, have any kids?" I asked him, my voice cracking.

He gave me a smile, one that didn't quite reach his eyes. "Unfortunately, I never got the chance to journey down that road. I'm married to my job, I guess you could say. My students are my children." I was sure he expected some marvelling response, but I didn't know what to say. He cleared his throat. "Any further questions?"

I blinked away the film that still glossed over my eyes and shuffled the papers in my lap. "Yes. Just one more." I shifted and straightened my back. "Who do you think will win the Program versus who do you want to win?"

"Well, that's an easy one," he exclaimed. "You. For both. Though it won't be easy. There's some steep competition this year, as I'm sure you're aware. I expect it to be the most challenging Courtship Program yet."

I nodded, my mind flashing to Nash. There were surely other strong competitors I'd face also, but Nash wasn't just a talented witch. He was ruthless and conniving. I might have a good shot if everyone played fair, but I couldn't count on Nash to do that.

"I'm so very proud of the witch you're quickly becoming, Lydia," the dean went on. "The moment I heard the results of your Sorting Ceremony, my mind raced with all the possibilities of what this could mean. But I didn't want to make a rash decision until I met you." He grinned. "Within seconds of being in your presence, I knew. There was absolutely no doubt in my mind that you could compete, and you could win. Try not to let your apprehensions get the best of you."

"And as for who would be by my side at the end," I said. "Have you put any thought into who that might be?"

The dean gave an indifferent shrug. "I'd much rather it just be you and Miss Stonerose. But that's not how things work in our world, is it? There's always balance, always a counterpart. So, if I had to choose, I would say Mr. Abernathy should stand with you at the end."

He'd said *should*. Not would. And I wasn't sure I wanted to ask him to clarify, wasn't sure I could handle any other answer.

I stared in awe at this man in front of me, the leader of our school. This elder in our Dark Faction. I saw him in a whole new light. He'd proved time and time again that he could be kind and cared for the students here.

I'd spent weeks resenting him for pushing me into this program, convinced that he was setting me up for failure. But now...I trusted him. He truly believed I could win against all the contenders. He saw the bigger picture...and I was in it, leading this faction and tearing down its walls.

And I saw it, too.

Finally. I thought of my mother in her younger years,

those rebel days when she wanted this very thing. How did she keep that from me for so long? What truly drove her off the path she was headed down before my dad died?

I'd probably never learn the answers to those questions, but one thing was for sure: Something about my mother's past was connected to my future.

I just had to figure out what.

CHAPTER 16

IDLE HANDS ARE the devil's playthings.

The saying never made much sense to me until now. I tried my best to occupy my time for the rest of the Solstice break. I paddled around my bedroom with books. Ate enough junk food to feed an army. Attempted to numb my brain with a movie. I even reorganized my closet by color.

But I wasn't the settling type.

Anson and Willa would be back in a couple days, and I had made a mental note a while ago to find a way back into the Midnight Circle's meeting place to discover anything I could about what Nash had done to my boyfriend.

As far as I knew, all the members had gone home for the holidays, leaving me the perfect opportunity to spend some time lurking around down in their meeting place. I had a nagging feeling that, if Nash truly did do something to Anson in the caves that day, it wasn't for nothing. The Circle had to be involved in some way, and I was betting I could find the proof I needed down there.

I just had to find a way in.

I slipped on my old black sweatshirt and threw the hood over my head, so it covered most of my face before setting out across the school. I didn't take the obvious way—through the mess hall and library—but hung to the winding corridors instead. There were only a few Wicked Born and a handful of teachers who stayed behind, but I couldn't risk anyone seeing me sneaking down the teacher's wing.

I glanced behind me as I rounded the final corner and peered down the long, narrow hallway that led to the enchanted entrance. I hugged the wall, creeping as quietly as I could.

It was late in the day, and the sun had hidden behind the school on the other side, leaving only a dim orange glow that hung lazily in the air, highlighting all the dust particles floating there.

I passed by numerous glass display cases containing priceless relics from our history: ancient tools, weapons, grimoires with pages so delicate they could never be opened again. Then the Urn of Osiris. A fake replica that only Anson, Willa, and I knew about. The original had been destroyed in that damn cave, and I cringed at the thought of anyone ever finding out. I couldn't imagine the repercussions.

Finally, I neared the end of the hallway, where it turned into a dead corner, and tucked myself into the little nook it provided before stealing one more glance over my shoulder. A cloaking enchantment would have been ideal, but I couldn't trust it right now. Not when the dean surely had his senses on high alert for my every move.

I gently pressed my palm to the rough stone wall and let my magic hum to the surface in search of a hidden keyhole. When I'd watched Nash do it before, he'd whispered the way in. But I would try every incantation I knew of before I gave up. I *had* to get inside.

The force of power pushed back on a stone near the middle of the wall, and I quietly called out every unlock incantation I could think of with no luck at all. But the power throbbed on the other side, taunting me. I stepped back and thumbed through all the possibilities and combinations in my mind.

"Come on, brain," I whispered to myself in frustration. "Think like them."

Nash was talented, but arrogant, and I assumed the rest were more or less the same. They'd probably choose a simple password, something easy to remember. But, also, something that would boast just how confident they were in their shady dealings. One word popped up in my mind, but I shook my head.

"No," I said to myself. "They couldn't be that arrogant, could they?" I pressed my hand to the cold stone once again and closed my eyes as I hummed the simple chant. *"Aperta sesama."*

Magic on the other side of the wall responded with a click, and I backed up a step as I guffawed in disbelief. Just like the first time, the stones lit up with a glow and began to rearrange themselves before my eyes until a narrow opening appeared and a set of stairs led the way down.

"Are you kidding me? Open sesame?"

I shook my head and took the first few steps down. The stairway was longer than I remembered, but I eventually reached the bottom.

My ears perked and listened for any sign of life, but I was only met with a cold silence. I grinned inside.

Perfect.

A few lanterns hung in corners with flames that cast the already eerie space in a haunting glow. Someone had clearly been here since Solstice break started, and I put my senses on high alert as I slowly wandered about.

The red velvet sofas with tufted backs sat untouched. Walls of black bookshelves with glass fronts stood like giants, watching me. I took my time to peer inside them all, noting all the Dark texts and relics enclosed. Most showed signs of age, while others seemed brand new, as if the Midnight Circle were erecting their own collection of new age tools for the future they envisioned.

Still, nothing seemed connected to the magic Nash had used in that cave. I felt a tinge of it that night, like a taste of poison on my tongue. I needed to look for something out of place, something...beyond the Dark.

I wandered farther into the space, opening doors to rooms filled with bunks and personal belongings. They must be for members who didn't attend the academy.

Just how far did this secret circle reach out there in our world?

I opened a thick, heavy door far from the glow of the lantern light and was met with pure darkness. I reached for my magic and snapped my fingers.

"*Ignis*," I said. A small flame danced from my fingertips and into a cold lantern on a table in the center. The space lit up, and I jumped back with a loud gasp.

The room was filled with people, looming in a line of black cloaks down a wall. But I quickly realized they were only that—cloaks hanging in wait for their owners to wear. I shuddered and closed the door, but my heart still raced from the sudden fright that struck my chest.

One last door waited at the very back of the vast, underground space, and I carefully stepped toward it. This door was different from the others: still wooden, but thicker with gaudy wrought iron hinges and a massive padlock on the black metal latch.

What could they possibly want to hide so badly? There had to be something behind that door.

I held the lock in my palm, heavy and real, just like the one on the restricted area in the library. No amount of magic was going to open it. Refusing to accept defeat, I searched around for something I could break it open with. But, then again, I couldn't very well leave behind such blaring evidence that I'd been here.

I ran my fingers over the rough wooden surface for any sign of a magical way in, but there was nothing. This door was solid. Then I eyed the iron hinges and noted how they were constructed—with thick metal loops held together with a heavy spike.

I pinched the top of it with my fingers and tried to wiggle it free. There was a bit of give, but it would take some work. I scraped away the years of dirt and rust that crusted around the cracks, breaking a few fingernails. But I didn't care. I was getting in that room.

Finally, after a few minutes of wiggling, I pulled the top spike free and then moved on to the bottom one. They slid from their loops with a loud scraping noise like nails on a chalkboard, and I cringed. Adrenaline pulsed through my veins as I set the metal spikes aside and gripped the sliver of edge that poked out and slowly worked the door from its opening. It moaned and scratched the stone floor, but I pried it open enough to slip inside.

The room was pitch black, so I snapped my sore fingertips and lit a lantern that sat on a little table just inside the doorway. Then I grabbed the handle and held it up as I examined the contents of the space.

More bookshelves with glass facings. They completely covered the walls from floor to ceiling, side to side. I approached them and peered inside. Papers. I moved the lantern to see more and found nothing but sheet after sheet of paper, covered in scribbles and writings. They filled the cases and lined the shelves side by side.

"What the…"

I stepped back and held the lantern out as far as I could while I took in the enormity of the strange collection. They were grimoire pages. An entire witch's handbook deconstructed and laid out for everyone to read. I leaned in and narrowed my eyes as I tried to read some of them. Words like sacrifice, necromancy, and other terms for forbidden spells filled the pages. No one should possess magic as dark as this.

Then a cold realization seared through my body and stole the breath right from my chest.

"No," I whispered and shook my head. "It can't be."

This was Talia Blackstone's grimoire. In its entirety.

The Midnight Circle must have copied every single page before returning it. Someone took it from the spot where I left it in the café that night and they could have easily kept it, but the book had mysteriously been returned.

It must have been Nash. He must have been panicked about getting caught. And no one had looked further into the grimoire's disappearance after it'd been returned. Maybe this group was smarter than I gave them credit for.

As I backed up, still gawking at the collection, I nearly knocked over a smaller display case that sat in the center of the room. A table with a glass box on top.

I moved the light and peered inside, only to find the complete ritual for resurrection—one of the most illegal spells of our entire world, in both factions. Witches were forbidden to mess with life or death. But here it was, a resurrection spell on full display.

These pages were clearly more important than the rest, as if they were...practicing it.

"No..." The word squeezed from my throat.

I couldn't let them continue. Who knew the chaos the Midnight Circle could create with this? Taking the spells away now might not mean much if they had already memorized them, but I had to at least try.

The glass box wasn't locked, so I carefully opened the lid.

The distinct padding of footsteps on the stairs echoed through the chamber. The lid nearly fell from my grasp.

Someone was coming.

I grabbed the sheets of paper and stuffed them in the pocket of my hoodie before I slipped out the narrow opening

I'd made in the door. With one heave, I put it back in place and jammed the metal spikes through the hinges.

The soft thud of footsteps disappeared, but no one was in sight. My chest heaved despite my efforts to stay calm.

I pressed my back to the wall and crept back up the corridor. When I reached the end, I glanced both ways to make sure the coast was clear before taking off the way I had come in. Adrenaline ran hot in my veins as the bottom of the stairs came into view.

"Stop!" a deep voice bellowed from behind me.

My heart protested in my chest, and I froze.

"This place is off-limits," he warned. "Turn around."

Slowly, I spun around, careful not to ruffle the papers in my pocket, and my mouth fell open when I found Hallowell staring back at me. What the hell was he doing here? Was Professor Hallowell a member of the Midnight Circle?

His face relaxed with a chortle, and he crossed his arms. "Lydia Laveau. I should have known it was you. You can't be here, you know?"

I shook my head. "Technically, I'm a member of this circle. I may not want to be, but it is what it is." My shoulders slumped. "So, why can't I be here?"

He examined my face as he held his hands at his back and gave an unsettling smile. "The prodigal daughter, first light born chosen for the dark." His eyes widened dramatically. "The girl with the *big* power. What else don't we know about you?"

My stomach soured.

"I'm leaving," I said sternly and tried to walk past him.

He grabbed my arm and I turned to him with a glare. "Don't let me catch you down here without a standing member ever again. Do you understand?"

Inside, I was a melting mess of fear and emotion, but I wouldn't let this full-grown man intimidate me this way. "Fine by me."

I yanked my arm free and took off for the stairs. My feet could hardly move as fast as my heart demanded. I didn't stop until I reached the mouth of my wing of the school. I rounded the corner and collapsed against the wall as I slowly slid to the floor, my chest heaving. I had to calm down.

Hugging my knees tight to my chest, I slowed my breathing. The pages crinkled in my hoodie, and I remembered that I held an illegal resurrection spell right in my pocket.

What was I going to do with it? I couldn't keep it, but I also couldn't give it up. Who would I trust with this? Willa and Anson, yes. But they weren't here. The dean? No, our relationship was too fragile, and I still wasn't sure if I trusted him.

I pressed my lips together and tilted my head back to the wall, tears brimming my eyes. That was it, then; there wasn't anyone I could rely on right now. I was stuck with the responsibility of this spell until the Solstice break was over.

I let it sink in. I could do it...

...as long as no one checked that locked room until then.

CHAPTER 17

I FELT LIKE A ROCK, heavy and mounted in place. Unable to move. My limbs hung from my body as my skin soldered to the chair I sat in across from the dean's desk, and my ears filled with a pulse that pounded on my brain, muffling the sounds of the world around me.

Something—a deep voice—beckoned me from the other side, gently pulling me from the depths.

"Lydia?" Mr. Blackwood said with anxious worry in his tone. I blinked away the haze over my eyes and stared at him in confusion. His brow raised. "Did you hear what I said?"

My head slowly bobbed up and down. "Anson...isn't coming back."

"It's just a few more days," he quickly assured. "But I thought you'd like to know, considering your relationship with him."

I thought of the blackened veins that spread outward over his heart. He promised they were nothing to worry about. He'd said his grandmother would fix him up with some silly potion. But now I worried that they had gotten worse. What else could it be?

"What did he say, exactly?" I asked, my voice cracking. "Did he say why?"

The dean leaned back in his chair with an indifferent shrug. "It was his grandmother I spoke to, actually. Mr. Abernathy is just a little under the weather and didn't feel up to the harsh effects of portal travel today." He smiled. "Probably all that hard labor around the farm. I'm sure his grandparents had a long list of chores for him to help with when he arrived," he said, making light of the situation. Part of me was grateful for the attempt, but it did nothing to soothe my nerves. "Don't fret. He should be back in a couple of days."

I wanted to stand and leave, but I leaned forward and bounced my foot on the floor.

"Is everything alright?" Mr. Blackwood asked.

I didn't move, didn't reply.

"You can trust me to be on your side with anything, Lydia," he said. "If something is wrong or someone is upsetting you, you can tell me. I can help."

The words tumbled around in my mouth, eager to be set free. To spill the burden of everything onto someone else. Let them share in the constant stress.

I think Anson is seriously ill!

Nash Crane is a psychopath who is leading an underground coven bent on resurrecting an ancient, evil witch!

Hallowell is in on it!

But I couldn't say it. Any of it.

I wanted so desperately, deep down in my soul, to trust the dean. I truly did. But something nagged in the back of mind each time I tried. There was still something he wasn't telling me. About my past, my future. Something. And I couldn't figure it out. Until then, I just couldn't bring myself to open that door of trust. This was a burden I'd have to carry all on my own.

I glanced at the clock. "I have to go meet Willa." I stood

and stuffed my hands in my pockets. "Thank you for letting me know about Anson."

I headed for the door and closed it behind me as the sound of the dean saying my name once more banged against it. I couldn't stay any longer. It was too tempting to spill everything to him and beg for his help. But what if he had a hand in all of it? What if he knew about the Midnight Circle and all the awful things Nash had done—and would do? What if the dean knew of my own secret, that I harbored some ancient magic inside of me?

He said so himself: nothing happened in his school without him knowing.

Worry and emotion toiled in my gut. I squashed it all down as deep as it would go and headed for the main lobby where all the Wicked Born were returning from their wonderful trips back home to the mundane world. I'd promised Willa I'd meet her.

I could hear the commotion before I rounded the corner, and the noise amplified once I did. Dozens of students filed in through the front doors from the portals outside, carting their luggage in hand, smiles on their faces. They all looked so refreshed. Happy.

Normal.

Willa's crown of brown curls bobbed through the crowd, and I smiled as I waved to her. She beamed and quickened her pace toward me. When she reached me, she set her bag down and dramatically placed her hands at her hips with a disapproving look.

"You look like shit," she said.

I flung my arm over her shoulder with a grin. "And you look like a total babe. Tom's been asking about you."

She rolled her eyes and let her backpack slide from her shoulder to hand it to me. "Let's get back to our room. I miss my bed. Mom and Dad wasted no time turning my old bedroom into storage. I slept on a roll out sofa the whole time."

Once back in our shared quarters, Willa threw all her luggage in the corner and collapsed on her bed. She rolled around in the pillows, clearly relishing in the comfort, then peered over at my side of the room with a curious look.

"Did you...*clean* your side?" she asked in mock disbelief.

I shrugged. "Having Mom here reminded me what a disaster I am sometimes."

She sat upright and dangled her legs off the side of the bed. "Tell me about her visit."

I shook my head. "Not until you tell me about yours."

"First thing's first." Willa hopped to her feet and rummaged through her backpack. She pulled out a stack of magazines and something wrapped in yellow paper.

The smell wafted across my nose as she handed me the pile of goods. A burger!

She grinned. "As per your request."

I set the magazines down on the blanket next to me and tore into the two all beef patties, special sauce, lettuce, cheese, pickles, and onions on a sesame seed bun.

My eyes rolled back in my head as I moaned in delight. "Oh, my Gods, this is exactly what I needed right now."

Willa chuckled and plopped back on her bed. "You know, you could just whip one up with magic anytime."

I stuffed the monstrous bite to the side of my mouth and shook my head. "Not the same. It needs the special touch only a group of teenagers working a fast food chain can give." I swallowed and took another bite as Big Mac sauce dripped down my fingers. "Spill. How was your trip home?"

"My dad was a bit quiet at first," she said. "Stern. Short answers. But after a couple of days, he warmed up." She chortled. "He's always been super stubborn, but he loves me; there's no question about that."

"Did you guys do anything special?"

"Not really." She kicked off her shoes. "I helped Mom

bake cookies. Helped Dad cut the tree down and drag it home. It was always our tradition." She sighed happily. "We went skating, sledding, shopping. It was nice to be normal for a while, you know?"

I nodded. "Yeah, I know exactly what you mean."

"So, tell me about your mom's visit," she chirped. "How did everyone react to having her here?"

"There weren't really a ton of people around," I told her. "A few students, some teachers. A couple of elders. But they all reacted the way you'd expect."

Willa rolled her eyes. "One day, the two factions are going to have to learn to grow up."

I chewed at the inside of my cheek. "The dean seemed to be happy, though."

"Yeah?" she said, her interest piqued. "Like how?"

"I don't know." My shoulders slumped. "He was ecstatic about the groundbreaking act of it. Having a Light Faction elder on campus. And my mother, no less." I inched forward and leaned on my knees. "He knows her. Like, they have a past."

Willa's eyes widened. "What do you mean?"

"They went to the same high school together. And their group of friends were these, like, hippie silent protesters for change. They all wanted this. Way back then, so many years ago. A group of young Wicked Born saw the blatant divide in our world and knew it was wrong." I sucked in a deep breath. "And he knew my dad."

Her expression blanked. "But you—"

"Don't know anything about the guy." I stood and began pacing. "I begged Mom to tell me something. Anything. And she did, but carefully and super vague. And the dean was no better."

"What did they tell you?"

"That my father was a good man, loved my mother deeply," I replied. "He died before she found out she was pregnant. But when she did, Mom abandoned everything she and her friends believed in and accepted her role in the Light Faction."

Willa's face pinched in. "What? Why would she do that?"

"To protect me. She didn't want to raise a child around such dangerous ideals." I grabbed the athame and ring from my bookshelf. "This was his," I said and pulled it halfway from its little sheath. "It's enchanted to only work for his blood." I stared at it admiringly, knowing his fingers once gripped it. "For *my* blood. Anyone else who attempts to wield it will be injured. And this ring," I added and held it out for Willa, "Mom gave it to me for Christmas. It's—"

She leaped from her bed and plucked it from my palm. "This is a syphon!"

"I take it you've heard of it?" I kidded.

She turned it around in her fingers as she stared at it. "Yeah, they're super hard to get. And can only be forged in the House of the High Council by the weapon's master."

I smirked. "You're such a nerd. I love it."

She handed me back the ring. "This is powerful, Lydia. And exactly what you need right now. This thing can syphon your powers and store them so you can use your magic during times when you can't trust calling to it." Her eyes urged me to catch on. "Like during the Courtship Program?"

I nodded and slipped it into my jeans pocket. "I know. It definitely makes me feel better about this whole thing. At least as good as I can feel about it, considering what's at stake."

We both went quiet for a moment. I'd bet Willa was thinking about the same thing I was: how dangerous the whole program would be. But panicking wasn't productive, so I stuffed my arm between my mattress and box spring to pull out the papers I stole from the Midnight Circle.

"Enough about that," I said. "Turns out we actually have something bigger to freak out about right now."

I handed the sheets to her, and she hesitantly unfolded them.

Her face paled. "What…is this?"

"I think you know."

Willa stared at me, fear washed across her frozen expression. "This is a Resurrection spell. That's…illegal. Where did you get this?"

I crossed my arms tightly across my chest. "I may have done some snooping around."

"Where?" The pieces seemed to click into place as her expression went from stunned to disappointed. "Lydia, do not tell me you snuck into the Midnight Circle."

"What?" I replied defensively, spreading my hands. "We're members, aren't we?"

She handed me back the papers with a stern look. "No, we're not. They think we are, but we can't be part of something like that. It's the opposite of everything you represent. I mean, what were you thinking, Lydia? Who knows what could have happened to you down there?"

"Everyone was gone," I said, and then thought of Hallowell. Best wait to tell her that part. "And I wanted to find a clue as to what Nash did to Anson."

"And?" she pressed. "What did you find?"

I sighed. "They have Talia Blackstone's entire grimoire on display in a locked room. Page for page. And this"—I waved the sheets of paper—"was front and center. I'm convinced Nash is playing around with dark magic he has no right or real ability to control. And he carelessly used that power in the caves that night. The hex has left some kind of residual effect on Anson and…it's doing something to him. Hurting him."

"We have to tell someone!" Willa's eyes bulged.

My arms slumped. "Like who? I don't trust *anyone* in this place. Not even Anson is telling me the truth."

"Where is he, anyway?"

Tears brimmed my eyes. "He's staying home for a few

more days. His grandmother said he's not feeling well. I'm..."
My lip trembled as I bit back the emotion that forced its way
up. "I'm telling myself I'll deal with it when he comes back.
For now..." I glanced at the papers in my hand. "I can tackle
one thing at a time."

Willa swooped over and sat next to me on the bed,
covering my hand with both of hers. "We, Lydia. *We* can
tackle this together. You say you can't trust anyone, but you
can always trust me. That much I swear."

I pressed my lips together as a single rogue tear escaped
and slid down my cheek to fill the narrow line that formed
across my mouth.

"Just tell me what to do," she added.

I took in a long, deep breath to calm my nerves and willed
away the tears that threatened to break free. I thought of
Nash and Ferris, the Circle, the grimoire room. How I
couldn't trust the dean, or even my own damn mother, to tell
me the whole truth of my own past. It felt like control was
slipping from my hands faster than I could scramble to hold
on to it.

But there was one thing I *could* control.

A grin spread across my lips as I turned to my friend. "We
practice until we can compete in this stupid Program with our
eyes closed," I told her. "We win and gain the power to bring
down the Circle ourselves."

"Bringing down a large group of evil, corrupt
witches...just the two of us?" Willa asked. "That's a tall
order..."

My chest heaved with anxiety. She was right. But what
other choice did we have?

CHAPTER 18

I WOULD NEVER ADMIT DEFEAT. It'd always been one of my faults, and this time, it might get me killed.

Then again, maybe it'd prove to be a strength, my saving grace. If anything, life had shown me that sometimes my stubbornness worked in my favor, and I was hoping like hell that would be the case this time around.

Either way, I would take my stubbornness to my grave. Just hopefully not anytime soon.

Willa and I needed to get the Morphium Elixir right, to perfect our shapeshifting technique, especially if Potions was going to be the first test of the Courtship Program. It would set us off with a bang and would be a sure win to the next round.

But the universe refused to let us get it right.

We spent the next two days trying over and over, adjusting the ratios of ingredients each time, only for it to fall flat and evaporate into thin air. Every. Single. Time.

I could feel the frustration Willa carried on her chest, but I wouldn't give up. The cryo spell was a colossal disaster, the tragic death of my cactus plant a sure sign not to try it out on anything else.

I let my obsessive tendency take over and pushed us to get the elixir right. It was a fine distraction from the fact that my boyfriend still hadn't returned, and I had no idea what state his health would be in when he did.

If he did.

No, I couldn't think like that. *Focus, Lydia.* I had to put everything I had into what I could control. Like this damn potion. Once we got the ingredient combo perfect, we could finally move on to practicing for another test.

Unfortunately, by our next Potions class, I could tell Willa was losing her motivation in the face of so many defeats.

"Gods," she whispered tiredly as Hallowell paced the front of our class. Everyone sat quietly at their tables as they wrote in their grimoires. "Maybe we'll never get this thing right."

I eyed the shady professor as he busied himself with something on his desk. "No, we'll get it. I think it's the order we're adding the ingredients."

I pulled out the box from under our table that held the evidence of three failed attempts we'd sneakily tried during class when the professor wasn't looking. A new vial now bubbled with our latest try.

"We've only got days until the Program starts," she whispered back. "Maybe we should try something else."

Hallowell paced the front again, eying everyone carefully. I waited until his back was turned and pulled out a small satchel of dried silkworms and added a pinch of the white dust to our vial. It began to fizz, and we held our breaths as it slowly settled.

But, instead of evaporating like all the rest…it held.

My breath squeezed in my throat, and we exchanged a look. Her eyes shone in a way that revealed she must be feeling that same sheer disbelief mixed with relief that I was feeling.

"That's it," she squealed under her breath. "Oh, my gods, Lydia. We freaking did it."

"Finally," I replied and let the reprieve settle.

"But how do we know for sure it's right?" she added.

A grin smeared across my face as I double checked Hallowell's location once again—lurking over someone else's table—and reached into my bag for the little vial of snakeskin Miss Haggy had given me.

I rolled it between my fingers with a smug look. "Well, one way is to sneak some into Nash's coffee later."

Willa matched my devilish expression, and I popped the tiny cork before adding a single scale of dried snakeskin. The potion accepted it and still held.

"What's this?" Professor Hallowell demanded from behind us.

A startled yelp barked from both of us as we turned to find him standing there, a pissed off look plastered to his face. When did he walk over this way? My heart crawled up into my throat as I shifted in my seat to try and cover the box that held our ticket to advancing in the Courtship Program.

I gave an indifferent shrug, trying to play it off with a smile. "Just practicing potions, sir. This *is* potions class, after all."

His expression pinched, and he snapped, "That's not the assignment."

Willa gawked at me with a slight shake of her head.

"Well," I replied and glanced back to Hallowell from my stool. "It's actually practice for the Program. Just trying to get as much as we can before it starts."

"That is to be done on your *own* time," Hallowell grumbled. He adjusted the button on the sleeves of his black shirt before rolling them up to his elbows. "Not mine."

I narrowed my eyes. "It's not like we asked to be in this stupid comp—"

"I would advise you to refrain from insulting the process in which we elect our leaders, Miss Laveau."

By now, all heads in the class had turned to watch the show. Anger boiled in my gut.

"What exactly have you made here, anyway?" he added and motioned to the large vial that sat in the box.

"It's a Morphium Elixir, sir," Willa admitted sheepishly.

I flashed her a glare at her betrayal, and she shrugged helplessly.

He chortled and crossed his arms. "Wasting class time trying to perform a potentially dangerous spell beyond your capabilities?" He scoffed. "If I were you, I'd be careful, messing with things you have no business messing in."

Gee, thanks for the vote of confidence.

Willa and I exchanged a glance of finality.

Hallowell held out his hand. "Give it here. I've no choice but to confiscate it."

My back straightened. "But we need this!"

Not to mention, the last person I wanted to hand this over to was Hallowell. Especially after that run in I'd had with him over holiday break. I didn't trust him one bit.

He shot me a look that said 'don't cross me right now' and wagged his upturned fingertips in wait. As a professor, he had too much power in this school for me to show insubordination in the face of his request. I had to hand it over.

A groan rumbled in my chest as I reluctantly bent over and fetched our one and only copy of the potion and popped a cork on the top before handing it to him.

"Thank you," he said, his tone staid. "I'll take the opportunity to remind you, Miss, Laveau, that your privilege will do you no good in my class. You'd be wise to keep that in mind."

Blood steamed in my veins as he tucked our precious vial into the inside pocket of his black vest.

"I suggest you don't try this again," he added. "Not in my class, *nor* in your own time."

Then he headed back to the front of class and impatiently dismissed everyone.

The room filled with the commotion of closing books and shuffling chairs, and I blew out an exasperated breath. "Gods, I hate that man. Guess it's back to square one."

Willa gave me a wink as she stuffed her things inside her bag. "I recorded every single version we tried. Including that one."

I beamed. "You're my favorite friend."

She shoved playfully at my shoulder as we strolled toward the door. "I'm your only friend, you freak."

"Thank the Gods for that."

AT THE END of the day, I stood in the shower and let the scalding hot water beat down on my body, washing away the stress and anger I harbored toward Hallowell for taking our only working potion. I knew a part of him delighted in it. I didn't want to waste my energy on the man, but if I let it go, it left a cavity for my worry over Anson to fill.

I tipped my head back and closed my eyes as the shower soaked my hair. A cool breeze blew over my skin, and I turned to find a small portal in the tiled wall. A wet scream forced from my throat just as Anson leaned in and cupped a hand over my mouth. My chest heaved with excitement, and he placed a finger across his lips.

I could hear one of the other girls pad across the floor in bare feet on the other side of the curtain.

"Are you okay?" she asked me.

Anson let go, and I cleared my throat. "Uh, yeah. Sorry, just got a shot of cold water come through."

I listened and waited as the sounds of her retreating footsteps disappeared and she left the bathroom. I whipped around to face my boyfriend who hung halfway through the portal with a satisfied grin on his face. A healthy face. He looked a thousand times better than he did the day he'd left to go home.

"Come here," he said quietly, a hunger in his charcoal eyes as he grabbed me by the waist.

"Feeling better, I see," I said carefully, hyper-aware of the fact I was stark naked.

He stared at me admiringly, the corner of his mouth twitching. "Yeah, my grandmother fixed me up a supply of healing potions."

I let my slick naked body press up against him, soaking his black t-shirt. He didn't seem to mind. My hands smoothed over his cheeks as my thumbs brushed under the skin around his eyes.

"You look well," I said.

His eager fingers slid up my back and pulled me even closer. I shivered as his warm breath tickled my skin and his lips dragged over the curve of my neck.

"Not as good as you do right now," he whispered in my ear.

Goosebumps scoured over me, and my nipples hardened just as his wandering hand brushed across them. He chuckled, and his mouth found mine. My body responded immediately, pushing against him, wanting him closer.

"I can't believe you're back," I whispered through heavy kisses. "I'm mad at you."

"Are you, now?" he replied as he panted, his mouth searching for more.

I nodded. "You took too long to come back."

His whole body hummed with desire, and his fingers squeezed into the soft skin of my backside. He pressed his forehead to mine. Without releasing me from his embrace, he reached down with one arm and flipped back the shower handle, and the water stopped pouring down on us.

"Well, guess I'll have to make it up to you, won't I?" he

said, and I shivered as his mouth touched my ear and his fingers dug into the tender flesh of my side. "Grab your stuff."

Without hesitation, I slipped my arm outside the curtain and grabbed my bag and towel from a hook. Before I had the chance to take a step forward, Anson's body leaned in further and scooped me into his arms to yank me through the portal to his quarters.

~

I LAID in a pool of contentment as moonlight filtered in through the wooden blinds and cooled my hot skin. Anson's fingertips mindlessly trailed up and down my bare arm as I draped half my body over his. I was my happiest when I was with him. In any form. We could be sitting on the edge of a cliff or wrapped in blankets as we made love. It didn't matter, as long as we were together. When I was with him, I felt like I could finally take a full breath. Could let my eyes drift closed without the jarring noise of the world to greet me in the darkness.

A sliver of moonlight cut through the dimness of his room and left a white line across his chest. My head rested in the crook of his arm as I stared at the hypnotizing patterns of black tattoos that covered his skin. They were beautiful, just like him.

"Did you have a good trip home?" I asked, my voice weak and tired.

His chest moved beneath me as he spoke. "Yeah, it was nice to get outside the school for a bit. See the world again." He sighed. "And my grandparents were happy for the extra set of hands around the farm. How was your visit with your mom?"

I traced the dark lines on his skin as I admired the artwork. "Good. As expected, for the most part." I rubbed my lips together. "I did find out that the dean and her go way back."

He chuckled. "Seriously?"

"Yeah, they went to high school together and had the same group of friends."

But I didn't want to talk about that, about me. I was eager to learn more about how he looks so much better.

"So, the potion your grandma made," I said. "Does that mean she knows what's wrong with you?"

He shook his head. "Not really. But she could tell it was the aftereffects of a dark hex, one she'd never seen before. She might have been able to develop a counter curse for it if she knew the type of magic Nash used in the caves that night."

I sucked in a bubbly breath and shifted my weight as I propped myself up on my elbow and looked him in the face. "We might not be able to find the exact hex he was throwing around, but I think we can trace back to the source of the magic he's been using." I swallowed nervously. "It's not good. And someone like him definitely shouldn't be toying around with something so ancient and unpredictable."

Anson tensed and hauled himself upward in bed. "What are you talking about?"

My gaze fell from his. "I, uh, I might have snuck into the Midnight Circle while you were gone."

"Lydia!"

My gaze pleaded with him for forgiveness. "I was fine! And I found what they've been up to." I slipped my hand in his. "Anson, they have a copy of Talia Blackstone's grimoire. The whole thing is on display for them to study. I think they're trying to harness the old magic she used, but I'm betting they can't. Which is why…"

Anson's eyes bulged. "Why what?"

"I think…they're trying to bring back Talia from the dead."

CANDACE OSMOND & REBECCA HAMILTON

His face paled in the moonlight, and his head dipped, letting half his long brown waves fall over his eyes.

"I know firsthand how dangerous that magic can be," he croaked through a whisper. Then he groaned. "That goddamn book."

He ripped off the blankets and shoved his legs through a pair of pants from the floor as he ambled across the room. I sat there, holding a sheet to my chest as he gripped the edges of his desk while his head hung low as if in thought. I wanted to ask, but part of me already knew what he was thinking of.

Norah.

I crawled out of the bed and draped the sheet around my naked body as I walked toward him. My hand caressed his back. His pulse beat wildly under my palm. Then I noticed a wooden box on his desk with dozens of empty vials inside. I plucked one out and held it to my nose. Remnants of thyme and raven's blood tickled my nose.

"Anson, have you taken all of these?" I asked, stunned.

He inhaled sharply. "Yes."

I balked. "But there's enough in here to last months. Maybe longer."

He shook free of my hand and stood straight, but his shoulders sagged. His face was awash with painful emotions I'd never understand.

"The hex is stronger than I thought, and now...I guess we know why." He grabbed a t-shirt from the back of a chair and hauled it over his head. "Have you told anyone about the grimoire?"

"No," I said honestly. "Just Willa. I mean, who could I even trust with something like this?"

He stared at me, his eyes glistening with doom. "No one."

CHAPTER 19

It was funny how I could be immersed in a sea of people and still feel utterly alone.

I sat in the Great Hall, Anson and Willa flanking my sides, while the entire student body filled hundreds of chairs and threw glances ahead at the stage in wait. My fingers gripped the edge of the chair beneath me, my knuckles white from pressure, my palms sweaty with stress.

Today was the first official day that every last Wicked Born had finally returned from the Solstice break. An assembly of sorts had been scheduled for this morning to welcome everyone back and also announce details pertaining to the upcoming Courtship Program.

The three of us sat near the back, and I scanned the hundreds of heads and stared unblinking at one in particular. Nash Crane. He was with Ferris and a few others, laughing and carrying on with that gross, entitled smugness he now wore without care.

"We're probably going to get called up on stage," Willa said.

I muttered a 'yeah,' my eyes never leaving Nash.

Anson sighed through his nose. "Be prepared to answer questions, too," he said. "The press is here."

"Mm-hmm," I mumbled.

I wished I could read Nash's mind, see what he was really up to. Get ahead of the Midnight Circle. Find a weak spot I could use to exploit them.

Figure out a way to make Anson better.

That final thought forced me to pull my gaze from Nash and sneak a glance at my boyfriend next to me. His hands trembled in his lap and the skin under his eyes was puffy, his hair unwashed.

"You okay?" I whispered.

He leaned back in the chair and crossed his arms tightly. "I could use a few hours of sleep."

I exchanged a worried glance with Willa, but before I could say anything, a hush fell over the room as everyone shifted in their seats and looked straight ahead. The dean had stepped up on the stage. He leaned into the microphone on the black wooden podium.

"Ladies and gentlemen." He addressed the crowd with an enthusiastic smile then motioned to the front row. "Faculty and Elders of the Dark Faction. We welcome you here today. I trust you had a wonderful Solstice with friends and family?"

The room filled with cheering as his gaze scanned the room and hovered over me for a moment before he continued. "I've brought you all here on this wonderful day to talk about the upcoming Courtship Program. As most of you are aware, our decennial event is a prestigious and highly coveted competition that kicks off in a few short days, and I wanted to bring everyone up to speed before I hand over the room to the press."

Half of the front row were Elders in pristine black and grey suits, while the other half consisted of hungry reporters who immediately adjusted their cameras in preparation at the dean's words.

Shit. Talk about being tragically underprepared for this.

"Each time around, we nominate our most promising Wicked Born to compete in a series of tests to determine a pair of winners to advance in their pledge and train to join the leaders of our great Faction. It's a fair and worthy process and has never failed us." He beamed over the admiring faces of the student body. "This year, our Game Designers have decided to announce the first three tests, while keeping the final fourth test open. They'll be planning that one based on the results our contenders provide during the first three. Each test will be a weekly event and held on Fridays. During that time there will be no classes in session. You are all expected to attend and witness the rise of your next leaders."

He turned to his left and motioned with a hand to a man and woman who stood in wait. Although they were the opposite sex, they looked the same: slicked black hair, pale flawless skin, and a cunning expression as they scanned the crowd.

"Our Game Designers this year are a sibling duo coming to us from Darkstar Academy, our sister school in Romania. With that, I'd like to hand the podium over to them. Let's give them a warm welcome, shall we?"

The dean stepped away as he clapped, and the rest of the room erupted in applause as the two designers stepped up and adjusted the mic. The brother of the duo leaned in, his expression stone cold.

"Hello." He spoke with a beautiful Romanian accent that reminded me of Dracula. "My name is Adrian Negrustea, and this is my sister, Adina. We are pleased to be here at Arcane Academy. Our family has contributed to the design of the Courtship Program for centuries, and we're very excited to curate the tests for you this year here in North America."

He moved aside and let his sister Adina take the mic. "As Mr. Blackwood has previously stated, we have decided, given this year's...unique circumstances surrounding the contenders, to leave the final test open. We want to ensure the highest level of fairness in the result of this competition. In order to gain the analytics we need, the first three tests will be Potions, Enchantment, and Conjuring. In that order."

The crowd cheered with excitement.

Adina gave a curt nod. "That is all."

They both stepped back, and Mr. Blackwood took to the stand once again. "Thank you, Adrian and Adina. We're all looking forward to seeing what you have in store for us." He turned his attention forward. "And now, we'll welcome our contenders onto the stage! Let's hear it for Carol Isadora and her supplement Addy Winters!"

The room erupted with a pounding applause as the two women skipped onto the stage and stood together at the dean's side. He called off the next few teams: Adam Arkin and Jane Mort, Arien Madden and Michael Lougheed, Nash Crane and Ferris Cooper, Jack Lynch and Chasity Broomfeild, and finally Kyle Jennings and his supplement pairing Althea Thornwell.

Aside from Carol and Nash's teams, I knew none of the Wicked Born chosen for this event. These were the very witches and warlocks I was expected to face in the coming days in a fight for leadership, and I was just seeing their faces and hearing their names for the first time. They all seemed happy and eager as the crowd cheered them on while they each took their place in the line on stage.

The dean then cleared his throat, his smile widening. "And our seventh team is a special one. Comprised of Lydia Laveau, the first light born chosen for the dark and youngest Wicked Born to ever compete in the Courtship Program, alongside her wildly capable supplement, Willa Stonerose!"

He waved us up and clapped loudly into the mic. I looked to Willa, expecting a rush of boos to flood our way, but we were only met with the eager embrace of cheery gusto.

I fished around for a smile in a sea of my rattled nerves as

WICKED CURSE

I took Willa by the hand and walked down the divide that sliced the center of the room, surprised by the uplifting roar of my peers.

Just like before, when the first announcements had been made, they proved me wrong. I expected the welcome to wear off by now, when they all realized I had no right to compete. But the majority of the student body beamed up at us on the stage—a sentiment not shared by the front row of Elders and special guests. They remained staid, unmoving in their seats, as if only barely tolerating my presence. I swallowed nervously and gripped Willa's hand.

The dean peered out across the room in search of Anson. "And our final team consists of a single competitor. Anson Abernathy is a third-year student here at Arcane Academy. He's shown great promise in every field of study and comes to us by way of volunteering. He has chosen to compete without the aid of a supplement. Let's give him a round of applause!"

All heads turned toward the back of the auditorium, where Anson peeled himself from the chair and strolled to the stage to join us. He didn't smile, didn't wave. Just stood with an indifferent, empty gaze and stuffed his hands in the pockets of his jeans. Alone.

Mr. Blackwood gripped the mic. "Thank you for being here today," he said to us on the stage. "I'll now leave you in the capable hands of our eager press. We've got representatives from every region here to question each of you."

He stepped away and took a seat in the first row with the Elders and faculty. I took a deep breath, but before I had the chance to even release it, a wave of noise jumped up from the group of journalists that swarmed the stage.

My heart pounded as all eyes pointed at me, along with half a dozen recording devices and camera flashes. My head spun under the pressure of noise that assaulted me, too

CANDACE OSMOND & REBECCA HAMILTON

chaotic to understand a full question, though a few key words jumped out at me.

Miss Laveau!

Are you sure you're ready?

Right to be here...

Unfair advantage...

My mouth gaped as my eyes flitted back and forth over the hungry, relentless reporters and their insulting questions. My ears filled with the pounding beat of my heart, and a hot sweat broke out all over my body. Panic took over.

"Lydia?" Willa nudged from my side. "Are you okay?"

I shook my head, my feet retreating before my brain even told them to. I bolted off the side of the stage and made a run for the door, the wave of noise turning and attempting to follow in a lightning cloud of camera flashes. My chest burned with a breath that wouldn't release as I sprinted across the school.

But where could I go?

I'd fallen into a complete flight or fight mode, and my limbs refused to quit until I'd fled as far as possible from the Great Hall. I turned down corridors I'd never ventured before, desperate to put as much distance between me and everyone else as possible.

An arm wrapped around my body from behind and spun me toward them.

Anson.

Without missing a beat, he waved his other arm in the air, and a portal formed, sucking the air around us into the void. He pressed his lips to my forehead as I let him take me and pull us through. The opening snapped shut behind us as we landed firmly in his room.

I struggled to take a full breath as my arms crossed firmly over my chest. Tears burned my eyes. Anson held me close to him, his body humming with mutters of assurance.

"It's okay," he whispered in my ear. "It's over. We're gone."

I pulled away enough to peer up at him; his face was pale and sweaty, his eyes rimmed with dark circles.

Immediately, my focus shifted from an inward panic to an outward concern for the man I loved. I regained control of my lungs and calmed my breathing as I reached up to caress the stressed skin under his eyes.

"Are you alright?" he asked.

I nodded. "I am now. Thank you." I kissed him. "Are...*you* okay?"

His hold on me relaxed, and he released a sigh. "I'm fine. It's just...taking a lot to recover from Crane's hex. But the doses are working."

I guffawed. "Working? Or just keeping it at bay?"

He turned from me.

"Anson, at the rate you are going through those vials, you'll run out by tomorrow."

He loomed over his desk and opened the wooden box that held all the empty glass tubes. "Don't worry. My grandmother showed me how to make the potion."

My eyes bulged. Exhaustion threatened to pull me down, but my concern for him gave me strength. "What? So, you're just going to keep taking the potion for the rest of your life?"

He rested his fists against the desk and leaned forward, letting his hair fall in front of his face. I could see the tension he harbored through the hard muscles that pulled under the surface.

"What else do you propose I do, Lydia?" he asked helplessly. He craned his neck to look at me. "Who can help us? We can't exactly go storming into the Midnight Circle and demand a counter curse, can we? No more than we can demand they stop whatever it is they're doing down there. We don't have that power. And those who do, like the dean or your mother, they only tell half-truths. If we come out with something like this, it'll be squashed before it spreads, and who knows what'll happen to us then."

He rubbed his hands over his face. "If we out the Midnight Circle, it'll only be a matter of time before everyone discovers our hybrid powers." He let out a puff of air and rolled his eyes. "Maybe some already know. But if that information goes public..."

Every emotion fled from my body, and a cold gasp froze in my throat. I'd never considered that maybe, just *maybe*, there were those who already knew our secret. Knew it because there really *were* others out there like Anson and me. Light Born chosen for the Dark, bestowed with an ancient magic with no instruction on how to use it.

"Anson—"

He held up a hand and closed his eyes, his limbs slightly trembling. "Look, I'm beat. The portal travel took a lot out of me. I don't have the energy to fight about this right now." He swayed over to the bed and laid down. "Will you stay?"

Part of me wanted nothing more than to curl up in bed with him and forget the world. Even for just a day. But I couldn't. Willa would be looking for me, and I had things to face. Things I couldn't run away from forever.

I stood there in the middle of his room, my fingers twisted together with uncertainty as I stared at him; he was already sinking into the pile of bedding, his body wrought with exhaustion.

I put on a smile and took two long strides toward him to sit on the edge of the bed and place a kiss on his forehead. "I'd love to stay, but I promised Willa we'd practice today."

Anson's sleepy eyes examined mine, but whatever reprieve was there melted away.

I put my mouth to his in a warm kiss. "Thanks for saving me from the mob." I chuckled lightly. "Get some sleep. We'll figure out the rest tomorrow."

"I love you," he muttered.

"I love you, too," I said and pushed off the mattress before heading for the door.

I had to keep my composure, reign back my eagerness to leave. Because I wasn't waiting until tomorrow to figure out what was wrong with Anson.

I was going to do it right now.

And as dangerous as it might be, I knew the perfect place to start.

CHAPTER 20

Rage, mixed with determination, fueled my limbs as I bolted across the winding stone floors of the school. Wicked Born littered the campus, enjoying the day off after the assembly, and their eyes lit up as I passed them by. Surely my exit from the Great Hall was all anyone was talking about. Crazy Lydia Light Born; it was all too much for her.

But I didn't care.

My days of worrying what everyone else thought was long over. No one truly knew the turmoil of my daily life here at the academy. They only saw me for what was on the surface: a fish out of water, something to entertain them in the weeks to come as I fought in the Program.

I finally reached the wing where Nash and Ferris' room was and beat on the door with my fist, my stomach hot with the anger that toiled there. Feet shuffled on the other side of the door, and the latch clicked as someone opened it a crack. Ferris' big green eyes peered out at me.

"Where is he?" I demanded.

"He's...indisposed right now," Ferris replied. A metal chain kept the door from opening any farther than just a few inches.

"Well, tell him to throw on some pants because I need to speak with him."

He pursed his lips with a hint of uncertainty. "He's in the shower."

I narrowed my eyes. "I'll wait."

"Lydia—"

I flicked my wrist, and the chain snapped as the door pushed open. Ferris jumped back with a startling shriek. I stormed inside and gawked around their quarters. Red and black satin linens adorned every surface, and the air choked me with the heavy stench of cologne. A bare-chested Nash appeared in a narrow doorway I assumed was a closet before but now realized was their own private bathroom.

I cocked an eyebrow. "Wow, third years get special treatment, huh?"

Nash looked away with a devilish smirk as he pulled a black polo shirt from his closet and slipped it on. "No more than a first year Light Born."

I crossed my arms. "What's that supposed to mean?"

He combed back his wet hair without a care in the world. "I thought you'd have run to the ends of the earth after that disaster with the press, yet here you are. Strolling the halls of the school as if nothing can touch you. As if the rules of our society don't apply to you."

I clenched my teeth as every fiber of my being seethed at his words.

He's deflecting, Lydia. Don't let him get in your head. He knows why you're here.

"They bombarded me," I said, despite myself. "I wasn't prepared—"

"You're gonna have to build a thicker skin than that, honey," Ferris said from behind me.

I turned to find him wrapped in a gold kimono as he sat and sipped from a teacup.

"That's just the beginning of the press tour for the

Program. They'll be like hungry dogs for this whole process."
He arched one ginger eyebrow. "And they're coming for *you*."

Great, one more thing to deal with.

I spun back to face Nash. "I'm not here to talk about the Program."

"No?" he replied with mock surprise, walking over to a little buffet table under the window to pour himself a cup of tea. "What else could you possibly want, then?" He flashed me a knowing glare.

"What did you do to Anson in the caves that night?"

Nash exchanged a glance with Ferris and gave me a weak shrug. "You were there. You saw for yourself."

My jaw protested as my teeth clenched harder. "You struck him with a hex. And now he's…"

His sly expression brightened. "What? Is the golden boy not feeling well?"

"You know he's not," I spat. "The hex you used, there's no known counter curse for it."

"Oh, I wouldn't say that," Nash replied and took a calculated sip from his cup.

My patience was running thin, and my magic hummed just below the surface of my skin, begging to be used. As if it had a mind of its own.

I grabbed hold of Nash's wrist and stared into his snake-like eyes. "Just give me the counter curse, Crane." My grip tightened though he never fought back. "Or I might be tempted to use a Truth Spell and force the answer I need."

His dark eyebrows lowered as his eyes deepened with intensity. "My, Lydia, that's a highly advanced spell, one often used by Light Born." The corner of his mouth twitched as he flicked his arm from my grip and wrapped his fingers around my forearm. His hold squeezed, and I fought back a wince. His head cocked to the side. "Now, you wouldn't know how to do something like that, would you?"

I wrung my arm from his grasp and stepped back. A chilly panic filled my chest. Nash knew I was powerful; I'd foolishly revealed as much to him. But he didn't know about my hybrid powers. At least, not surely.

I stole a glance over Nash's shoulder at Ferris who hung quietly in the background. His pleading gaze offered a warning, one I was surprised to find. What was he trying to tell me?

I took in a deep breath. "Look, I know you were using illegal magic in the caves that night. Magic you have no right to use, and probably can barely handle." That elicited a slight guffaw from Nash. "You hit Anson with a dark hex, and we couldn't figure out how to counter it because we had no knowledge of the magic's origin." I swallowed nervously. "But I know the origin now. I promise not to tell the dean if you just hand over the counter curse."

The room filled with Nash's loud, guttural laugh. "The dean doesn't scare me. Look, princess. If you want the cure for your precious boyfriend, then return the pages you stole."

"You have no idea what those pages can do!" I argued. "The Midnight Circle shouldn't be messing with Talia Blackstone's magic. It's dead. Leave it that way."

Nash calmly set down his cup and strolled over to the door. He opened it wide and waved a hand in the empty space it created. "If you won't comply, then leave."

Fury seared across my skin, and I clenched my fists. A small whiff of energy pulsed from my body, and the knob ripped from Nash's hand as the door slammed shut. A split second of shock flashed across his face, but he masked it with a confident grin.

I closed my eyes for a moment and calmed myself with a few deep breaths. "Please, Nash. I think he's...dying. Do you really want that blood on your hands?"

Ferris stepped forward, but Nash held out a hand of

warning to stay back and then jabbed a finger in my direction. "You have until midnight before the final test to return the pages. If you want to leave Prince Charming to suffer until then, that's on you. Not me."

He opened the door again and stood by as he waited for me to leave. Knowing I wasn't going to win this argument, I picked up my dignity and left the room. But the second the door shut behind me, the weight of it all crashed down on my shoulders. I leaned against the wall, bracing for the impact of emotions that came erupting to the surface.

I was torn.

I had the ability to help the man I loved. But it came at a colossal price. Handing back the resurrection spell to the Midnight Circle would be letting the bad guys win. Talia's ancient power in the hands of the Midnight Circle could potentially destroy our whole world. On both sides.

But Anson's life depended on it.

This was it. I had to finally admit it to myself: I needed help. I couldn't do this on my own. I had to tell someone.

If only I knew who to trust.

I HAD to regain control of my emotions. They constantly kicked open the door that contained my hybrid magic. That darkness, that unknown source of power that usually laid dormant under my skin, was thriving after my encounter with Nash. It uneased me.

I stuffed my trembling hands under my armpits as I stormed across the school to my quarters. As I neared the mess hall, an odd commotion of noise fell over my ears. I slowed my pace and peered around the corner of one of the wide entrances and groaned.

All the press was there.

I couldn't face them right now. Not like this. Not when I was so close to the edge.

I glanced around and threw my hood up over my head in an attempt to hide my face as I skirted around the mess hall, taking the long way back to my room. I could only hope no one told them where that was. The corridor on my wing was clear, so I raced toward the door and slipped inside before locking it.

"Lydia!" Willa said with a squeal as she jumped from her desk chair, her eyes wide with concern. "Where have you been? Are you okay?" She held up her hands which trembled the same as mine.

I cringed. "Oh, Gods, I'm sorry. You can feel it, can't you?"

She nodded. "It only bothers me when you get like this." She swallowed. "When you get worked up. What's going on? Where did you run off to? The whole school has been looking for you."

I paced the floor as beads of sweat broke out all over my skin. "I just…I had to get away. They bombarded me."

Willa let out a deep sigh and sat on her bed. "I know. That was totally unfair. But…I think we can expect more of it as the Program goes on."

I tipped my face to the ceiling and closed my eyes, working to calm my breathing. "Yeah, that's pretty much what Ferris said."

"Ferris?"

I opened my eyes and looked at her. "After I ran out, Anson grabbed me and portaled us to his room. I could see then how much his health is rapidly deteriorating. He's…sick, Willa. He needs help. I…*I* need help." I spun around and plopped down on the edge of my mattress. "I went to Nash to demand answers."

She inched forward. "And?"

"He basically said I had to return the resurrection spell

before he would help me." I wrung my fingers through my hair and thrust myself forward on bouncing legs. "I have to tell someone. The dean. Anyone. I just…I can't do nothing."

She came to me and kneeled at my feet as she placed calming hands on my trembling knees. "You and I both know you can't do that. Not yet. We don't know who to trust, and Anson made you swear not to. Just think about it, Lydia. Think it through. If you confide in the dean, he's going to have a slew of other questions that you can't answer. At best, Anson will be disqualified from the Program for his health. At worst…he could be sent away to be treated and they'll discover he's been hiding hybrid powers all these years."

A moan of agony vibrated in my throat, and I fell back on the bed. Willa was right. I'd just be handing him over to the very people we were trying to hide from. Tears burned my eyes as a stream of sobs bubbled in my chest.

"I don't know what to do, Willa," I muttered through the wave of crying that erupted.

She hauled herself onto my bed and sat up straight. "If you have to give them a resurrection spell in exchange for the counter for Anson, then that's what we do."

I bolted upright and stared at her incredulously. "We can't—"

She gave me a cheeky grin. "I didn't say *which* resurrection spell."

My face twisted, tugging my eyebrows together.

"The pages you took," she said. "They're just photocopies from Talia's grimoire, right?"

I nodded and wiped my running nose with the back of my hand.

"Then we make another photocopy of the pages you have, adjust just one of the ingredients or steps, make a copy of *that* one, and use it to trade for the counter."

I combed over the details in my mind. I could see how it might work.

"We can do it," Willa urged. "At the very least, it'll buy us some time to make sure Anson gets better before they realize it's a fake."

"You think it will really work?"

She shrugged. "I don't know. But it's all we've got right now."

CHAPTER 21

"ARE YOU SURE YOU KNOW IT?" Willa asked for the hundredth time.

"Yes, yes," I replied through short breaths.

We raced around our room, pulling on clothes and whipping our hair back into elastics.

We'd slept in. Today was the first Courtship Program test and we'd stayed up most of the night memorizing every single step and ingredient for our Morphiem Elixir.

"Read it again," she said. "Just to be sure."

"Willa." I stopped and looked at her with tired eyes. "I know it. We practiced a million times."

"Are you sure?" She glanced at her watch. "The test starts in less than half an hour. We don't know what the extra challenge will be. The designers might have us do it blindfolded, or with one hand tied behind our back. *If* we're lucky. We can't waver on this."

She opened the door and waited for me. I chewed at the inside of my cheek and then sighed, holding out my hand.

"Give me the recipe," I said. "I'll read it again on the way to the Hall."

She grinned triumphantly and handed me the piece of

paper, worn from the oils of our fingers and the thousand attempts we made at perfecting it.

I read it over and over as I followed her through the school toward the Great Hall. The commotion of the waiting crowd met my ears and my heart sped up. We turned a final corner and I saw dozens of Wicked Born loitering around the entrance. They erupted with cheer at the sight of us, and I gasped, startled.

Willa grabbed my hand, and we met them all with smiles as we weaved through the crowd. The double doors swung open, revealing rows and rows of empty chairs waiting to be filled with Wicked Born eager to witness the start of the Program.

Willa and I stopped just a few feet inside to take in the enormousness of it all while everyone else swarmed in and sat down. Black banners hung from the cathedral ceilings, boasting the details of today's event. The stage near the front of the room was lined with eight tables, each one holding an equal number of small cauldrons and tools, as well as a heavily stocked shelving system behind it all.

"This is it," Willa said, glancing at me.

I inhaled deeply and tipped up my chin. "No turning back now."

The other contenders appeared and took to the stage with us as the Game Designers stood at the end. Their crisp black suits and slicked back hair made them appear almost robotic. Willa and I chose a table just as Anson stepped on the stage and claimed the one next to us. I noted his pale expression and disheveled appearance.

"Are you alright?" I whispered to him.

He only gave a weak nod as the dean took to the podium near the end where the Game Designers stood. The Great Hall was filled from side to side with eager faces.

Mr. Blackwood cleared his throat. "Welcome, everyone!" He held his arms out as the room became heavy with applause. "I know we're all excited for the first official test of our decennial Courtship Program, so I won't delay for long. As per our lovely Game Designers' decision, the first challenge will be Potions, and it will be performed by our eight talented teams without the aid of a recipe."

The fifteen contenders all exchanged a variety of glances: confidence, worry, determination. Willa was right to push me to memorize ours.

"That's right," the dean continued. "Our Wicked Born will carry out a potion of their choosing from memory. It must be a potion that will wow our judges, or risk not advancing to the next round." He waved his fingers in a circle on the surface of the podium, and a clear, crystal bowl appeared, filled with pieces of paper. "This contains the names of each team, and the order will be chosen at random." He fished out a slip of paper and unfolded it. "First up, Carol and Addy!"

Everyone cheered, and the dean raised his arms in the air before snapping his fingers. The tall, ornate windows disappeared as long banners rolled down and blocked out the sunlight. Another snap of his fingers, and dozens of torches blazed to life, lining the walls with massive flames and casting the entire hall in firelight.

Mr. Blackwood leaned into the mic one last time. "Let the games begin!"

He stepped away and turned toward all of us, clapping along with the crowd for Carol and Addy. We all stood by as the two women fetched a slew of ingredients from the shelves behind us and filled their table. Carefully, they added each item in calculated measures to their steaming cauldron.

After about twenty minutes, the two stepped back, pleased with the result, and Addy jumped off the stage to grab one of the many indoor plants that graced the room. She set the short and stubby succulent with large purple leaves on their table as Carol addressed the crowd.

"We all know how to cast an invisibility enchantment," she

called out and scooped a vial into the cauldron with a pair of metal tongs. "But an invisibility *potion* can render a living thing completely undetectable from the inside out. No sounds of breathing, no heartbeat to be found." She began gently pouring the concoction over the plant, and it disappeared before our very eyes. With a grin, she waved a hand through the air where the plant should be. "Just totally gone."

"Or is it?" Addy opened a small satchel and sprinkled its contents over the void. The plant reappeared, as if it had always been there.

The Great Hall boomed with cheer as the judges—a mix of faculty, elders, and the Designers—all exchanged looks of mild approval from the front row. We stood in wait as they whispered among themselves. Finally, they settled back into their seats, and one of them gave a nod toward the dean who stood idly at the edge of the stage. He smiled and leaped for the mic.

"Carol and Addy, congratulations! Your winning potion has advanced you to the next test!"

We all clapped and cheered for Carol's team. I didn't dislike the woman and wanted to see her succeed, but I really hoped her talent didn't bring her to the end. I wanted to stand there, with Anson and Willa. Then again, anyone would be better than Nash at my side.

Four more teams went before us, leaving just me and Willa with Nash's team and Anson. Two of the four failed to perfect their potions and were immediately disqualified. My feet began to protest standing still for so long, and my patience wore thin.

I just wanted to make our potion and move on so we could slip back to our room before the press swarmed us again. I peered out over the crowd in search of them. It wasn't hard to pick out their extra eager faces, with cameras and notepads clutched in their grips.

Anson was the sixth, and he wavered as his hands gripped

the edge of the table. He took a few deep breaths before slowly collecting the ingredients he needed and concocting them inside the cauldron. Before long, his potion steamed like a perfect brew, which he gently ladled it into a large vial.

He held it up to the room. "As most of you know, it's rare for a Dark Born to hold weight over an element. Rare, but not unheard of. I was lucky enough to be given a natural affinity to water." He poured the contents of the vial over the table, covering it in a thick, aqua-colored blanket of liquid. He grinned. "And ice."

He slapped his hands together loudly, and the enchanted, watery veil turned to solid ice, encasing the table and the items on top in a frozen state. With another booming clap, the entire thing shattered to millions of pieces and scattered across the stage onto the floor.

Wicked Born cheered as the judges convened once again, and I held my breath. Within a few seconds, they came to a decision and one of them gave an assuring nod to the dean.

The dean pulled the mic closer and said into it, "Anson Abernathy, you have qualified for the next round."

My lungs relaxed, and I turned to Anson. With nothing to lean on, he lowered himself to the floor, cross-legged. My eyes widened, and my instinct was to go to him, but he gave me a discreet shake of his head.

Willa held my hand. It took every ounce of my willpower not to run to my boyfriend, but it would only raise suspicion around me and the people I'm connected to. And that wasn't good for any of us.

The dean stood at his post on the podium and selected another name from the bowl. He turned and smiled at Willa and me before leaning into the mic.

"Our seventh team will be Lydia Laveau and her supplement Willa Stonerose! I'm excited to see what you ladies have to show us."

With hundreds of eyes fixed on me, my cheeks filled with

warmth. I lit the flame under the tabletop cauldron and organized our tools while Willa grabbed all the ingredients from the shelves at our backs.

Whispers and curious gasps of breath trickled up from the crowd as we worked to add each ingredient to the mix. A pinch of this, a sprinkle of that, a spoonful of another. All carefully measured and added at just the right times, in just the right order.

The Morphiem Elixir was one of the most delicate potions I'd ever seen or attempted. There was no room for error, no forgiveness for any missteps.

Willa held two vials as I carefully spooned the potion into each one. The final touch was a drop of our blood in each glass tube. I pinched a needle between my fingers while pricking our thumbs. The two drops of blood mixed with the contents, and steam billowed up. We exchanged one last look and gave one another a nod. We were ready.

In unison, we downed the potions and then spoke together, "*Et fiet vobis.*"

I knew the spell was working by the reaction of the room. Loud whispers and sharp intakes of breath met my ears, and I beamed with pride as Willa's face slowly morphed into mine. Like looking in a mirror, only I knew it wouldn't match the reflection of the face I now wore: hers.

We turned and faced a room of stunned expressions, and a deafening silence covered us like a blanket. My chest heaved with anticipation. Was it too much? Was it too advanced? Could we possibly be disqualified for using such an expert potion, or worse, did it reveal too much about our abilities? *My* abilities, the ones I wasn't supposed to have?

I stood frozen while Willa gripped my fingers under the table. My eyes fixed on the judges below. They took longer than they did with any other teams to discuss our entry. Finally, they dispersed to the seats again, expressions of staidness painted on thick.

One of them gave that coveted nod, and I felt my body dissolve into relief. Willa squeezed harder and turned to hug me.

"I feel like vomiting," she whispered in my ear.

I pulled away and already saw the effects of the temporary potion wearing away. Her beautiful caramel skin bled through the mask of my paleness.

The final team left waiting was Nash and Ferris. The dean didn't have to select their names from the bowl and instead encouraged them to proceed.

I caught Nash's sly stare as he adjusted the red velvet blazer he wore. Ferris fetched all the ingredients from the shelves and filled their table with dozens of bottles and sacks of things. Just a few feet away, I could hardly make out their movements among the mess.

Once their cauldron bubbled and steamed, Ferris held an empty vial in his hands while Nash spooned their potion into it. I tried to keep track of the items they used, to determine what they were about to do, but it was chaos on their table. I was sure they didn't even use all the things they grabbed.

Willa nudged my arm and motioned with her chin. "Look," she whispered. "Nash's jacket."

While one of his hands slowly poured spoonful after spoonful of the mixture into a vial, his other hand reached under his jacket into his pant's pocket. My eyes widened when I witnessed him slip out another large glass tube and swap the cork top to the clearly fake potion. No one else seemed to notice. But I did.

Nash was cheating.

"Oh, my God," Willa whispered again and narrowed her eyes. "Is that…"

I examined the new glass tube with extra care, trying to see what she saw. When Nash held it up for the crowd with a boastful grin, I realized what she meant. The rim, the way it bowed and waved. Hand-blown glass. Not rare, but that particular vial came from Willa's personal collection. Hand crafted by her mother. I knew this because that was the exact vial we'd been using in Potions class.

The one Hallowell had confiscated from us.

Willa tensed and opened her mouth to speak, but I held her back.

"Don't," I whispered. "That's the one with the snakeskin in it. It would have changed Nash's appearance to snake-like features but...if they add drops of their blood..."

Willa brightened. "They'll literally turn into snakes."

"Only if the right words are spoken," I muttered under my breath. "Just wait."

Just as I suspected, Nash and Ferris added drops of their own blood to the potion, probably assuming they could just copy our winning entry and advance. They each sipped from the same tube in turn and, before they had a chance to utter a single word, I called out for everyone to hear.

"*Anguis!*"

The entire hall shuffled in their chairs as the judges tensed and stood, clearly angry that I dared interfere with the test. Nash and Ferris gawked at me with a mixture of confusion and worry. But I didn't care. They were the ones who were about to get disqualified.

Anson was by my side. "What did you do?"

I shushed him. "Watch."

Within seconds, they both buckled over and convulsed. Like a wave, the crowd inched forward to see what was happening, and the judges jumped to the edge of the stage in a panic.

Nash and Ferris' figures morphed and shrunk, their clothes slipping to the floor. I stood, filled with glee at two snakes that coiled into piles.

They got what they deserved.

The dean ran over, bolts of silver magic crackling over his arms. He waved them around in a fright of anger and urgency, releasing the boys from their self-inflicted punishment. I watched Mr. Blackwood's face, waiting for the appraise I expected for flushing out a cheater, but was surprised to only find malice in his eyes.

"What have you done?" he bellowed and stormed across the stage while Nash and Ferris—already back to their human forms—frantically shoved on their clothing.

"That should teach them to mess with magic they know nothing about," I replied.

The dean pinched the bridge of his nose. "Lydia, you cannot disrupt an entry while it's in process. That's grounds for disqualification."

My hopeful expression fell into despair. "They're the ones who should be disqualified! Not only did they *steal* that potion from me, they cheated and copied us!"

The male Game Designer, Adrien, stepped forward from the floor below and peered up at us. "Do you have proof of this?"

My stare immediately fled to Hallowell, but he only narrowed his eyes. There was no way in hell that man was going to take my side in this. He probably gave the potion to them to begin with.

I motioned to Willa. "She can attest."

One of the Elders piped in with a deep eye roll. "Anyone else aside from your biased supplement?"

My lungs squeezed with panic as my mind fought for an answer, a way out of this. How quickly everything turned around on me. If this were any other situation, Nash would be seen for what he truly was: a conniving, lying, stealing, cheat of a snake. But, as I took in the grim expressions that faced me in the Great Hall, I realized...that was never going to happen.

Reluctantly, I gritted my teeth as I shook my head in admission.

The judges huddled together for a few moments before

Adrien and his sister took to the stage. Adrien leaned into the mic.

"It has been decided Mr. Crane and his supplement will advance to the next test."

I clenched my fists at my sides, allowing my powers to flood to the surface. But Anson's sudden touch, his hand wrapping around my waist, kept me grounded.

"As for Ms. Laveau and Ms. Stonerose, take this as your only warning," the judge continued. "You are not to interfere with another contestant's demonstration again or you will be immediately disqualified." He let his gaze pan across the remaining contestants. "That stands for all of you."

Hallowell sat smugly in his chair, and the rest of the panel sat down with tight lips. They wouldn't even offer me so much as a glance. In that moment, I realized two things to be true. My presence in the Program was tolerated, at best. And…

They want Nash to win.

I knew then, there was nothing I could do to get him and Ferris kicked out of the Program. Rage filtered through my entire body. Anson's grip around my waist tightened as he gently pulled me back toward him, reminding me to keep my composure. The dean stood at the mic once more to congratulate the winners and invite everyone back next Friday for the second test: Enchantment. The press rushed to the stage, and Nash gave me a sly wink from the corner of his eye before giving the camera his attention, charm dialed to full blast.

"What the hell was all that?" Willa asked as other reporters jabbed recording devices our way and spewed a stream of inaudible questions.

"Hallowell must have given the potion to Nash." I shook my head. "The game is rigged."

Anson sighed at my back. "Then that means this just got a whole lot harder."

CHAPTER 22

IT WAS hard enough to walk these halls as an outcast, avoiding the stares and doing my best to ignore the rude whispers at my audacity to roam the same floors as them.

But I'd take silent stereotyping over the forceful and invasive presence of the Wicked Born press. They were everywhere. Hallways, dark corners, lingering outside the bathrooms. Even the mess hall was a live zone of reporters, prying students for information about the school, the event, and us contenders. They'd yet to get their hands on me, and I knew the hunger for my exclusive words was deepening.

"It's ridiculous they're even allowed to be here," Willa said as we waited in the shadow of a blind corner for Anson. He glanced over his shoulder before slinking into the slim protection the little nook provided. "I mean, it's a *school.*"

"Yeah, but we're not kids," he pointed out and handed us both coffees. He had taken the risk of braving the mess hall for us. "We're adults, and this isn't the mundane world. We're not protected under any laws of minors. The Courtship Program is one of the most respected events of our culture. The press have a right to be here and report to the world what's going on."

I rolled my eyes and held the warm paper cup between my hands. "We're nothing more than spectacles." Anson's hand pressed comfortingly at my back, and I smiled. "Did you run into any trouble?"

He sleepily shook his head. "No." The corner of his mouth twitched. "But they're not looking for me."

A moan rolled around in my chest. "So, what's the plan for today? Are we practicing for the next test?"

"Enchantment?" Willa piped in. "I'd like to. But I'm not as worried about this one as the others. You're pretty confident, right?"

I grimaced. "About enchantments? Yeah. I've been enchanting things since I was seven. Clothes, books, food, my appearance. I could do an enchantment spell with my eyes closed. But about the test? With what happened at the last one...not so much."

She took a big gulp of her coffee and glanced at her watch. "All the more reason to over-prepare for the test. I'm going to head to the library and study all the past Programs that had Enchantment as a test and see what extra challenges are most common."

I grinned. "I've got a quick meeting at the paper. Meet up in a bit?"

"Sure," Willa replied and looked to Anson. "Make sure she gets there unscathed?"

He gave her a quick salute before she ducked out and mingled with the passing crowd. I took another sip of my coffee as Anson pulled me closer and moved us further into the shadow of the crook.

His lips found mine, and I happily accepted them. We hadn't had a moment alone in what felt like forever. The unexpected heat of his body wrapped me in a blanket, and I relaxed into the embrace. His mouth slid from mine and brushed against the skin of my cheek, resting near my ear as his warm breath tickled.

"You'll have to show me some Enchantment pointers later," he whispered.

My hand wrapped around the back of his head, my fingertips combing through his hair, and I gazed into those dark voids that stared back.

"Yeah?" I replied with a smirk. "I think I could teach you a thing or two."

He pressed his forehead to mine, and a deep hum rolled from his throat. "I look forward to it."

"You look well today."

"I took a dose this morning," he told me. "I tweaked my grandmother's recipe to double the potency. Seems to work a little better."

My brow pinched with worry. "Is that safe?"

The heat suddenly left our embrace, and he pulled away. "It's just herbs, Lydia. Not poison."

My gaze fell to the floor. I wanted to beg him to be more careful, to maybe even let me help him. It killed me to not tell him about Nash and the fake resurrection spell. He'd demand me not to do it. He knew first-hand what Talia Blackstone's magic could do in the wrong grips.

Sure, trading a fake spell for Anson's cure would fix his situation, but it was only a band-aid. It would only be a matter of time before Nash and the Circle figured out it wasn't the real spell and they'd come for me. For him. For Willa. I didn't want to risk that.

But I couldn't let him die.

Maybe I was being dramatic, but the dark hex that lived in Anson's body didn't seem to be letting up, and I feared it would only get worse. Willa and I were nearly done constructing the fake resurrection spell. So, the question I had to ask myself was: do I do it? Trade a lie for a cure, and risk the backlash?

I looked at my boyfriend, the man I loved, and saw the dark circles around his eyes and the pale, clammy skin hidden just under the thin veil of a weak potion...and I knew I'd do anything for him. Whatever retaliation Nash and the Circle threw my way, I'd handle it.

A burst of Wicked Born passed by the opening of the nook we stood in, and he sighed as his hand slipped into mine.

"Let's get you to the newsroom."

Before I could say anything, he gently tugged my arm and glanced both ways before pulling us out of the corner and blending in with the Saturday morning crowd. Vendor tables lined the halls, selling Arcane Academy merchandise, Program t-shirts, and magical themed cupcakes with dancing sprinkles, all taking advantage of the increased traffic on campus and the historical event that was playing out before us.

I paused at one table that sold novelty mugs. A row of large white cups caught my eye among all the mostly black merch, and I scooped it up.

"It...color changes when it gets hot," the lady on the other side of the table said.

She picked one up and wrapped her hand around it, warming the surface. Anson stood by my side as the mug changed from white to black, and the woman stared at me with wide eyes. Was she...afraid?

"I made them...uh, they're inspired by..." She cleared her throat. "You."

My heart thudded in my chest. She was scared of my reaction.

I turned the cup over in my hands as I admired the clever idea. I exchanged a glance with Anson, and he lightly shrugged.

I smiled at the woman and held out the mug. "How much?"

"What?" she replied, startled.

"For the cup?" I said. "These are cool. I want one."

Her shoulders relaxed under the curtain of blonde curls that covered them. "Uh, you can have it."

"Really? No, I insist on paying. Please."

Her pale cheeks filled with pink. "It's yours if you would, maybe, *sign* a few of them?"

I laughed. "Seriously? Like, autograph them?"

The woman gave a nervous shrug. "Lydia Laveau merch is pretty hot right now. Autographed merch would sell like crazy."

At my side, Anson chuckled and looked away as he sipped his coffee. Was this chick for real? People would actually buy things with my name on it? The idea was ridiculous. Still, I wanted the mug and part of me wanted to help out the woman.

"Got a Sharpie?" I asked.

She brightened and pulled one from her pocket. I scrawled my signature on the bottom of a few of the color changing mugs and thanked her for mine as I stuffed it in my leather shoulder bag. Anson took my hand as he led me through the congestion of people that filled the hallways.

"Come on, Miss Famous," he said jokingly.

I guffawed. "Hardly."

We rounded a corner and came face-to-face with a swarm of reporters who flew into a cavalcade of questions and camera flashes. I shielded my eyes and winced as Anson pulled me back.

"Lydia! Lydia!" they called to me. "How do you feel about the Potions test? Did Nash Crane really steal the potion from you? Who do you think will win?"

My ears rang from the noise, and Anson pulled me tight to his chest. I buried my face against his leather jacket as the air around us tightened and he waved his other arm at his side. A portal opened, and the noise level increased, crashing down on us like a tidal wave as he pulled us through.

In a split second, everything was silent again as we came through the other side and landed with a hard stomp on the stone floor. We were in the office wing, just down from the dean's office and right outside the newsroom. One of the only places on campus the press wasn't permitted to venture.

My chest heaved, and I buckled over to calm down.

"Hardly famous, you say?" Anson joked.

"They're relentless," I replied and straightened. "Willa thinks I should get it over with and talk to them."

He shook his head. "They'll chew you up and spit you out, Lydia. They don't care about you. They only want the story. *A* story, even if they twist it into something it's not." His lips pursed. "You should know that."

"Well, I know *I* won't be that kind of journalist," I argued. "I have dignity and respect. So, what am I supposed to do, then?" I added with a shrug. "Have you portal me around everywhere?"

Anson quickly wrapped a hand around my waist and pulled me to him, our noses touching as his fingers pressed firmly at my back. "Whatever it takes to keep you safe."

A grin smeared across my mouth before I stretched up to place a kiss on his waiting lips. "Thanks, but I can handle myself."

His chest hummed with a quiet laugh. "I know. But can you blame me for trying?"

I shook my head and kissed him again. Gods, I loved this man.

"I've got to go," he whispered in a single breath that caressed my face. "TA duties to catch up on. *Actual* TA duties." He let me go and gave me a wink. "See you later for that Enchantment lesson?"

I nodded, giddy inside. Our fingers remained entwined as he began to walk away, and I held on to the last second before he headed down the hall. At his departure, my arm fell to my side. Today was a good day. Anson seemed well enough that I forgot about the hex for a moment. But he was doubling the dose of his grandma's potion, and I fell back into the usual pit of worry as I watched him disappear.

I had to get that counter curse from Nash.

There would surely be retaliation once they figured out it was a fake. And they would figure it out when they eventually attempted to bring Talia back from the dead with the ancient spell.

How would the retaliation come? An attack on me? On those I loved? Or would it be more subtle? Like the hex Anson now carried. Something else they could leverage over me.

As I stood alone in the corridor outside the newsroom and pondered over all the uncertainties that faced me, I knew then what I had to do. If I were to swap the resurrection spell for a counter on Anson, then I had to have a backup plan in place. I had to tell someone about the Midnight Circle and the things they were doing before they figured out it was a fake.

I just had to decide who to tell.

"Lydia?" Tom's voice spoke from behind. I turned to find his head poking out the glass pane door. "You coming in? We're about to start."

I inhaled with a smile. "Yeah, I'm coming."

I followed Tom inside where four others sat around the large narrow table that anchored the space. Two women, two men, and dozens of papers in front of them. I stood in the doorway and held my breath as they peered up at me, but I quickly relaxed when they welcomed me in with greetings and a wave of hands.

Tom walked around to the front end of the table and faced us as I took a seat directly across from him, everyone else sitting along the sides.

"Lydia, welcome to the first official Arcane News meeting of the new year," Tom said. "This is Janie, Tyler, Marley, and Adam."

I nodded at each of my fellow journalists. "Hey, guys. Thanks for letting me join."

"Happy to have you," Marley replied. "We could use some fresh blood."

Tom ruffled some papers. "You can relax here, Lydia. These are your people. There will be zero talk of Light Born or Dark Born politics toward one another. Just a group of intelligent, like-minded individuals who love the news with an unbiased point of view."

I settled back in my seat with a sense of warmth in my stomach. "Great."

"Right," he said to the table. "Let's get started, shall we?"

We all opened notebooks and clicked pens, ready to proceed. I could sense they didn't see me as everyone else in the school did: the Light Born daughter who was chosen for their dark, secret Faction. I was just Lydia here.

"I hope you all had a nice break at home with your families over the holiday," Tom said. "But obviously things are moving pretty fast here on campus. The halls are filled with guests and vendors. The big guns press are everywhere. This New Year's edition of the paper won't just be sent out to our school. Digital copies will be sent to every Dark Wicked born across the globe, and hard copies will be printed and sent to all seven academies."

My brain immediately flew into a mode of plotting. The words I contribute to this particular paper would be read by *every* single Dark Born in the world?

"Marley." He turned his attention to her with a clipboard in hand. "You've got History. I need you to really dig into the details of past Courtship Programs. Tests, contenders, who won, who lost, casualties. Whatever you can find."

Marley nodded and began jotting down notes.

"Lifestyle," he continued and pointed the tip of his pen toward Janie. "You've got that covered, right?"

Janie gave a confident wink. "Absolutely."

"Adam, I need you to gather up individual interviews with each contender and their supplement," Tom said. "Tyler, you're on layout, but can you maybe jump in and help Adam with that? Eight teams, fifteen interviews. That's a lot, and it might be hard to get an exclusive with the teams that have already lost."

I was included on that master list, but they never once alluded to it. I wasn't a contender here in this room. I was just me, a budding journalist. But not just that. I was suddenly filled with a new sense of hope that I could find a place in this school.

"Lydia," Tom called across the table. "How's that feature with the dean coming along?"

I moaned inwardly. "I, uh, started it. Just need to steal him for one more interview to finish some of the questions I had. The piece should be ready soon."

He clapped his hands together with a cute smile. "Excellent. I won't keep you guys any longer. We've all got work to do on this lovely Saturday. Let's make this a paper they won't forget."

The team jumped from their chairs and dispersed to the smaller desks while I sauntered around to Tom.

"Hey, can I ask a favor?" I tapped my pen against my thigh nervously.

"Yeah, totally," he replied. "Always."

I glanced around, making sure everyone was preoccupied before I leaned in, lowering my voice. "I have this lead on a...potentially explosive story. Like, world-changing."

He raised his blond eyebrows. "Do tell."

"There may be an underground coven forming here on campus, but I can't divulge too much. It's...a bit risky. But I want to pursue it."

Tom shifted uncomfortably as he leaned against the edge of the table. "Well, I don't know if I can give you the go-ahead to put yourself in danger, Lydia." He chuckled. "Anson may kill me."

I put on a playful smile. "No, no. It's not like that. I'll be fine. But this coven, it's...they're playing around with things they shouldn't be touching. And I have reason to believe that members of our faculty are involved."

Tom rubbed his hand over his jaw, then let it sit there as he shook his head. "Gods, that would make a great add-on to this edition," he said, though he paused a long moment before continuing. Finally, he exhaled. "Okay. Pursue it. *Carefully*. And report on it anonymously."

"Anonymously?"

"Yeah, I can say the story was sent in without a name," he replied. "But I'll need proof to go along with it."

"Like, what kind of proof?"

"Pictures, videos, items," he said. "Anything tangible that can both prove the coven's existence and the involvement of professors." He cleared his throat and cracked open a water bottle he grabbed from the table. "Can you do that?"

I had the perfect opportunity to expose the Midnight Circle and walk away unscathed. I grinned widely. "Yeah, I can do that."

"Awesome." Tom happily shoved off from the table. He lowered his gaze in a serious manner—an expression that didn't quite fit on his sweet and kind face. "But I want you to report back to me. *Often*. Before you make any risky moves, anything at all. I want to know you're safe, or where I can help if need be."

I gave him a mock salute, releasing him from the attempt of seriousness. "Roger that."

I left the newsroom, grinning from ear to ear. I had a whole new sense of hope and could see a way to the end of this. Through all the leverage that hung over my head, past the bullshit that Nash Crane continued to pile up in front of me.

I had a plan.

All I had to do was break into the Midnight Circle one more time and get the stone-cold proof I needed to back up this story. If I could pull it off, then I wouldn't need to worry about finding someone to trust with the information. I wouldn't need help from the dean or my mother, or people I constantly second guessed. First, I'd trade the fake spell for Anson's counter curse. Then I was going to expose the Circle and bring them down.

I was going to tell the whole world.

And all I had to do was not get caught snooping this time.

But how was I going to do that?

CHAPTER 23

ANSON WAS SICK, a fact I could no longer debate. He wasn't getting better, and the potion his grandmother had given him was already weakening against the dark hex that Nash had cursed upon him.

But now I had hope.

Thoughts formulated in circles in my mind as I strolled across campus toward my boyfriend's quarters. The late evening sky cast the school in a dark blanket, and moonlight slipped across the floor through the many archways and windows.

The castle really came to life at night, reminding me that it wasn't just a school for witches, but an ancient structure that would be here long after we were all gone. Torches lit the way as I skirted around the common areas and took the less travelled route to the wing where his room was located.

He knew I was headed over, so I knocked once and let myself in. His long, lithe frame suffocated a large bean bag chair, a sketchbook and charcoal in his hands. He glanced up at me with a weak smile.

"Hey," he greeted, setting his things on the floor before pushing himself out of the bean bag.

My heart kicked up a notch. "Hey, to you, too."

A pit in my stomach warmed at the sight of his shirtless torso, littered with tattoos, flexed and gleaming in the candlelight that filled the dim room. Anson was the most beautiful creature I'd ever seen in my life. He had this tragic beauty about him that he wore without care, making it incredibly hard to formulate a coherent thought in his presence. Especially in times like this, when I had him all to myself.

He sauntered over to me, the black tendrils of the dark curse that surrounded his heart pulsating on the skin of his chest. At least they hadn't spread much further than the last time I'd seen them. Part of me relaxed knowing his grandma's concoction was at least keeping the hex's damage at bay.

"Come to teach me a few things about Enchantment?" His lips curled as they inched closer to my face.

I tipped up my chin and welcomed his mouth on mine, relishing in the warmth that exuded from his skin. His breath. His very presence.

Simply put, Anson was intoxicating.

I pulled back with a slight gasp, my head swimming. "I hope you've saved some energy. It can be…exhausting."

My back pressed up to the door as Anson's body leaned against mine, his arms trapping me in a cage I never wanted to escape from. His dark eyes flashed with a hunger that matched my own as his gaze raked over my body. His finger trailed down my neck, following the thumping artery that gave me away, and he placed a smooth, lingering kiss there.

I wrapped my arms around his shoulders. Goosebumps covered my hot skin, and his face nuzzled my neck as his breath cascaded against my earlobe.

"Can I tell you a secret?" he whispered.

I moaned in response.

"I don't need any help with Enchantment."

I leaned back and grinned. "My, Mr. Abernathy. Luring

me to your bed, then, are you?"

My hands slipped from his shoulders and caressed the soft curves of his torso, cascading down, and I hooked my fingertips in the waist of his grey sweatpants. A slight tremble rocked through him, and he pressed against me with a deep groan. Our mouths came together and locked in a passionate kiss.

Nothing could sever us at this point. I wanted to devour every inch of him. But I knew his energy wouldn't last—not with the way it wavered lately, coming and going like a fleeting breath.

I grinned against his lips. "Guess I'll have to teach you a thing or two about something else then."

With one swift movement, Anson's arms scooped under my thighs and hoisted me into his arms. I wrapped my legs around his waist and pulled at the back of his hair while our lips smashed together in a heated embrace.

He lowered me onto the bed and crawled over my panting body, and I grabbed his arms and forced him onto his back as I climbed on top of him.

My shirt came off quickly, and I peered down at him with a devilish smirk. "Just sit back and enjoy the ride."

His hips rolled upward, driving a warm purr from my throat. "Whatever you say, teach."

I LEFT behind a sleeping Anson and crept through the empty corridors of the school. I had an hour until midnight, and if the Circle was gathering tonight, then I had to sneak into the meeting place now and get the proof Tom needed. I couldn't trade Talia's fake resurrection spell for Anson's cure until I had everything in place.

I glanced over my shoulder before rounding the corner to the professor's wing and, when the coast was clear, I summoned an invisibility enchantment and sped down to the end of the massive hallway to where it rounded into a dead corner. The hidden entrance.

But as I placed my hand against the stone wall and didn't feel the same magical energy pressing back as before, I knew it was no use.

They'd moved the entrance.

"Damnit," I said under my breath.

I searched around the wall, hoping to pick up on that energy signature. Defeat hung heavy in my gut, and I gave the stone a kick. I needed to get in there. I needed that cold, hard proof of the illegal coven's existence.

And there was only one other place I could think of to look.

Nash's room.

I snuck across the school and headed for the third-year wing that held Nash and Ferris's quarters. I stopped at the mouth of the corridor and peered down the long, dark hallway. Only a couple of torches lit the narrow space, and no one was around.

I crept along the wall, holding on to my invisibility cloak as I approached their door. *Closed.* I pressed my ear to it and listened for any sign of life, but only silence echoed back. I took a deep breath and slowly turned the knob before slipping inside.

I stood there frozen, my chest heaving with anxious breaths as my ears perked for any proof I wasn't alone. But the room was totally empty of life. I checked the bathroom they shared, just in case. Also empty, though humidity lingered in the air, telling me someone had recently showered. A sure sign that Nash and Ferris were not long gone.

I wasted no time in searching around. I had no idea what I was actually looking for, but I figured I'd know it when I saw it. Paperwork, writings, pictures, anything at all that proved the Midnight Circle existed and were up to no good.

The click of the door unlatching alerted me someone was coming in. I flexed the enchantment that protected my appearance as I stood straight and held my breath. Ferris walked in and stopped just inside the door. He peered around curiously, as if noting the disrupted belongings in their room, and then sniffed at the air.

He sighed dramatically. "Show yourself, Lydia. I know you're here."

My heart squeezed in my chest. *Just stay still. Wait for him to leave.*

Ferris rolled his eyes and flipped back a long red curl from his face. "I can smell your perfume, girl. Just come out." He locked the door and turned back to face the room. "I won't tell anyone. But Nash is going to be back soon, so it's best you leave now."

Hesitantly, I dropped the glamour of invisibility and crossed my arms. Ferris's eyes widened as I appeared out of thin air, and he smiled. A genuine expression. I hated how he could do that. Make me still believe he cared, even for a split second.

We stared at one another, letting the silence and tension mix around us.

Finally, Ferris caved. "If you're looking for a way in, they've moved the entrance."

I failed to hide the surprise on my face.

"Must have been after you stole that spell everyone's been going crazy over," he added.

I arched an eyebrow. "For a coven that wanted me to join so bad, they sure work hard to keep me out."

"Tricking you into joining was all for show, you know that, right?" he told me. "It was a test for Nash."

I pursed my lips. "Figures."

"Kudos on that little trick you pulled during the first test," he said. "I told Nash not to use it." He chortled. "Guess it serves us right for stealing."

"And cheating," I added.

Ferris's freckled face pinched with a grin. "And cheating." He shrugged. "But, hey, it got us to advance. So all is well."

"Is it?" I challenged.

He tipped his head to the side and urged something with his eyes. Something he wanted me to see, but couldn't tell me. "What do you think?"

"I think everything's a Goddamn mess, and you guys are using Anson's life as leverage over me."

His eyes widened, and he took a step closer. "For the record, I wanted no part in that. I've tried to reason with Nash to stop. I don't want that blood on my hands."

I shook my head. "Why are you telling me this?"

"Like I said before, I *am* your friend, Lydia. Whether you believe it or not. I'm loyal to Nash, yes, but the friendship you and I, and even Willa, formed…that's real to me. It still is."

I firmed my arms across my chest. "Then help me stop the Circle."

He heaved a helpless sigh. "I can't do that."

"Then shut up and stay out of my way."

He wavered in place before reluctantly stepping aside and unlocking the door. I stomped over to it and grabbed the knob, but he placed his hand over mine.

My eyes shot to his, and I fought with my resolve. I liked Ferris. Truly. It seemed like forever had passed since I'd admitted that, though I couldn't ignore the fact I honestly thought of him as a close ally once.

But there was no way I could ever trust him again—not while he was so close to my enemy.

His hand trembled over mine as he seemed to fight with his thoughts. "I can't help you. I'd be dealt the same fate your boyfriend has." He inhaled deeply. "But I can tell you where they moved the entrance."

Was this a trap? I chewed at my lip. Even if it was, it still sounded like the only shot I had. "Where?"

"In Haggy's apothecary."

My eyes bulged with disbelief. "Miss Haggy is a member of the Midnight Circle?"

"The Circle runs deeper than you think, Lydia." He leaned in front of me as he poked his head out the door and glanced back and forth. "Go, now. Nash will be here soon."

I wanted to say thank you for the intel, but I stifled down the urge. I couldn't show any sign of weakness to Ferris, or anyone else for that matter. While I felt better about him than I did Nash, I still didn't have an ounce of trust for either of them.

Ferris might claim to be my friend and seem to want to help, but he could also be leading me right into a trap.

MY PLANS TO sneak into the Midnight Circle and gather the proof I needed came to a screeching halt once Ferris divulged details of the new location of the entrance. I couldn't exactly poke around Haggy's shop without her watching my every move. And now that I knew she was a member of the coven, I had to even be careful when going there for supplies.

The rest of the week flew by in a series of classes, practice, and stolen late nights with Anson. Friday rolled around in the blink of an eye, and I now stood on the stage in the Great Hall for the second test: Enchantment.

My fellow remaining Wicked Born contenders flanked each side of the table Willa and I waited behind. It was a huge turn out once again, the giant room filled from side to side with eager onlookers.

The dean took to the podium and breathed into the mic. "Welcome, everyone! Thank you for coming to witness the second stage of our beloved Program. Our six remaining teams will compete against one another in a display of enchanting abilities." He turned slightly and gave us all an encouraging smile. "The Game Designers have decided to deepen the difficulty by adding the challenge of a blindfold."

An audible gasp swarmed through the crowd, and I dared a glance down at the front row where the designer duo sat with the judges. Hallowell glared up at me, almost smugly. As if he thought this would be hard for me.

Little did he know, I could enchant with my eyes closed, and I was quite literally about to prove it.

"In front of each of you is a sheet," Mr. Blackwood continued. "Underneath it is a series of predetermined objects. Once you're all securely blindfolded, you'll begin in unison and attempt to enchant each item in succession. Once you fail to animate something, you'll automatically be disqualified as the item will disappear."

Willa and I exchanged a glance. This *should* be one of the easiest things we'd done all week, but with the way things had been going in my life lately, I couldn't help but worry. Too much was at stake.

"Time to put your claim to the test," she whispered to me and playfully nudged my arm.

I mean, I had told her I could do an enchantment spell with my eyes closed. But I'd also told her I was worried the tests were rigged, and I couldn't shake that feeling, even now.

I grabbed her hand and squeezed tightly. "We got this."

I hope. But now wasn't the time to pass my worries onto my supplement.

The Game Designers came behind each of us and made sure the blindfolds were secure and completely covered our eyes.

"Contenders," the dean said, "remove your sheets and begin with the item farthest to the left, then make your way through the line. You cannot move on to the next item until you've successfully enchanted the one before it. But there's another twist. Only the first four teams to complete the task will move on, so you mustn't fall behind. Good luck!"

My ears rang as the crowd erupted into a quick cheer, but I held Willa's hand tightly between us. As much of an advantage Enchantment was for me, it could easily become my downfall. Even with the help of my sieve ring, I could quickly slip deep into my magic, letting too much out because my guards weren't up.

Despite my best efforts, Willa seemed to sense my worry as she tightened her grip on my hand. Her other hand removed the thin blanket that covered our unknown objects.

My free hand reached out and smoothed over the things in front of us. A mix of hard, sharp, soft, and cold touched my fingers. I moved back to the first item, a small candelabra, and, one by one, Willa and I successfully enchanted each object, making our way through the dozen or so things before us.

When we got to the eighth item, an oversized button up shirt, I felt a block of some kind. The garment didn't match the space and energy around it. Almost as if...it was already enchanted.

"You feel that?" I whispered to Willa.

She hummed a response while reaching over, and I heard the gentle sounds of her pulling the shirt through her hands. "Yeah, it's not a shirt. It's—" She squeezed my fingers and smoothed out the item on the table. "It's a scarf. This must be a trick of some kind. Like an extra challenge."

I guffawed under my breath. "As if blindfolded wasn't enough of a challenge?"

I took the enchanted scarf and doused it in my own magic, removing the illusion that covered it. Within a few short moments, I could feel the sparkly sequins that wove into the fabric and I wiggled my fingers, making the garment dance in the air.

The crowd watched silently, and I wished I could see their faces, see their reactions as Willa and I seemingly worked with ease. How did we compare to the others? Were we going too fast? Did everyone else have an enchanted object to deal with or was this a low-blow attempt by Nash to cause us to fail?

My ears perked at the soft thud of footsteps approaching the mic.

"Miss Broomfield's team has failed to get past the eighth object," the dean announced. "We're now down to five teams remaining." He waited a few breaths as we all continued to focus. "And we have our first to move on to the third round! Mr. Abernathy has successfully enchanted all thirteen objects!"

The room filled with a roar of approval, and I sucked in a deep breath of relief. Anson was moving on. He must have figured out the enchanted eighth object. Willa and I just had three more items left, and if Anson was done without raising any suspicion, then we weren't moving too fast.

But did that mean we were moving too slow?

Together, we picked up what felt like a doll of sorts. Arms and legs, a bulbous head with plastic hair. I pictured it in my mind's eye, willing my partner to sense what I could see, and I felt her assuring hand squeeze. Our connection was unlike anything I'd ever heard of, and I was certain it was stronger than any of the other teams.

We worked in unison and enchanted the doll to dance on the table in front of us. The sound of the crowd's awe and light applause told me we were successful, and we moved on to the next item.

"And another team has failed to move on," the dean said into the mic, and I swallowed nervously. "Kyle Jennings and his supplement Althea Thornwell. Thank you for your participation. Kindly step back while the others continue."

My heart raced as Willa and I worked to enchant our last object. When I felt the wings flap on a taxidermy bird, the breeze tickling my face, I let go of the tension I'd been holding onto as the dean announced our advancement.

I ripped off the blindfold and embraced Willa until my

breathing calmed.

"It's okay," she whispered. "You did it."

"*We* did it," I replied in her ear.

I stared at Anson over her shoulder, and our eyes locked in understanding. We were both closer to the end. Closer to our goal. I wanted nothing more than to run into his arms right there on the stage, but we'd agreed to put on the show of hardly knowing one another. If the press caught wind that we were dating, there'd be a frenzy of intrusive questions.

"And there we have it, ladies and gentlemen!" Mr. Blackwood called out across the room. "Anson Abernathy, Lydia Laveau and Willa Stonerose, Carol Isadora and Addy Winters, and Nash Crane with Ferris Cooper! Our final four teams will move on to the third test next week: Conjuring. Let's give them all a round of applause, shall we?"

I stood next to my peers and waved for the crowd with a smile. But inside, I was seething. Nash and Ferris passed. They'd move on. The longer they stayed in the Program, the more chances they got to take out Anson.

At this point, I could only hope they weren't great at Conjuring. It was a highly advanced specialty that very few young Wicked Born could even attempt, let alone master. It took a great deal of strength and concentration, and the will to hold your power over the circle you cast.

My throat tightened as I craned my neck to sneak a peek at my boyfriend. The signs of wear and tear that the hex was wreaking on his body were evident: the pale skin, the dark circles, the way he moved his limbs as if they weighed a thousand pounds.

Anson went through the motions of his days by using up every ounce of energy he could spare. And now a part of me worried…would he be able to endure the physical toll that Conjuring would take on his already beaten body?

I knew then, in that moment, I only had one choice.

I had to get Anson's cure before the final test.

CHAPTER 24

THE IRONY of life as a Wicked Born would never cease to astound me. Here we were, sitting in the comfortable atmosphere of soft guitar tunes and torchlight that the Crow's Nest provided, as we discussed which dark entities we would conjure on Friday.

All the while, true evil roamed the surface every day. I had enemies every which way I turned, but instead of facing them head-on, I was forced to sit and ponder over what demon would be easier to handle than others while the entire student body watched.

Willa jabbed me in the arm with the edge of an open book. "Look, this one here. It's not super hard, but it's really old. I bet no one's conjured it in decades. We could totally do it."

I sipped my latte and peered down at the pages. "A kappa?" I pondered on it. It *was* an easy conjure, almost too easy. But that didn't matter. The test was to hold the circle until the end. It didn't matter how hard or easy it was. Then I realized a Kappa was a water demon. I turned to my left where Anson sat watching the guitarist sing quietly on the little stage. "Might be a good one for you. It's a water origin."

He seemed nonplussed by my words, his eyes not really focusing on anything. Just sort of drifting, wavering in place. What was he thinking about?

"Yeah, sure," he replied and rubbed a hand over his face as he set down his untouched tea. "Sounds good."

I caressed his thigh. "You okay?"

Finally, he brought his gaze to mine, exhaustion behind those black holes. He managed a half smile. "Yeah, I'm fine," he assured me and kissed the corner of my mouth. "I'm going to head back, though. Get some sleep. I've got a ton of TA classes tomorrow, and Friday is just around the corner."

"Okay," I replied, unsure. My hand reached for his as he stood from the chair, and I gently pulled him back to me for another kiss. "I'll see you tomorrow?"

He held my chin between his finger and thumb as he admired my lips. "Sure."

I stretched my neck and gave him another quick peck before watching him leave the Crow's Nest, then turned back around in my seat, soaking in the warmth that exuded from my skin. A warmth only Anson could stir up.

"You guys hurt my teeth," Willa muttered beside me as she flipped through more pages of her Conjuring book.

I chuckled. "Sorry. I don't mean to get like that. It's…hard not to, though."

She tipped her head back and stared at me with a mocking gleam in her eyes. "Young love. Who am I to challenge it?"

I playfully shoved at her shoulder. "Have you talked to Tom since the Solstice Dance?"

"Tom?" Her eyebrows wrinkled together. "The hot, nerdy blond guy?"

"Yeah," I replied. "He's so into you."

Willa guffawed and tried to hide her blushing cheeks in the pages of the book. "Funny, his lack of phone calls says otherwise."

"Maybe he's shy," I said. "I think you guys could seriously hit it off. Come by the newsroom this week and hang with me. It'll give you guys an excuse to talk."

"I thought we couldn't trust letting anyone in our little trio?" she reminded me.

I shrugged. "I think—" I pressed my lips. "I feel like, maybe, we can trust Tom."

"Really?"

She didn't seem convinced.

"I mean, I want to," I said. "He's helping me release the story on the Circle. And Anson seems to trust him."

Willa rolled her eyes. "I still can't believe you're going ahead with that."

"What else am I supposed to do? Take them down myself?" I watched her fiddle with the edge of a page. "This way, I can put it out there for the world to take care of. There'll be zero trace back to me. Or us."

Willa regarded me with worry. "Except that they'll know only you and I have been down there. Only *we've* seen the grimoire."

I exhaled a shaky breath and downed the rest of my beverage. "Yeah, but the entrance has been moved and they won't suspect anyone would tell me. If the story leaks, they'll be pointing fingers at each other for a while. It'll buy us even more time to make sure Anson is cured."

She snapped the book shut and stuffed it in her bag. "Then we have very little time to trade that fake spell for his counter."

"Is it ready?"

She nodded. "Yeah, I finished it last night."

"Okay, I just need to find a way to sneak into Haggy's shop and find the new entrance so I can nab some evidence for the story first. Then we can arrange a meeting to swap it. Because, once they get it, I'll surely never get back inside."

"Do you think Ferris was telling the truth?"

I mulled it over. "Yeah, part of me does. The hell if I know why he's helping us, though. It's probably a trap. But the door is gone and moving it off campus would be smart."

She moaned and slid back in her chair. "What if we ask Nash when the next meeting is? Say we want to attend."

I shook my head. "Not a chance. Apparently recruiting us was only a test for him to prove his loyalty and abilities. They all know we want no part in the coven. It'll seem suspicious if we suddenly show an interest."

"Well, we don't have a ton of time to pull this off, Lydia," she said. "We've got more than one deadline facing us. Nash said return the spell by midnight prior to the last test, and that's next week. But you've got to get this proof first."

I pinched the bridge of my nose. "Then I'll have to sneak into Haggy's while it's closed."

My stomach tightened.

"Okay," she said, the word trailing off with uncertainty. "And, while I'm behind you one hundred percent in whatever you want to do, have you thought this through? Like, really thought about what happens after all this?"

She shifted upright and faced me as she leaned in. "Say we're successful. We find the new door, get the proof we need for your story, then swap the fake spell for Anson's counter curse. It'll be a matter of days before the entire Dark Faction knows about the Midnight Circle, and the coven will be out for blood. *Your* blood." Her hands fidgeted in her lap. "And by then, if we win this thing, we'll be up and coming leaders of this faction. Are you sure you want to release that kind of chaos? There will be those who won't know how to handle this information. There'll be riots, uprisings, other covens forming. At best."

My limbs tingled with fear, but I squeezed my fists to will it away. "I don't see another way, Willa. I can't let Anson live with this hex that could very well one day kill him. And I can't in good conscience let a secret coven resurrect an ancient, evil witch from her grave so they can overthrow the Dark Faction."

We sat in the heaviness of the facts for a few moments as the rest of the world continued to move around us. Our peers didn't know all the dangers that lurked just below their feet. My plan was the only way. It would save the man I loved, while also exposing a potential threat to our world. Two birds with one stone, so to speak.

The only alternative wasn't really an acceptable alternative at all. If this didn't work, I would be forced to choose between Anson and the rest of the world. And I wasn't that strong. I'd choose Anson. Always and forever.

But what kind of person would that make me?

I STARED into the back of Nash's head as the four remaining teams strolled through the crowd toward the stage as if we were parting the sea. Everyone cheered under the cover of torchlight and incense smoke, but I didn't offer them a single glance. I was too busy willing Nash to lose.

Conjuring wasn't an easy task. Not even for a well-seasoned witch. I was shocked to learn it would be one of our tests, but I realized now why the Game Designers chose it. The contenders weren't everyday Wicked Born. Myself, as a former Light Witch, had proven time and time again that I was a smidge more powerful than the average First Year. But it was expected, given my background.

If only they really knew…

Then there was Anson. The talented Third Year who was foolish enough to volunteer. Solo, no less, which as far as the Game Designers must have been concerned, should have put him at a disadvantage. Dark Witches weren't supposed to reach full power without a supplement, and yet, he'd proven strong enough to stay in the competition. I knew it was because he also had Light Witch powers—a dual, like me. But the Game Designers didn't know that, since that wasn't supposed to be possible. He must have thrown a wrench into any early plans they'd had.

And then, Nash. The privileged and indisputably talented Third Year who would literally do anything to win. Even cheating. And they knew that. They created a Program fit for his abilities and turned a blind eye when I proved how blatantly he broke the rules.

Willa, Anson, and I just *had* to win this one. It was no secret Nash wanted to stand next to me in the end. But if our two teams failed, then Nash and Carol would win by default, and I was betting the snake already had a back-up plan in place to pull Carol over to his side. Maybe she was already in the Midnight Circle. I wouldn't be surprised. Nothing shocked me anymore.

The four teams walked up the few short stairs and stood on the stage to face the whole school. My lungs refused to fully inflate as my nerves choked down any ability to calm my breathing. I mindlessly twisted my enchanted cuff ring around my middle finger, hoping it would be enough to control the power I knew I'd have to tap into in just a few moments.

Conjuring was...challenging. It required the utmost control and an immense amount of power just to maintain a hold over a casted circle. And a circle was often cast with a coven.

I swallowed nervously and smiled for the onlookers. But I knew, deep in my gut, things were going to get intense. This was an attempt to really cut down the remaining teams.

"Welcome!" Mr. Blackwood called into the mic and held his arms out proudly as everyone erupted into cheer. "We gather here today to witness the third test in the decennial Courtship Program. Our Arcane Academy was delighted to learn we were chosen for this highly coveted event, and our contenders are definitely not disappointing." He craned his neck to glance back at us with a smile before pointing his attention back to the crowd. "Are they?"

The level of noise increased and boomed in my ears. Feet pounded on the floor and clapping pierced the air. It made me feel…wrong. They were clearly entertained and excited to watch us conjure demons, but I felt like cattle standing on a stage awaiting auction.

"Today, we'll witness the four remaining teams perform Conjuring. Each team will have to cast a circle, then conjure an entity while binding it there. It cannot escape, and our contenders mustn't lose control. The challenge our gracious designers have constructed for this particular test is that the teams must hold the circle for thirty minutes."

Thirty minutes? That was insane.

An audible wave of shock filled the room as the countdown numbers of a digital clock appeared in the air, large enough for the whole Great Hall to see.

I glanced at Anson to my left and noted his continually declining health as it flooded to the surface. The potions he'd been taking weren't working like they had just days ago. His skin was so pale it almost appeared translucent in some places. His eyelids hung heavy over his distant gaze. But I couldn't say anything. He'd never forgive me for getting him disqualified.

All I could do now was hope he could get through the next half an hour.

"A salt circle will contain our teams in a protective space," the dean added as the Game Designers began pouring a thick line of salt around the perimeter of the stage. "Along with the ashes burned on the previous full moon. This will provide safety for everyone as we watch our Wicked Born contenders battle it out for a place in the final round."

Next to me, Willa quietly guffawed. "Cool. Trap us inside with the demons that could potentially kill us. Sounds good. As long as everyone else can watch. That's all that matters, I guess."

Mr. Blackwood cleared his throat and leaned closer to the mic. "This isn't just a game today. Conjuring demons and casting circles is serious, and possibly life-threatening. If any of our contenders, *my students*, wish to back out then now is the time. Once the ward is cast around you, there will be no way out and *no* way in to help you until this is over."

The line of contenders all exchanged a worried glance, but no one said a word.

"Very well," the dean said with a hint of disappointment. "Proceed."

We all stepped inside as Adrien and Adina continued laying the ring of salt. I felt the invisible wall of protection solidify around us, holding us in, but also sealing our fate, should it come to that.

I caught Carol's nervous gaze.

"Are you guys confident in this?" I asked. "We can't let the entities get loose, or the seven of us will be demon lunchmeat."

She held her chin high. "Don't worry about us. We can hold our own."

Nash sneered my way. "It's you we should be worried about, princess. Do they even conjure demons in the Light Faction?" He gave a mocking sad face. "Or is that too dark for your precious white hats and your purist morals?"

Anson tensed and stalked forward. "You'll watch your tongue, Crane. Unless you wish me to rip it from your mouth."

I discreetly touched my fingertips to his hand and felt the tension wash away from him as he stepped back toward me. I'd like to think my touch had the power to calm the man, but I could see how he simply didn't have the energy to hold onto it.

My stomach twisted with prickles of nerves. Anson was never going to make it thirty whole minutes.

My chest heaved with anxiousness as my mind raced

through my options. I could halt the test right now, out my boyfriend as unfit to compete, and risk exposing our shared secret. They'd dig so deep to find that hex, they'd surely discover his hidden abilities.

But what if he could hold on? What if he bound his demon and made it to the end? Then he'd be able to advance to the final test, and we could very well win this whole thing. Together.

I didn't know what to do, but the chance to speak up was taken as the Game Designers completed the salt and ash circle. The dean announced the start of the test, and Anson dove for the table of supplies that sat in the center of the stage.

"Come on," Willa whispered and tugged at my arm. "He'll be fine. We have to start."

Tears stung my dry eyes. "Will he, though?"

She shrugged helplessly. "He'll have to be."

I followed her over to the table, and we grabbed our supplies. We retreated to our corner of the stage where I laid the candles as she used chalk to draw a pentagram enclosed with a circle.

I was highly aware of the actions of the other teams— Anson in particular—but I took a deep breath and reminded myself that I had to focus. I had to keep my head in the game that Willa and I were playing. She was my responsibility, and I owed her every ounce of concentration I could muster.

"Ready?" Willa whispered to me as she stood by my side and we peered down at our handiwork.

I nodded. "Yeah, let's get this over with."

She rounded the other side, and we tensed our arms at our sides as we mentally reached to one another. Quietly, we recanted the spell that we'd studied all week.

North, East, South, and West.

We call ye forth to this circle, blessed.
Earth and Air. Fire and Water.
Come to join these two daughters.

THE FIVE CANDLES flickered to life with a flame on each corner of our pentagram.

BODY, Mind, Spirit, and Heart.
Make sacred this space, a world apart.
Mother of Earth and Father of Sky.
Join with our heart, the time is nigh.

I COULD FEEL my dark magic rolling around under the surface of my skin, where it always laid dormant. It sprang to life and gave me a rush of energy that I witnessed funnel through Willa. She held it with grace.

GREAT SPIRIT, Divine One, Creator of all.
Answer our most reverent call.
The circle is cast, the light unbroken.
So mote it be, our magick spoken.

THE CONFINES of our circle cast pushed against our open arms, testing its limits. We stood strong. Never wavering.

Nothing was getting out.

I opened my eyes again and shared a fixed gaze with my partner. She gave a slight nod, and I knew we were ready to summon our demon.

But were we ready to face it?

CHAPTER 25

SINCE ANSON WAS GOING to try the kappa, Willa and I had decided on an equally ancient entity, rooted in the element of fire. Abaddon the Destroyer. Aptly named for its relentless desire to forge through the world and set it ablaze.

If we could prove our ability to contain it, we'd surely advance to the final round. If we couldn't... Well, I didn't want to think about that. I just wish we'd known there was a thirty-minute expectation attached to this test.

This was going to be one of the hardest things I'd ever done.

Together, we silently chanted a call to the demon and immediately felt its reply. A wretched sour taste filled my mouth, and I fought back the bile that threatened to rise from my stomach.

Abaddon manifested a presence in our circle—not in bodily form, but there, nonetheless. I could feel it testing the limits of the binding, looking for a way out. It shouldn't be able to find one. Willa and I were solid. But we hadn't planned to contain it for thirty minutes, and doubt was starting to creep in.

I looked at the countdown clock. Fifteen minutes had

passed. Halfway. We were halfway to winning this round and advancing to the final test. I fortified my magical grip and subconsciously reached out to Willa until she flexed her powers, reaching back. It was our way of reassuring one another.

I dared steal a glance to my right where Anson stood in the corner with his circle cast. The kappa demon's essence, formed in water, writhed inside the confines he created.

Anson's face dripped with sweat, and I caught the slightest twitch in his stance. I looked to Willa with alarmed eyes, and she followed my gaze back toward my struggling boyfriend. His hands trembled as he held his arms out in the air, desperately holding the bind.

That demon should have been easy for him. He really was bad off under the effects of that hex.

Another minute ticked down on the clock.

"He's not going to make it," I whispered to Willa.

She stared at him, and her face paled. "Oh, my Gods... he's not."

The kappa demon let out a fierce, watery cry and one of Anson's candles doused. Without a second thought, I dug up more of my fledgling dark magic and reached toward his circle to relight it. He struggled to turn his head my way, and his face, red with strain, fought back tears as his eyes pleaded with me. He needed help.

My head whipped toward the crowd and scanned the front row of judges and elders. They sat unbothered, but the dean tensed in his seat, leaning forward and ready to jump in at any moment. He was the only one who seemed to care. And why would the others? A salt and ash circle had been cast. Only the Wicked Born contained inside would be in danger.

"Anson?" I whispered.

He didn't budge. Every ounce of his strength was focused on keeping his demon contained. But it wasn't enough. A

CANDACE OSMOND & REBECCA HAMILTON

choked moan bubbled from his throat, and I watched in horror as the man I loved crumbled to the floor like a rag doll.

The kappa demon flexed the restraints of the circle, and two candles went out.

Panicked, I flicked my wrist and relit the candles again. The crowd were in their seats, eager and hungry to witness failure. Some were even standing now to get a better look. To see someone die.

Disgusting.

I strained my hand toward the kappa, stretching mine and Willa's bind to include Anson's circle. The dean jumped onto the stage, ready to enter our protection of salt and ash, to disrupt the other teams.

"Don't cross the salt ring!" I begged him as tears squeezed from my eyes and streamed down my reddened face. I glanced at the clock. Only seven minutes remained. "If I let go of his circle, I might lose control of ours, too."

Mr. Blackwood's expression was soaked in concern. "Lydia—"

"No!" I demanded. "Let me do this. I have to win." My eyes flickered to Willa's. "*We* have to win."

The kappa let out an agonized moan, like a petulant child wanting to break free of its mother's firm grasp. I flicked my wrist again, tightening the hold. Our own entity grew within our circle cast, as if it were aware of the way Willa and I struggled.

Anson's lifeless body lay in a heap on the floor, just a few feet away, and it killed me that I couldn't run to him. That no one could. The medical team stood close by, poised and ready to jump in.

The two demons fought for release, matched by the effort we used to maintain control over both circles. I could feel the strain beginning to wear me down, stretching my skin and pounding against my head. One of our own candles shook, and the flame threatened to go out. But it didn't.

Five minutes remained.

My dark magic wasn't enough…and neither was my light.

My stare locked with Willa's, and I could tell she knew it, too. But could I tap into my hybrid magic and not lose control in front of all these people? While my body was already suffering from exhaustion?

All five of our candles shook, and I knew then, I had no choice. We needed more.

"Can you do this with me?" I whispered to Willa through the pain. "Can you hold it with me?"

"Yes," she replied with confidence and flexed her outstretched arms. "I can do it if you can."

I widened my stance and reached with my arms as far as I could while Willa did the same. I awakened my dormant and unpredictable hybrid magic, calling to it and begging for help. Willing it to heed my authority. I felt it crawl to the surface. From the corner of my eye, the emerald in my ring glowed and pulsated with the power it now filtered.

The kappa from Anson's circle must have sensed a taste of the strange, ancient magic, because it threw itself at the invisible confines. The force pushed at us, and we rocked back on our feet. The whole crowd gasped, but I focused on the demon, lowering my posture and widening my legs as I tensed my wrists to hold everything in place with all my might.

Suddenly, Abaddon's presence grew before us. The circle we'd cast erupted with a thick tunnel of flames that shot up to the ceiling like a volcano exploding just inches from us. The dense heat seared my skin, and I let out a guttural scream, followed by Willa's matching cry.

But I would not waver.

My hybrid powers remained intact and refused to relent— a fact that I would be eternally grateful for, should we make it through this. The whole room filled with tension and whispers of awe.

Mr. Blackwood stood at the edge of the salt and ash ring.

His unease and anxiousness were evident in the way he paced back and forth. I begged him with my eyes once again, and he met me with a look of disdain.

This must have been torture for him, to watch a student suffer this way and there be nothing he could do about it. Of course, he could break the protective ring and jump in to save us, but that would endanger everyone in the room, and risk getting me disqualified for messing with another contender's entry. He wanted me to win.

And I wanted it, too.

Finally, the clock began to tick with a final countdown from sixty seconds. The end was in our grasp. But Willa was shaking with every inch of her body, and she looked at me with tears of agony.

"Lydia," she struggled to say, "I-I can't—"

"Yes, you can! You *have* to."

I reached to grab her trembling hand. The instant our palms met, my fingers wrapped around hers in a desperate grip, and a thunderous bolt of power shook through us. My ring warmed and quickly turned hot, burning the skin beneath it. But I fought through the pain. The demons twisted and groaned within their confines, pushing at the walls of power that held them in place.

Thirty seconds.

I drudged up one last handful of hybrid magic, bringing it to the forefront of my very being, willing it to do as I wanted it to. My veins lit up with an electric green and seared through my skin, crawling toward my fingertips that were entwined with Willa's. The emerald veins continued across to her, and we both threw our heads back as our guttural screams filled the room.

The sounds eliciting from the crowd became muffled to my heat-filled ears. Every ounce of me shook as Willa and I fought to maintain the hold on both circles, on both relentless demons. My eyes locked on the clock. My breath fell in sync with the declining numbers as they went down from ten.

When it hit zero and the enchanted device disappeared from thin air, I pushed my arms through the empty space between them, fighting against the strain like a taut elastic band.

"*Prope circulo!*" I managed to say as my hands came together in a painful clap, sending the demons back to where they came from.

A dense wave of energy pulsed outward from the space between me and Willa, knocking everyone in the Great Hall to the floor. Uncontrollable sobs bubbled from my mouth as we collided in a shaking embrace.

"A-are you okay?" I spoke to her ear. She wept on my shoulder, and I felt her head move in a nodding motion. I squeezed her tighter. "I'm so sorry. I shouldn't have made you do that. But..."

I pulled back and glanced at Anson on the floor. The medical team was already surrounding him.

Willa wiped the wetness from her face with her sleeve. "It's okay. Really. It had to be done."

"Lydia?" the dean said as he broke through the ring of salt and ash. His trembling hands felt my shoulders and arms as he inspected me with a desperate expression. He glanced to Willa and ran a hand over his distraught face. "Are you both alright?"

I nodded. "We're..." I held out my arms; burn marks left blackened evidence all over my skin. Matched on Willa. "We'll be fine."

He whipped his head around, frantic. "Can we get medical over here, too!"

Two doctors rushed over and immediately began treating our wounds with a mix of magic and first aid supplies. They pulled at our limbs and ripped away cumbersome bits of clothing. My eyes were locked on Anson's body as they worked to treat him and secure him to a stretcher.

The press swarmed the edge of the stage, peering up at the contenders through lenses and bombarding us with questions. The other two teams stood off to the side, blank looks on their faces. Even Nash appeared in shock. Surely it wasn't easy to hold their circles while this was happening just a few feet away.

"Back up!" Mr. Blackwood scolded the press. "Have some Gods damn decency."

I was eternally grateful for him in that moment. Regardless of the trust I constantly fought to find for him, the dean truly did care. I could see it now. In desperation, our true selves come to the surface.

The medical team hoisted Anson's stretcher in the air and began moving him off the stage toward the back.

"Where are they taking him?" I asked.

"To the infirmary," Mr. Blackwood replied. "They'll...they'll do what they can, Lydia."

There was something about the words he left unspoken that crashed into me.

My panicked eyes fled to Willa's equally concerned expression.

Willa leaned closer. "Go with him. I'll stay and talk to the press, keep them from coming to look for you."

Hot emotions burned in my throat. "Are you sure?"

She nodded, and the dean gently squeezed my arm. "Go. I'll stay with Miss Stonerose and make sure she's okay." Then he lowered his brow. "If anyone asks, it was hell fire from the demons that singed you both. Not Lydia's magic." He glanced between us. "Do you understand?"

A pit turned over in the gallows of my gut. *He knew.* This whole time...Mr. Blackwood knew my secret.

Of course he did. It explained so much. But I didn't have time to explore that right now. They'd already left the room with Anson, and I couldn't leave him alone with the Elders and medical team for long.

I grabbed Willa's face and pressed my forehead to hers. "I love you."

"I love you, too," she replied with a grateful smile. Then she pushed at my chest. "Now, go."

I turned and ran out of the Great Hall, leaving everything behind me. The mess, the aftermath of what my magic had done, the relentless press who called my name.

All but Anson had advanced to the final round. Willa and I still had a chance to win this thing and move on to lead this broken faction out of the shadows and into a new light.

But none of that mattered to me right now.

I had only one thing on my mind.

Was the man I loved still alive...or already dead?

CHAPTER 26

"LET ME IN!" I screamed as I beat my fists on the double doors of the infirmary.

I stared in through the little round windows. I'd been standing there for at least fifteen minutes, but the Elders and medical team in the room just ignored me. Tools and potions and incense smoke moved around the flat surface that Anson's body laid on. I could see, through the kerfuffle of people, his naked chest exposed to the ceiling.

Blackened veins completely covered it, like brambles of malicious tattoos. Tears burned the stressed skin around my eyes while adrenaline still coursed through my body. I'd just bound two demons at the same time, while holding two cast circles.

But I couldn't think of that right now.

I let out another frustrated cry as I kicked the thick, wooden door. My chest heaved rapidly, uncontrollably, as I backed up. Magic coiled in the pit of my stomach, barreling outward through my limbs, green static crackling in my palms. I braced my stance, ready to blast my way through those damn doors.

"Lydia!" Mr. Blackwood bellowed from the end of the corridor.

The distraction was enough to reel my magic back, just for a moment. But that's all he needed. He came running down the hall and grasped my upper arms, panic in his steely eyes.

"That won't help anyone," he told me in a huff.

My lungs were still rampant, and I struggled to calm myself. He gently squeezed my shoulders.

"It's okay," he said quietly. "It's alright now."

"They won't let me in there," I said through uncontrollable sobs. "They won't let me be with him."

"It's policy, Lydia," he replied. "You're not immediate family."

I shoved at his chest and stepped away. "The hell I'm not! I'm all he has here!"

Mr. Blackwood sighed and threw a calculated look between me and the doors. "Not all. I've watched over Mr. Abernathy from the moment he arrived here."

I guffawed. "Yeah? And giving him Talia Blackstone's grimoire and covering up his supplement's death? That was watching out for him?"

His back stiffened. "You've no idea what you're talking about, Lydia."

I narrowed my eyes. "I know enough."

His gaze averted to my exposed arms, and he stepped closer while shrugging out of his silver blazer. "Your magic isn't subsiding."

I glanced down in panic. My veins. They were alight with the strange emerald glow once again. It wasn't unheard of in the Wicked Born world to have magic manifest in such ways. But it was rare and did indicate immense power. More power than I would want anyone to see in me, especially as a first year. Enough power to draw suspicion.

My mother once told me there are those who use their

magic, and those who become consumed by it. I flexed my fists and the veins pulsed under my skin.

I guess I was the latter.

In all the commotion and cover of hellfire, I doubted anyone in the Great Hall even noticed. But here, in the empty hallway…I was totally exposed. I glanced up at him and tried to look as surprised as I could.

"W-what could it be from?" I asked innocently as I shook my head. "The demons?"

He tipped his head and gave me an impatient look as he flung the jacket over my shoulders. "I think you and I both know what happened out there."

He sighed and glanced at the doors again as I slipped my arms through the sleeves.

"Luckily, no one else seems to have put the pieces together," he said. "Too much was happening. They think it was all the demon magic affecting the three of you."

My breath came in stifled bursts, and I turned my gaze toward the doors, too. "That's not what happened to Anson." The words came out in a barely audible whisper. "He could have done it. He could have passed the test."

"Lydia," Mr. Blackwood lowered his voice, "if you know what happened to Anson, or what's been plaguing him these last few weeks, you can tell me. I can help."

My eyes bulged as I whipped my head and stared up at him. "You knew he was sick this whole time?"

"I suspected something was amiss," he replied. "Mr. Abernathy had skipped several classes, and I could see it in his appearance. How something was ailing him. I'd asked him several times if he was alright. He insisted he was fine, just weighed down by the stress of preparing for the Program."

I wanted to tell the dean everything. I truly did. The truth burned in the back of my throat. But if Anson didn't see fit to confide in the man, then how could I on his behalf? I needed to talk to Anson first. But he was in some strange, magic-induced coma.

"I...can't tell you," I admitted. "It's not my secret to share." My fingertips gripped the deep edge around the little window in one of the doors as I peered inside. They were drawing blood from him. "But...they can't pry too deep. They can't..." I fought for the right words. "If they look too far into the source of his magic then...then..."

Mr. Blackwood raised his eyebrows encouragingly. "Then what?"

I shook my head. "I don't know what will happen," I said, swallowing hard, "but it won't be good for either of us."

A strange sense of understanding flickered in the gleam of his eyes as he examined my face. Almost as if he were searching for the truth in my words, a truth that maybe he already knew. Or assumed, at least.

He'd given Anson and Norah that grimoire years ago for a reason. He must have known about Anson's past and the swift cover-up of his Sorting Ceremony. It was the only explanation.

He gripped my arms and leaned down to my height as his voice dropped to a whisper. "I'll go in. I'll watch over Mr. Abernathy. But you need to go back to your quarters and stay there. Lock the door. Willa appeased the press with a few statements, but they'll be hunting the campus for you."

I chewed at my lip. The dean's hands gripped my upper arms, and I stared at the two round windows in the doors. How could I leave? How could I just let the vultures poke and prod at my boyfriend's body while he lay helpless to speak for himself?

"Lydia, dear," the dean said calmly. I dared look at him, fright in my expression. "I promise. Anson will be safe. I'll see to it." His brow lowered. "Do you trust me?"

My hands trembled at my sides. Finally, I nodded. But I still wasn't sure I did.

Mr. Blackwood stepped back and waved an arm in the air. The empty space began to shimmer and ripple with the tear he was creating. A portal formed, and I could see my room on the other side.

"Go," he said. "It won't be long now. The press will be at these doors the second they're done interviewing the other contenders. I'll keep them at bay, and I'll make sure the people in that room are only treating Anson's illness. I won't let them pry any further."

Could I trust him? I thought of my options and realized... I had none.

With a sniffle and a wipe of my face with the back of my hand, I nodded and then stepped through the portal the dean had created for me. It closed behind with a hasty snap, and I fell to the stone floor of mine and Willa's room. She rushed over and came to her knees at my side.

"Lydia!" she exclaimed. "Are you okay? Where's Anson?"

I shifted and moved my legs underneath me to sit up straight and looked at her with the heavy blanket of defeat weighing on my shoulders.

"He's in a coma," I replied, my voice hoarse. "They're examining him in the infirmary and wouldn't let me in because I'm not *immediate family*." I rolled my eyes and brought my knees to my chin to hug my legs tightly.

She shook her head through my words. "But, if they——"

"The dean is with him," I said. "He promised to not let them look too deep. To make sure he was only being treated for the hex."

She rubbed her lips together.

"What?" I asked.

Willa tipped her head sadly. "In order to treat the dark curse that lives in Anson, they'll need to know the origin of the magic used to make it. They'll *have* to dig deep. Or risk him dying."

My mouth gaped helplessly. "Well, I guess all we can hope

for is that what they find leads them to Talia Blackstone's grimoire and then to the Midnight Circle."

"Lydia," she said softly and touched her hand to my knee. "Most of the people in that room probably already know about the Circle. From what we know now, I'm betting most of the Elders are even members. We thought this coven was something new, but I'm starting to believe it's something…older."

I inhaled a shaky breath. "Then we have to get that proof and expose the story now. We can't wait for the Arcane paper. Tom's not sending it out until after the Program is done." I mulled over our options. "But the international media is already on the grounds and desperate for a feature, especially from me. If they want a juicy story, then I'll give them one."

"But what about the risks?" Willa asked, the space between her eyebrows puckering.

I spread my hands. "I think the situation at hand just shifted the scales on that one."

She rocked back and crossed her legs. "Then that means…"

We shared the same nervous look, and I added, "We have to sneak into the Circle's meeting place tonight."

Before we could dive into a plan of attack, the giant arched window that divided the space flung open, and a tiny flame came whipping through the air. A fire message. I reached out and snatched it before shaking away the bits of ash and flames. My shaky fingers unrolled the enchanted parchment.

Willa leaned in. "What's it say?"

All words evaded me as my exhausted eyes stared unblinking at the message.

"Lydia?" she urged. "Who is it from?"

"It's…a ritual," I whispered and read it again in disbelief, rubbing my thumb over the words at the very top. "*Quia anathema est anima evigilare faciatis*. Awaken a cursed soul. I can

CANDACE OSMOND & REBECCA HAMILTON

free Anson's soul from the hex with this. It alludes to using both dark and light magic but…" I looked at her. "We both know that means hybrid magic."

"What?" she exclaimed and slipped the paper from my fingers. Her eyes scanned the words contained there and she began reciting them. "Dried petals of black dahlia, crushed silphium, blood of phoenix, bones of a red witch—Lydia… these are impossible ingredients. I mean, silphium alone is an extinct herb. And the bones of a *red witch*? What the hell is a red witch?"

"Good question," I chortled and vigorously rubbed my hands over my exhausted face, before tucking my disheveled hair behind my ears. "But that's not the question we need to be asking here."

In a matter of seconds, our luck had mysteriously turned around. We possibly possessed the very cure Anson needed. A spell to awaken a cursed soul is exactly what he needed. I should be ecstatic. I should be running off to perform the spell right now. But my mind now flooded with a hoard of brand-new worries and questions.

How were we going to find these ingredients?

What was a red witch?

Was the whole thing a trap?

Which then led me to the biggest question of all…

Who sent the note?

CHAPTER 27

"I GIVE UP," Willa grumbled, exhaustion heavy in her voice as she closed another book. "There's nothing, Lydia."

Though she spoke quietly, her words echoed off the library walls as the pitch-black evening sky covered us through the solarium glass ceiling. It was late. No one else was here.

I closed the grimoire I'd been reading through and shoved it to the center of the table where our massive discarded pile sat.

"I know. There's no mention of red witches *whatsoever*. Red cloaks, spells to turn things red, red dawn..." I sighed and let my head lull backward as I cast my face upward. My dry eyes demanded to stay closed, but I forced them open and returned my attention to Willa. "I need coffee."

"No," she said and stood from her chair. "You need sleep. It's three in the morning, and we've had a horrible day."

"But I need to figure this out," I replied. "Anson's on a deadline. He's slipping away, and there's nothing anyone can do without a counter curse, or the origin of the hex."

Her sleepy gaze fell to the floor, and she gently shrugged. "We could always do the trade with Nash now. Get the counter curse."

I chewed at my lip for a moment. "No. As much as it kills me to say it, I *can't* choose Anson over the entire world." I chortled and rocked back and forth in my chair. "I want to. *So* badly. But what kind of person would that make me? The girl who saves her boyfriend and lets an underground coven, bent on chaos, slip away in the night?"

"You're stronger than I am, then," she said. "I would have given in long ago."

I let out a frustrated groan. "I need that damn proof. I should be poking around Haggy's shop right now, not here, wasting time chasing a dead end." My gaze flitted over to the iron gates of the restricted area. "Or finding a way to get in there."

"The restricted section?" she said, unsure.

"Yeah. I bet my life that the information we need is in there."

Willa shook her head and came around the table to stand next to my chair. "Maybe, maybe not. Either way, we're never getting back in there after what happened with Nash and the stolen grimoires."

I sighed. "Then I guess we're back to square one. Tomorrow night, after the village closes down, I'm sneaking into Haggy's to look for the Circle's new entrance. I have to get that proof now, so we can trade the resurrection spell for Anson's cure. We have no idea what to expect once they figure out it's fake. But I'm betting it won't be good."

Willa smiled through a yawn as I stood and gathered my things. "Then that gives me all day tomorrow to research more about this mysterious spell and red witches."

I chuckled, then winced as my beaten body protested. Today was one of the hardest days of my life, both physically and mentally. Heck, even emotionally. I was dead on my feet.

"Mysterious spell or elaborate trap to tempt us to break into the restricted area again?" I reasoned. "Whoever sent it must have known we'd never find this stuff on the library shelves. They knew we'd realize we need in *there*." I pointed at the black metal gate. "And what if that's what they want? To get the upper hand and blackmail me? I refuse to be under the thumb of anyone else at this damn school."

Willa sighed as we strolled back to our quarters. "Who knows, Lydia?" She gave me a sideways look of utter exhaustion. "For now, let's sleep on it and tackle it tomorrow with fresh minds."

We walked in silence until we rounded the corner to our hall, and I smiled. "You know, you were a total badass today."

She laughed quietly. "Hardly. I was barely hanging on. You carried us that entire time. You were the badass that saved everyone in that circle. If you didn't think fast, and take control of Anson's demon, we'd all be toast."

I reached over and took her hand. "No way. I needed you." We stopped, and I flung my arms around her. "You're my rock in all this, Willa. I couldn't do any of this without you."

Her reassuring hand patted my back. "And you'll never have to."

~

DESPITE BEING UP HALF the night, I couldn't sleep once my head hit the pillow. I laid wide awake in a cloud of fatigue and stress while Willa's mouth gaped open, snoring softly.

At least one of us was getting sleep.

I was so proud of her. For a half-witch, she was more powerful than most seasoned Wicked Born I knew.

I sat on the edge of my bed, waiting for the moment the sun filled the morning sky, and then slipped out of the room. The castle was slowly waking up with sleepy Wicked Born emerging from their quarters and shuffling toward bathrooms and the mess hall. I made a beeline for the infirmary wing, avoiding the tempting aromas of fresh coffee and breakfast. I didn't have time for that.

I was hoping they'd let me in to see Anson today.

As I turned the corner, the sickening scent of medical potions accosted me. It reminded me of when I broke my leg as a child. Sure, magic healed the bone pretty fast, but I was still pumped full of gross concoctions and oils to make the magic hold. I'd despised it.

I glanced inside the little round windows of the exam room I'd last seen my boyfriend in, but it was totally empty, scrubbed and reset as if nothing ever happened in there just a few hours ago. The wing had a dozen other doors lining the halls, and I peered inside each one until I found him. I pushed at the door, and a wave of relief washed over me when I realized it wasn't locked.

I took a few steps into the room, and the breath squeezed from my lungs at the sight of him. Limp and lifeless, still as a statue as his frame filled the entire length of the bed. His exposed chest still sported the mess of blackened veins, but now strange symbols and salves peppered the skin as well. He didn't look alive, but I took comfort in the fact that his chest slowly rose and fell with labored breaths.

"I was wondering when you'd show up," spoke a sleepy voice from a far corner.

I whipped my gaze toward the back of the room as Mr. Blackwood removed a thin blanket from his lap and stood to stretch.

"Did you…Were you here all night?" I asked him.

He took his silver vest from the back of the chair and threw it on over the black collared shirt he wore.

"Yes," he replied and came toward me. "I promised you I'd watch over Mr. Abernathy. I can assure you, they only treated his symptoms. They never pried any further." His shoulders slumped. "There wasn't much more they could do anyway, without knowing the origin of this peculiar curse."

Grace filled my heart. I hadn't expected him to do that. My eyes locked on Anson lying there.

"Thank you." I took a deep breath. "So, what are they saying? Will he wake up?"

The dean froze, and I turned my gaze to him as he shook his head. "Not without a proper counter. And his condition, I'm afraid, will just worsen. Slowly, now that they're treating him. But it's a mere band-aid. It will only keep the damage at bay for a short while."

Just like his grandmother's potion.

"I see you're feeling more...like yourself," he added and gestured to my bare arms. The green veins had subsided sometime during the night, after I'd calmed down and reeled my magic back.

"Yeah," I said, and tried my best to play dumb. I stuffed a hand in my jeans' pocket to hide my syphon ring. "Wonder what happened there?"

He gave me that look again. The one that said he wasn't buying any of it.

"You don't have to hide from me, Lydia. I'm aware of what truly happened out there." He glanced at Anson. "Like Mr. Abernathy, you're a very...talented witch. It's not a crime. But it does paint a rather large target on both of you, should that knowledge spread."

I narrowed my eyes. "If you know so much, then why do you do the things you do?"

"Such as?" he challenged gently.

"Like with Anson and Norah. Why did you push them to do magic they clearly weren't ready for? Illegal magic, to boot. For such a dangerous text as Talia's grimoire, it seems careless to hand it over to a couple of First Year witches."

He sighed, but I could see the resolve coming to the

surface. "There's so much you don't know, that you just don't understand."

I opened my mouth to argue, but he held up a firm hand.

"*Yet*," he amended

He grabbed another chair and dragged it over to the one he had been sitting in and motioned for me to join him. We sat together, and he wiggled his fingers over the surface of the small side table until two steaming cups of coffee appeared. He handed one to me. The warmth seeped into my fingers and soothed my weary bones.

"There have been wheels in motion in the background of our world for years, Lydia. And I've been working in secret with a silent organization to help carefully move the Dark Faction into a better light. Mr. Abernathy had the potential to move us to the next step. To...create the beginnings of a bridge."

Secret organization? Please tell me he didn't mean the Midnight Circle. Was there some other underground coven at work here? And, if so, was it a force of good? Or was it just as bad as the group Nash tricked me into?

Part of me truly wanted to believe it was good, that the dean could actually be someone I could finally trust. I wanted that, so badly.

"So, how much do you know about Anson's parents, then?" I pried, knowing fully that my light born boyfriend was chosen for the dark and his ceremony was covered up faster than you could say conspiracy theory. On paper, he was adopted by a light faction family. I knew the truth, but what did the dean know?

"They were lovely people," he replied. "From what I'm told. It was a tragedy, the accident. They couldn't conceive children and adopted Anson without the knowledge of his birth parents. So sad to have gone through all that to get a child, only to leave this world so shortly afterward." He patted my leg. "But his grandparents raised him wonderfully. To be a good man. So, you can imagine my interest in him. A boy with dark magic, raised by light witches? It was unheard of."

I chewed at my lip; the damn thing was raw inside my mouth lately.

"Is that the true story?" I challenged, searching for a crack in his shield.

"Story?" he replied, his face twisted in confusion. When it was evident I wasn't falling for it, his expression turned stern, and he leaned closer, lowering his voice. "It's the only truth that really matters right now. For Mr. Abernathy's sake."

So, he did know, then. Which meant he probably knew *my* secret, too. Or some assumption of it. Some part of his plan to help the Dark Faction evolve had something to do with Light Borns chosen for the dark and the special abilities we apparently possessed.

It made me think that Anson's theory about there being more of us out there was truer than I first thought. Maybe the dean was trying to help us. Part of me wondered if it was him who'd sent me and Willa that fire message yesterday. He would have been here in the infirmary, but he could have easily slipped away for a moment.

But if it was him, why would he give the spell to us? If it could save Anson, why wouldn't he just do it himself? Perhaps it really was a trap then. To lure us into performing a shady spell and catch us in the act. More blackmail.

I refused to put myself in that situation again.

The door swung open, and a nurse strolled in carrying a tray of bowls, potions, and other tools. She regarded us with surprise.

"Oh, I didn't expect anyone to be in here," she said and set the tray down on a table. "I'm just going to change out the boy's salve swabs. I shouldn't be more than a few minutes."

The dean waved his hand and motioned to Anson's sleeping body. "Please, by all means. Don't let us keep you."

She seemed hesitant, as if she expected us to leave, and

my paranoia wings flapped loudly in my mind. I watched her intently, unblinking as she removed the large spots of salve and linen that peppered his body. Each one pulled away with a blackened bottom, and she expertly replaced them with new, white cloths soaked in medicine.

"Is that good?" I asked her. "The black on the cloths. Are they working?"

She gave me a sympathetic look. "It's…We're keeping him comfortable. The salve treatment is like…" She seemed to search for the right words. "Like skimming off the surface. It'll buy the Elders time to find a counter."

They'd never find it. Not without knowing it was specifically found in Talia Blackstone's grimoire. Or…right in my pocket.

Was the mysterious fire message real? Could I even trust that the spell would work? If I handed it over to the Elders, it would come with a hoard of questions I couldn't answer. Like how I even got it in the first place. And if it *were* real, and someone was risking everything to help me…would I be exposing them?

I glanced at the dean from the corner of my eye. If it were him that sent the note, I could be throwing him to the wolves. I mean, one of the ingredients was the bones of a red witch. But what on earth was a red witch? Something made up? Something outside the realm of our fragile, clandestine world?

The nurse left, and I set my cup of untouched coffee down on the side table before I stood.

"Leaving?" Mr. Blackwood asked.

"Yeah, I'm, uh, I still haven't slept since yesterday," I replied.

His face twisted with a look of disappointment. "Lydia, you should be taking care of yourself. Now, more than ever. You've got a big week ahead of you."

"I know, I just…" My glossy eyes fixed on Anson.

"Go," he said. "Get some rest. I'll stay with Mr. Abernathy."

Again, my heart filled with gratitude and urged me to give in and trust the man. But there was so much he wasn't telling me. "Don't you have, like, deanly duties?"

He smiled and sipped his coffee. "It's Saturday. My assistant is taking care of clerical tasks. And she knows where to find me if I'm needed."

I nodded hesitantly. "Okay. Then I'll be back later to check on him."

"Of course."

I wanted to leave a kiss on Anson's cheek, but I felt terribly exposed there with the dean watching. So, as much as it killed me, I walked away. I left the room in a cloud of fatigue and a heart full of pain. I felt like I had the solution in my hands but so many roadblocks in my way.

I could get the cure for Anson from Nash, as long as I handed over the resurrection spell I'd stolen. I had a fake one to trade, to keep something so dangerous out of the hands of the Midnight Circle, but I couldn't even hand *that* over without the proof I needed for the paper to out their existence. Because the second I handed over the spell, fake or not, the Circle would disappear, and I'd never get back in.

My only other option was to use the mysterious spell that was delivered to our room via fire message. We knew nothing of the sender or their intent. And the ingredients were all rare or extinct. I could hand it over to the Elders, to let their experts find the ingredients, but then they'd want to know where I got it. And it would alert the Circle members that may be hiding amongst them that I have a cure for Anson, and they could retaliate to protect their only leverage over me.

I was lost.

Before I knew it, I was walking down a familiar corridor on the other side of the school. I'd made my way across campus in a state of bewilderment, moving by sheer muscle memory. I snapped out of my daze halfway down the hall to my room.

With so much stacked against me, I only knew one thing to be certain: I was running out of time.

I had to make a choice.

CHAPTER 28

I FLUNG the door to my room open and swiftly closed it behind me. Willa, still asleep, bolted awake in her bed in a panic, her crown of curls flopping about messily.

"What's that?" she muttered sleepily and rubbed her eyes. "What's happening?"

Her mattress sunk with my weight as I perched on the edge. "How much do we know about this weird spell that was sent to us yesterday?"

She blinked away the remnants of sleep and struggled to focus on me. "Uh, well, it uses ingredients that may or may not even exist."

"So, you think it's fake?" I asked.

Her expression froze. "I hadn't considered—"

"Is there a way we can determine if it's real or not?"

She examined my tired face with concern then noted my clothes. I still wore the same outfit as yesterday. "Lydia, have you been up all night?"

I inhaled long and deep. "Just tell me. Do you think we can figure out if this soul awakening counter is an actual spell that will work?"

Her hands scrubbed the soft morning skin of her face, and she held her hair back as her gaze drifted in thought. After a moment, she looked at me. "Yeah, I think so. I mean, it would take a little research, but I'd just have to theorize the chemistry of each one and how they'd potentially interact with each ingredient."

"And if it proves to be real, can we find substitutes for the extinct items?" I asked, hopeful.

Willa shook her head in confusion. "What's going on, Lydia?"

My bottom lip trembled as the reality of the words formed in my mouth. "Anson isn't getting any better. They can't help him without knowledge of the hex's origin, or a straight up counter. Neither of which I can give them until I have the proof I need to expose the Midnight Circle before they figure out how to resurrect Talia Blackstone."

Willa blew out a long breath, and her eyes widened. "Our life is messed up."

I nodded. "Yeah." A comfortable silence held the air between us. "So, the ingredients. If you can confirm it's real, can you find substitutes for them?"

She slowly nodded. "Yeah, I think I can."

"Good," I replied and pushed off her bed.

"But what about the bones?" she reminded me.

I turned and fixed my gaze on hers. "Leave that part for me to figure out."

CONFIRMING the legitimacy of rare and extinct items was harder than one would assume.

Willa and I spent days tracing lineages of herbs and flowers, testing the hypothetic reactions of the combination of ingredients from the mysterious counter spell. After only a few short months at Arcane Academy, I felt like I'd read just about every damn book in the grand library. But, after four days of research and tests, Willa and I could confidently determine one thing to be true.

The spell to awaken a cursed soul was, in fact, real. And we'd put together a list of alternative ingredients that, in theory, should produce the same result.

That was the good news. The bad news was that we'd spent day and night confirming the spell, and it was now Wednesday. The final Courtship Program test was barely two days away, and I'd yet to find the new entrance to the Midnight Circle to get the evidence I needed against them. And I still hadn't found out anything about red witch bones.

It was time to make a trip to Miss Haggy's.

"Are you sure you don't want me to come?" Willa asked.

I grabbed my leather jacket from the back of the door. "No, you stay here. You've done enough to help. Besides, I have a feeling Haggy might be more inclined to divulge information if there's less of a risk of too many people knowing."

"But I could be a distraction for her while you snoop around for the new Circle entrance," she argued.

I shook my head. "I'm going back tonight, after closing, to do that."

"Then I'm going with you for that," she replied and firmed her expression.

She wasn't taking no for an answer. I hated putting her so close to danger like that. She didn't deserve to get wrapped up in all my shit. But here she was, loyal to a fault.

I gave her a smile as I stood in the doorway. "I'll be back soon."

I snuck through the lesser used corridors of the school and headed for a side entrance. I didn't dare try the main door, where there'd surely be a team of hungry reporters, thirsty for my story—for that exclusive interview with the girl who knocked them all on their asses.

I found the side door and bound across the vast fields that divided the space between the school and the little village it supported. The hood of my sweater was tucked down inside my jacket, and I pulled it out to throw over my head in an attempt to conceal my face.

I wandered the busy, stone-paved streets until Haggy's Apothecary came into view. A quick tug on the brass handle, and I was inside. The dense smell of various incense and candles filled my nostrils and made my head swarm.

Haggy was there, standing behind the counter as she scooped something from a large woven sack into several smaller ones.

She glanced up and grinned at the sight of me.

"You're a brave one to be venturing out and about," she said.

"And why is that?" I asked as I pretended to be interested in a particular shelf of assorted reptile eyes.

"The girl who tames demons and is unburned by hellfire?" she said. "Everyone in town will want to speak with you, dear."

I guffawed and rubbed at my arms. "I wasn't unburned. Trust me. Don't believe everything you hear."

"Hear?" she replied and closed the large sack with a drawstring. "I saw it with my own eyes."

Of course Haggy was in the audience. Who wasn't? I didn't reply. Just kept perusing the shelves for any indication of witch bones.

"And how did that Mors Velox spell go?" she asked, changing the subject.

The cryo spell? My chest tightened with panic. "Uh, what do you mean?"

She chuckled knowingly and tightened the sash of her silk

kimono as she came around the front of the counter. "I knew the moment I saw your list of ingredients. You can't fool me, dear. I've seen it all." She sauntered toward me, as though examining my every breath. "The only question I had was what would two first year students be doing with an ancient spell like that? One that hasn't been found in any modern grimoire."

It didn't matter; the damn spell hadn't worked anyway. I held my composure and gave her an indifferent glance. "I think you're mistaken."

She tipped her head back and forth. "Perhaps. But I doubt it." When I didn't reply, she moved the conversation. "Is there anything in particular I can help you with today?"

I reached into my pocket, pulled out the list Willa created of alternative ingredients, and handed it to Haggy. "Do you have these on hand?"

She studied the words on the page, then eyeballed me. "I do. I can prepare them for you while you wait." She cleared her throat and arched an eyebrow. "Is there...anything else you need?"

"Yes," I replied and continued scanning the endless shelves of jars and bags and boxes. "I'm also looking for bones or dust of bones." I purposely left that item off my shopping list so I could peruse the selection myself.

"Of course. I have bones from just about every creature known to Earth." Miss Haggy took a few strides over to a far wall and snapped her fingers. A small table of candles lit up and displayed a dusty shelf lined with jars of various sizes. "What exactly do you want?"

I took in a nervous breath. "Bones of...Wicked Born?"

Her eyes bulged, and she clapped her hands, causing the candles to go out again. "Using the bones of our kind is forbidden." She then narrowed her gaze and regarded me curiously, circling around as her navy kimono billowed at her feet. "I imagine the whereabouts of such a restricted ingredient as witch bones would surely be locked away in the restricted area of the school."

So I was, once again, back to square one. I had to get in the restricted area.

Once she'd prepared the rest of the items I needed, I pulled my hood closer to my face and headed back through town toward the school. Even with all but one ingredient in my hands, fear still held me prisoner. Without the red witch bones, this spell wouldn't work. It wouldn't save Anson.

I had to get in the restricted area.

Tonight.

I stuffed the tiny satchels inside the inner pocket of my jacket as I rounded the corner to the hallway that led to Nash's room. I stood outside the door and took a deep breath. My knuckles tapped against the thick wood.

The lock made a *click* as someone opened the door a crack. Ferris.

I pursed my lips. "Is Nash here?"

He stared at me, unblinking. Almost as if he were trying to read my mind…or get me to read his.

I raised my brow impatiently. "Well? *Is* he?"

Ferris rolled his eyes and opened the door wider, wordlessly inviting me in. I took only one step inside, refusing to go any farther inside the cologne-soaked room where the devil himself lived. Nash was sitting in a chair by the window, a clear glass of what looked like whiskey in his hand. He peered up at me with that godawful sly smirk.

"Lydia," he cooed and motioned to an empty chair. "Join me for a drink?"

I crossed my arms and reminded myself I was here for a favor. I had to play nice. "No thanks. I'm here to ask"—I groaned inside —"for your help."

He gave a mock look of surprise and sipped his drink. "*My* help? Well, I would have thought you'd come to make that trade. The final test is almost here."

"I'm not ready to hand that resurrection spell back," I lied. "You guys shouldn't even have it. You don't know what power like that can do."

"Well," he replied and set his glass down on a small table as he crossed his legs. "That may be true. But if you want that counter to save precious Prince Charming, handing back the spell you stole is your only option."

I seethed inside. "Do you still have the key to the restricted area?"

He exchanged a curious glance with Ferris, who stood off to the side.

"Of course not," Nash said. "That was confiscated immediately."

I wasn't buying it. "But you made a copy. Didn't you?"

He failed to hide his smug expression. "Maybe. Maybe not."

"I need the key, Nash."

He stood and came toward me. "Come to the Midnight Circle meeting tomorrow night."

"Why would I do that?"

"Come to the meeting," he repeated. "I'll make sure you're released from any ties to the coven. If you hand over the spell, I'll give you the key to the restricted area *and* the counter you need to save your boyfriend."

I tried to stifle the flood of disbelief that punched me in the chest. Why would Nash just hand everything over like that? I didn't trust him, but this was an opportunity to kill many birds with one stone. Hand over the fake resurrection spell and get not one but two chances to save Anson. If I couldn't find anything in the restricted area about red witches, then at least Talia's counter would surely reverse the hex.

Plus, it was my chance to get the proof I needed to expose the underground coven and their seedy doings.

I made a show of it being a hard decision, but I finally held out my arm.

"Fine," I replied, and Nash happily shook my hand. "Where do I meet you?"

And just like that, I made a deal with the devil. It was the best shot I had, and yet, fear trembled up my spine that I was making a terrible mistake.

CHAPTER 29

EVERYTHING BUILDING up to the eleventh hour was weighing on my nerves. The final Courtship Program test was tomorrow morning, and we had no idea what it even was. At least with the other three, they gave us something to practice. But the Game Designers said the final challenge would be one that'd truly test us all on a fair level. I just wish I knew what to expect.

But that was the least of my worries. Anson lay near death in a bed back at school, and I had two possible cures for him in my grasp, of which neither might work. And all I'd had to do was make a deal with the devil to secure them.

A deal I would have to carry out while also, discreetly, collecting solid proof that there was a secret coven operating under our noses that had infiltrated the academy, our Elders, and maybe even more.

The Midnight Circle wanted to resurrect an ancient evil in the form of Talia Blackstone: a mentally insane witch who, hundreds of years ago, wanted to watch the world burn. Why on earth would they want to bring someone like that back from the dead?

I stood in the blanket of shadows that the tree line offered as I waited for Nash and Ferris. It was close to midnight, and the village fell quiet with locked doors and darkened windows as everyone retreated to their homes or back to the school. Nash had said to meet him near the apothecary, so that's where I stood. Waiting impatiently.

Two figures moved along the tree line, making their way toward me. I squinted to make them out, and the conceded sway of Nash's gait was a dead giveaway he was one of the people approaching. One of the street torches cast a wide veil of light over the grass and illuminated Ferris at his side.

"You're late," I said when they reached me.

Nash gave a mocking bow. "Apologies, princess. We had to take care of a few things."

I rolled my eyes. "Let's just get this over with."

He stepped closer.

"Of course. Right this way," he purred as he leaned in and passed me by, letting his gross breath touch my face.

I cringed and swatted at the air. Ferris waited for me to take the middle, wordlessly gesturing to proceed. I followed close behind Nash until we stepped up to the front door of Haggy's shop.

"Can we just go in her store?" I asked, uncertain.

Nash turned his head and gave me a cunning smile. "We're not entering the apothecary."

Confusion swept through me as his crimson colored magic drifted around his hands like smoke to draw strange symbols on the door with his fingertips. The markings disappeared as fast as he drew them—too fast for me to make out—and then he opened the thick, wooden door and stepped inside.

I followed, with Ferris on my heels, and stopped just a couple feet past the threshold. It wasn't Miss Haggy's apothecary at all. We were inside the stone walls of the Midnight Circle's meeting place. The door must have been enchanted to be a two-way entrance.

"Impressive," I offered.

Nash raised his eyebrows. "Is that a compliment?"

"Not for you," I snapped. "I'm sure you had nothing to do with it."

He snickered. "My, Lydia, for a woman who wants so much from me, you're not very generous with your words."

"After what you've done," I told him, "you're lucky to only get my words."

He heaved an exaggerated sigh. "Very well, then." He motioned to the red velvet sofas. "Have a seat. Let's make the trade."

I followed him over to the empty seating area and noted how no one was around. Didn't he say there was a meeting? I sat on the sofa, a couple feet between us as Ferris made himself comfortable on the smaller adjacent one. He was unusually quiet. Not like the Ferris I knew at all. But I couldn't read his distant expression.

"Did you bring it?" Nash asked, stealing my attention.

I blinked away the daze. "Uh, yeah."

I reached into the inside pocket of my jacket and pulled out the small stack of folded papers that Willa and I worked so hard to make. I could only hope they'd pass as the real thing. Sweat beads broke out under my arms as I handed the papers to Nash.

He seemed pleased with himself as he gave the first sheet a glance over. Suddenly, someone appeared from behind the sofas, emerging from one of the narrow hallways that continued the underground space.

"Nash," said the tall, older man I'd never seen before. His bald head gleamed in the torchlight. "We need you for a moment."

Nash smiled at me. "Stay here. I have to deal with something first, then I'll grab your counter."

He moved to stand, and I swiftly grabbed his wrist. He peered down at me with a startle, and I glared up at him, clearing my throat. "You'll have to leave those with me until you return with the counter."

I had to play like I still needed it, after all. If he knew I already had one, he'd wonder why I was really here, and I didn't need *him* getting suspicious of *me*.

His mouth twisted into a grin. "What, don't trust me?"

"Hardly."

His grin turned to a sneer, and he tugged free of my grasp with a sharp shrug. Then he waved the papers at me. "You're on my turf now, princess. These stay with me."

He stared at me for a moment, letting his calculating gaze bore into me. Finally, he looked to Ferris and cocked his head toward the hallway, signaling his supplement to follow. With a sigh, Ferris stood, and they both disappeared down the dimly lit corridor.

Immediately, I sprung into action. I pulled out my phone and snapped pictures of whatever I could: displays of ancient relics, charms, and tools the Circle had no right to have in their possession. Then I took a quick panoramic video of the main area where they left me.

Distant voices muffled by the walls caught my attention, and I cautiously followed the lure of it down one of the dank corridors. Toward the end, a door was ajar, and I crept over with my back against the wall. Within a few minutes, at least a half dozen voices had weighed in on their discussion, but it was too early into my eavesdropping to follow along just yet. I didn't, however, miss the low, urgent tone of their voices.

I slid a little closer so I could make out the words more easily.

Nash's voice rose above the others. "So we're performing the resurrection tomorrow evening?"

"Now that we have Talia's spell back in our possession, yes," someone replied. "Good job, Mr. Crane. We were running out of time."

"I knew she would come around," he told them. "Lydia is weak."

Rage boiled at the bottom of my belly, ready to launch. But I kept my cool. My phone was still on video, and I held it close to the door.

"She mustn't be weak for long," someone else said, this time a female voice. "Once we summon Talia's soul, more red witches will be awakened. Lydia needs to be ready. Can you ensure that, Mr. Crane?"

"Well, we still don't know for sure if she even is a red witch," Nash replied. "How will we confirm?"

"From what she's displayed thus far, and with her background, we're certain Lydia Laveau is a powerful red witch, worthy of wielding Talia's power. She's the key to all of this, Mr. Crane. You must uphold your duty to rein her in."

My throat squeezed tightly, and the phone shook in my trembling hand as their words seeped into my ears, planting in my mind, attempting to form a visual. This couldn't be...

They couldn't already know my secret. Let alone moreso than I ever did.

And yet, it seemed they knew what I was.

And all this time, I'd had it wrong.

I wasn't a hybrid witch. Or at least, if I was, there was a name for it. I was a *red* witch.

The very thing I'd been searching for.

And apparently, Talia Blackstone had been one, too.

The thought made me ill. The final ingredient I needed for the counter spell that I did possess was...me. But I couldn't very well use my own bones to perform the spell.

"What are you doing?" a voice said so quietly I almost didn't hear them.

But I did hear, and it was enough to make me jump. I pressed my free hand over my mouth to stop the sound of a gasp from getting out, nearly dropping my phone in the process. I quickly stuffed it, still recording, inside my pocket and turned to find Ferris standing in the hallway behind me.

"Uh, w-what are *you* doing?" I whispered as I tiptoed a few steps farther from the door.

He thumbed over his shoulder as he regarded me curiously. "I was using the bathroom."

He eyed me, then the crack in the door, and gave a reluctant sigh as he grabbed my sleeve and pulled me back toward the main gathering area.

"How much did you hear?" he whispered angrily.

I stood straight and crossed my arms. "Enough."

He pinched the bridge of his freckled nose. "Lydia, you have no idea what you're getting yourself into—"

"Sounds like I don't really have a choice over what I'm *into*," I cut in and arched an eyebrow. "Do I?"

He didn't reply, only glanced around nervously.

"I would almost say you guys are the ones in over your heads," I went on. "Bringing back Talia Blackstone? Really? Ferris, that's *insane*."

"Don't you think I know that?" His eyes bulged. "Why do you think I've been risking my ass to try and help you?"

My expression turned blank as we stared at one another. Him urging me to put it together, me struggling to understand.

Then it hit me.

It all made sense and washed over me with a mix of relief and panic.

"The counter spell," I said quietly. "You sent that fire message, didn't you?"

He half-grinned and gave a shrug as he flipped one of his ginger waves away from his face. "Don't I always look out for you?"

My hands trembled as I worked through all the details. "But why send it to me if you knew I was still going to trade the resurrection spell I stole for Talia's real counter spell?"

He tipped his head to the side. "Lydia, that *is* Talia's counter."

"But why——" The realization and betrayal hit me in the gut. "Nash was never going to give it to me, was he?"

Ferris shook his head solemnly.

The crushing sensation of defeat pushed at my chest, and I fought back tears of frustration. I didn't know what to do. Nash was never going to give me the counter, which probably meant the same for the key. He just wanted the stolen resurrection spell back.

My ears rang with the pressure of my quickened pulse. My chest shook with half breaths, anxiety closing in. I couldn't go on like this much longer. Like I was constantly treading water, barely able to keep my head above the surface. The promise of safety was constantly put just within my reach and then yanked away the moment I came near.

I cleared my throat. "Uh, I need to go." I searched for an exit; the long staircase I'd ventured down a few times before was no longer there now that they moved the entrance to Haggy's shop. "How do I get out?"

"Nash is going to ask——"

I grabbed Ferris' silk shirt, which pulled a little at the seams with a slight ripping sound as I hauled him close. "*Where* is the exit, Ferris?"

I fought to calm my breathing, but it wouldn't relent. I needed air. I needed to get above ground. Ferris sighed and pointed at one of the three doors on the far wall, where the bottom of the stairs would have been.

"The middle one. That's the door we came in through," he told me. "But if you're going to leave, do it now. Nash will be back any second."

I released him with a shove, and he stumbled back a step. I didn't give him a final word as I turned and bounded for the door, bolted for the door, and thrust myself out into the cool night air. I fell to the ground where everything wretched from my stomach with violent convulsions.

My life was a lie. Everything I ever thought I knew was now only a fuzzy haze in my memories.

I'm not even a light born witch, I thought. *I never was.*

No, I was this strange, unknown breed of something called red witches. Not only did that turn my entire world upside down, but it also alluded to the fact that my bones were the key to saving the man I loved.

The very bones *in my body* were the last ingredient for the counter curse, the only counter in existence strong enough to rid him of the dark hex.

I finally got the proof I needed to expose the Midnight Circle, but what good was any of it?

I could out them to our world, let the information reach the right people and let them take the coven down. But where would that leave me? The coven possessed the only information that would give me the answers to what I truly am.

A...red witch.

But a sliver of hope found its way into my mind at one thought.

The Midnight Circle only had a *copy* of Talia Blackstone's grimoire. The real book lay in the restricted area of the school, behind those iron bars, and contained all the knowledge I needed—maybe even where to find bones of a red witch that wasn't myself to save Anson. And almost definitely more about what I am. What *both* Anson and I were.

I pushed myself up off the ground and took a deep breath.

I had to find a way into the restricted area.

Tonight.

CHAPTER 30

"Lydia!" Willa cried as she followed me around the room in a trail of my determination and hastiness. "You can't. Not tonight. Not with so many eyes on us during the Program!"

I stuffed my athame in my saddle bag, along with various things I'd thrown in there that might help me break into the dean's office. I could use any help I could get.

"Lydia!"

I threw the strap of my bag over my head and spun around to face her. "Look. I'm breaking into the dean's office. Right now. I'm going to use his personal entrance to get into the restricted area and find out anything and everything about red witches." I sighed. "With or without you."

Her hands slapped helplessly at her sides. "But why? Because of something Nash Crane said? You don't even know if any of it's true."

"But I do," I replied, my voice nothing but a shaky whisper. I pressed my hand to my chest. "I can feel the weight of its truth. I need to know more. And I need to figure out where to find the bones of my...kind."

She paced the floor.

"So, what's it going to be?" I asked her as calmly as I

could. "You have no obligation. I won't make you do anything you don't want to."

She came to a halt and pursed her lips as she stared at me. Her elbows pointed outward as she gripped her hips. Finally, a sigh pushed from her chest. "Of course I'm coming. That's not even a question. I'm just…worried about you. You haven't been sleeping. And the final test is tomorrow."

"Nothing else matters to me if Anson dies," I said. "If I didn't do everything I could to save him…I wouldn't be able to live with myself." I stepped closer to her, my jaw tight with determination. "And the secrets to my hybrid powers are possibly hidden in that place. Secrets that shouldn't be kept from me. I have a right to know what I am."

She grabbed her jacket from the bed. "Then let's not waste any more time."

Under the protection of my trusty invisibility enchantment, Willa and I crept across the school toward the office wing. Straight through the library was the fastest, easiest way, and I knew we could cling to the shadows the stacks provided. Not that we needed it, but just in case.

As we were passing through, Willa stopped and gasped, grabbing my arm.

"Lydia, look," she said and pointed toward the iron gates of the very area we were planning to sneak in the back of. "It's…"

"Open?" I finished, my voice filled with awe and a hint of skepticism.

We both stood stiffly, staring at the slack padlock that hung open in the metal loop. So discreet, we may have missed it.

"Did someone maybe forget to lock up earlier?" she said.

That didn't seem right. "Smells like a trap."

All that could be heard in the empty vastness of the library were our rapid breaths echoing in the air as we contemplated.

"Well," Willa said hesitantly, "if it *is* a trap, then it

wouldn't matter which end we sneak in. Someone would be watching us either way. But if it's not a trap…"

"Then someone's watching us, but on our side," I added. "Could it be Ferris?"

Her mouth pinched for a moment, then she shook her head. "No, he wouldn't have the ability to open it. It's protected against magical temperament, which means he would have definitely needed the key."

"Which we know he and Nash don't have."

"Exactly," she replied. "Because he would have bribed us with it by now."

I little voice in the back of mind whispered the idea that perhaps it was the dean, doing what he could to help us along. I still didn't fully believe the man, but he'd proved this week just how much he wanted my trust and what he was willing to do to earn it.

He stayed by Anson's side when I couldn't.

And he'd divulged bits and pieces of secrets he'd been hiding, almost as if he wanted to tell but couldn't.

Some of the last words he said to me suddenly rang in my ears.

There's so much you don't know, that you just don't understand. Yet.

I sucked in a deep breath. "Well, should we take the leap of faith?"

Her big brown eyes gleamed at me. "What have we got to lose?"

With a quick look around, we snuck inside the gate, and I quickly pushed the lock back in place, securing us inside the restricted area. Willa looked alarmed, but I held a finger over my lips.

"We'll sneak out through the dean's office again," I whispered. "This way, anyone wandering about won't follow us in here."

Her shoulders slumped with relief. "Good call." She

turned around and took in the endless, dust-covered shelves and stacks of old trunks. "So, where do we start?"

"The same shelf we found Talia's grimoire and that other one," I replied quietly as we crept along the narrow space. "I bet there's more texts on red witches there."

It only took a few minutes of skimming the spines to find the single shelf that once contained Talia Blackstone's ancient grimoire and the other one we'd stolen—the one with both light and dark magic practices inside.

But now, with what I so far knew, it wasn't light and dark mixing at all. It was hybrid magic. Red witches, working together with no confines on their abilities. Like me.

If these texts existed, and I was proof that this rare, unknown magic was real...then where did the rest of them go? Where were the red witches in our society today? Why weren't they mentioned? Why didn't we learn about them? And better yet... where was their faction?

"It's gone," Willa noted as she read the spines for a second time. "The grimoire. It's not here."

"What? That can't be right." I sidled up next to her to read them for myself. Sure enough, Talia's book was gone. I groaned. "They must have taken it somewhere else after the whole ordeal with the caves."

"Makes sense." She shrugged. "They should have locked it away after Norah's death, if you ask me."

"You're not wrong there," I said. "That would have saved us a lot of trouble." I tipped my head and read more of the spines on other shelves below it. "There's gotta be other texts, though."

We searched every book in the maze of shelves for over an hour, but all we managed to put together was a small stack of texts about other witch cultures that, over the centuries, decided to exist outside our Wicked Born world. Like the Celtic royalties and Romanian Travellers. Like Anson's birth mother.

Those witches operated without the domain of factions and strict rules that divided them by birth. They followed a completely different set of values and rules, managing to remain hidden from the mundane world, but live in it at the same time. Just like us.

I admired them for their ability. It proved we could exist without the confines of biased factions that stuck us in boxes before we even knew who we were ourselves.

It still told us nothing about red witches, though.

I let my weight slump on a large trunk and leaned forward on my lap, hanging my head. Exhaustion was breaking me down. I needed sleep. I needed a proper meal.

But it was like I couldn't slow down. Couldn't take a breath until everything was okay. With the final test in just a few hours and the man I loved laying on his death bed…the end was near, and I had to ensure it didn't end in disaster.

"Do you think, maybe, that the others are red witches?" Willa entertained.

"What, like, the Romani and the Celtics?" I said and shook my head. "No, I don't think so. Although, Anson's mother was one. But…it doesn't *feel* right. That idea. There's something we're missing."

She plopped down on the dusty floor where she heaved a deep, tired sigh. I felt it, too. The impossibility of it all. We were just two young Wicked Born, fighting our way through our five-year pledge while simultaneously trying to bring down a rising coven and save our loved ones. It was too much.

Willa's eyes drifted with the temptation of sleep, and I wanted to crawl onto the floor and join her. But I couldn't.

"You should go back—"

"What about the trunks?" Willa exclaimed as a new sense of hope seemed to bring her back to life. She pushed herself across the floor toward me. Her hand smoothed over the symbols on the trunk I sat on. "What we're looking for, it wouldn't be out on display on a shelf. Even in here."

She pulled herself to her feet and brushed the dust from her pants. "If the dean had to lock away Talia's book and that other one we stole, then he'd have to lock it *all* away. Everything pertaining to her magic, red witches, and whatever else that proved they existed. Right?"

The possibility gave me a rush of energy. "Right."

"Well, it doesn't make sense they'd move it all across campus. So it could still be here. Just...better locked away."

I stood from the old chest I'd been sitting on and looked down at it, noting the Wicked Born symbols it showed. We immediately set to work, studying every single trunk we could find for anything familiar. But most weren't even locked and only contained items too delicate to have out on display.

The others, the locked ones, lined the walls and stacked in piles on the floor in every corner. If the protected books were anywhere, it would be in those locked trunks.

We quickly deciphered that the carvings and symbols on most of them indicated houses of Wicked Born. Famous, important houses throughout time that birthed leaders, Elders, previous deans. If we were in the West side of Arcane Academy, there'd probably be one for the Laveau family. But here, on the East side, we read names like Crane, Blackwood, Hallowell, Winters, and more.

Something in my gut told me we were close. The trunk we were looking for was here. Somewhere.

I closed my eyes and firmed my arms at my sides as I tapped deep into my mind, concentrating on the idea of my hybrid magic. My...red magic. The one that could wield both light and dark, if I wanted. Or could let loose and dominate everything.

"Lydia!" Willa whispered with caution and touched my arm. "You shouldn't use magic down here. It could be warded. You might set off an alert."

I shook my head, my eyes remaining closed tightly. "I'm not using magic, I'm using...my gut."

"What?"

I broke the thin string of concentration I made and looked at her. "It might be stupid, but sometimes...I can *sense* things. When they're connected to me, or my magic. Things like, what to do, where to go. When I broke into the Midnight Circle, before they moved the entrance, something told me I *had* to get behind that door. The door guarding Talia's grimoire, which now I know why. Because it was tied to my magic."

She slowly nodded, then her gaze flitted around the dank space. "And you think you can sense the trunk we need?"

"It's worth a shot."

Without hesitation, she took both my hands, and we stood across from one another as we closed our eyes in unison and sank comfortably into concentration. The quiet hum of our breaths circled between us. That strange, invisible cord that connected us when we touched pulled tight. I could feel it vibrating, searching as we pushed. My heart sped up as the scent of the dank, musty space became tainted with a sweet scent of...knowing. It lured me.

Like one, our eyes flew open and fled right to an empty spot on the stone wall. Willa's expression twisted as if she was confused that nothing was there, but I immediately noted something amiss. I knelt down and brushed my fingers over the jagged stones held together with haphazard grout lines of chunky cement.

"Look," I said and continued to feel along the cracks. "These few stones right here—the mortar is new."

I hopped to my feet and took a deep breath before driving the bottom of my boot into the stones. I could feel them give, just a little, and reeled back to do it again.

"Lydia!" Willa shrieked under a whisper. "You can't do that."

"I don't care," I said curtly and stomped at the rocks again. A crack formed along one of the mortar lines. "I'm past the point of caring anymore. The secrets to what I am are in *there*." I pointed. "The key to finding the final ingredient we need to cure Anson is in *there*." My chest heaved with anticipation. "I'm not stopping until I have it. Now stand back."

She did as I said, and I continued to kick through the newly placed stones. It took a few minutes and every bit of strength in my legs, but finally one rock came loose. I pried my fingers around it to yank it free. The noise of crumbling stone echoed through the cavernous spaces that made up the restricted area. But I didn't care.

When I dropped to my knees, they protested, but I ignored the ache that thrummed from my ankles to my hips as I grabbed hold of the surrounding rocks and heaved them loose. Willa finally joined me and helped pry the last one away, leaving a hole large enough to crawl through.

"Well, holy shit," Willa blew out in a huff as she stared at the hole. "There it is."

A mid-sized trunk sat behind the wall, upholstered in black leather, kept together with wrought iron fittings and hinges. The symbol of a pentagram on its curved lid told me it was exactly what we were looking for.

We'd found Talia Blackstone's family trunk.

My fingers, torn and bloody, grabbed the chest and hauled it from its hiding place. Willa helped me pull it out onto the floor, and we both knelt before it.

"This is crazy, Lydia," Willa said shakily. "If we're caught—"

"If we're caught down here, with all of this, I think we'd be the ones with more questions than them," I told her. "And I'll just deny you had anything to do with it, anyway. I'll say I forced you."

She tipped her head to the side. "Lydia…"

"You're risking everything to help me," I replied. "I won't take you down with me if this goes south."

She inhaled nervously and glanced at the trunk. "Well… let's do this quickly so we can get out of here and never have to worry about that."

The lock was in place, but it was rather old. I hastily fetched my father's athame from my bag and slid it through the lock's loop. It took a few heaves, but the blade proved stronger than the rusting padlock, and the thing finally popped open.

My hands, shaky and weak but filled with anticipation, pushed the lid open. A creaky screech echoed through the space as billows of dust wafted up in our faces. We wasted no time digging in. But, immediately, one thing was evident.

It was mostly filled with books.

"What the…" Willa pulled out a small stack, just a few among the dozens or so. "These are all grimoires."

I rifled through the front pages of a stack I pulled out, and my heart raced. "They're *all* Talia's."

Willa's eyes widened. "No witch has ever kept this many. What could she possibly have recorded in these pages?"

I flipped one open—a newer grimoire compared to the others—to a random entry and began reading. My thumb gently brushed over dark fingerprints that once soaked into the delicate paper.

"My sisters have all perished at the hands of our oppressors. I am but the last red witch known to still roam this wretched earth. Some have fled into hiding, but most are nothing but ash under the boot of the other kinds. They are as clever as they are ruthless in ensuring our extinction.

"I refuse to relent. I will take my vengeance to my ashen grave. But not before I leave behind a piece of me for my future sisters to use and rise up to reclaim our birthright. A piece of my rib, hidden where only the worthy can find, will be the crux needed to awaken the red witches who've been so wrongfully diminished. A ritual sealed by my willing death. I shall have my revenge, and it will be through fire and blood."

I rocked back on my bottom and sank to the floor with Talia's startling words in my shaking hands as I stared unblinking at the pages, unable to believe what I'd just read. Talia Blackstone, as evil and insane as she may have been, sacrificed herself to save her kind.

My kind.

"Lydia?" Willa said gently.

I tore my eyes from the book. "They were...massacred."

Her hand slid over mine and gave a comforting squeeze. "As world shattering as this news is, we have to focus on the task at hand. The sun will be up soon. The final test will start, and Anson is still relying on us to save him."

I wiped at the wetness that leaked from my eyes and nodded. She was right. We came here to find out more about what I am, and to find where the bones of red witches might lie. The final ingredient needed to save the man I loved. But there was still one problem.

They were all burned to death.

I shrugged helplessly as more tears of exhaustion pushed through. "The bones..."

"There's none to be found," Willa finished with a sigh.

I stared at the books filled with Talia's life. "No."

"No?"

"There's *one* bone out there. Somewhere," I replied with a sliver of hope. "Talia said so herself. Right here. She took a piece of her ribs and left it behind for the rest of us to find."

Willa's mouth gaped wordlessly. I knew what she was thinking.

"We just need to read through her grimoires," I said. "I bet the answer to its location is in these pages. Somewhere."

"Lydia." She tipped her head pitifully. "There's dozens of grimoires here. That will take weeks. At best. And what if she hid the bones on the other side of the world?" Her hand squeezed mine and demanded my attention.

I looked at her, refusing to see the reason and grace in her eyes.

"We need something *now*."

My mind raced with questions that had no answers. With possibilities that had no hope. All I could do was move forward, to the next step, the next...anything. I refused to lay down and give up. Not here. Not when I'd come so far.

I flew into a frenzy, stuffing the grimoires into my bag. As many as I could. The rest I'd carry in my arms. I'd stick them down my pants if I had to. These were the last words of my kind, and they belonged with me, not locked behind a wall of stone, hidden from the world.

"What are you doing?" Willa shrieked.

I shoved a pile in her arms. "We're taking these."

"Lydia, we don't have time——"

"Then I'll make time!" I snapped but quickly reined myself in. "Sorry." I shook my head. "I'm...on edge." My shaking arms gripped the books tightly. "If time is what we need to read through these, then time is what we'll make."

"What——how?"

My mouth widened with a grin as the idea seeped into my mind. "Mors velox."

Her expression pinched. "The cryo spell? How——" Realization struck her back. "No. *No*! You can't be seriously thinking about using it on Anson? Lydia...we destroyed that plant. It didn't work."

"If we don't at least *try*, he dies anyway," I reminded her. "But if it works, we buy the time we need to read through these and find Talia's bone. At least this way we have a *chance*."

She groaned and cast her face to the stone ceiling above. "Yeah, but is that a chance you're willing to take?"

My chest rose with a heavy sigh. "I...don't know what else to do."

A moment of silence hung between us.

"Fine," she finally said, and my heart skipped a beat. She took the pile of grimoires from my hands with a hopeful grin. "Let's Mors Velox this bitch."

CHAPTER 31

THE THREAT of sleep was imminent. My parched eyes fought to close as I stood over Anson's seemingly lifeless body. The black veins had spread even farther, covering his neck and most of his face. His chest, under the brambles of the hex, rose and fell with labored breaths. Barely noticeable unless you stared at him unblinking. Which I did. My body swayed on my feet.

"Staying up the rest of the night to perfect this potion probably wasn't the best idea," Willa said from the other side of him.

"But it was the only option." I took a deep breath and braced myself on the edge of balance bars attached to the sides of the hospital bed.

"Well, it's now or never," she said and cast a glance at the door. "The final test is about to begin. We have to hurry."

I hated hurrying. We'd only gotten the spell to work fifty percent of the time. Which meant there was still half a chance this wasn't going to end well.

Willa was right, though. We were out of time.

I pulled out the vial of potion we'd concocted back in our room and popped the cork top, ready to pour it into my boyfriend's slack mouth. The sound of the door pushing open startled me. I quickly hid the glass tube in my hand.

"You ladies ready?" asked Mr. Blackwood as he poked his head inside. "We're about to begin."

I plastered on a smile. "Yep. Just, uh, saying goodbye to Anson first."

"We'll be right out," Willa added.

He regarded us for a moment, as if he sensed something was afoot.

And it was.

He'd once told me nothing happened in this school without him knowing. I wondered just how true that was. I'd hate to have to explain the poor attempt to seal Talia's chest back in the wall that Willa and I left behind last night. Or the stack of illegal grimoires we tucked away in the back of my closet. Or the vial of Mors Velox I held in my hands.

Regardless, he said nothing.

The door closed tightly, and I dropped the fake smile as I leaned over Anson's body and carefully coaxed the potion into his mouth. I gently tipped his head back, hoping that would help it go down easier.

Willa held her hands out over the bed. "Ready?"

I took them in mine. "Ready."

We secured our stance and held one another's hands tightly as I called to my magic, letting it roll to the surface until it coiled down my arms and into our touching palms. We chanted together.

O virtus potentia. Ego sum eos.

Apud eundem ictum ac vitae est in me verberat terræ.

Usque ad tempus donec tenere relatorum permiserunt ut iterum fluant.

I opened my eyes and peered down at Anson. There was no sign of change.

"Did it work?" she asked as her eyes raked over him.

"I-it had to," I replied, unsure. "We did everything right

this time, didn't we? And we tested this batch before coming here."

"Yeah, but we did everything right the first time, too."

The doubt in her voice killed me. The door flung open again, and the dean stepped inside.

"Ladies, do not make me drag you out of this room," he told us sternly. "They are waiting."

I wanted to argue, but Willa chimed in with a defeated sigh. "Come on, Lydia." She began to walk toward the door then stopped and waited for me to follow. "It's time to go. The rest is up to fate."

I stuffed the empty vial into my jacket pocket and leaned over Anson to place a kiss on his lips. I wouldn't leave this time without it.

"I love you," I whispered in his ear.

Walking away pained me. My chest was tight with panic; my mind raced with worry. But I followed Willa and the dean down the corridor toward the Great Hall where hundreds of Wicked Born waited for my arrival. To watch me compete against two worthy opponents in a fight for leadership. I still didn't believe they actually wanted me to win, and part of me whispered doubts through my mind.

They want to see you fail, Lydia.

I held my breath as Mr. Blackwood opened the double doors to the Great Hall, and a wave of noise rushed over me. I kept my gaze to the floor and walked with Willa up to the stage to take our place next to Nash and Carol's teams. I tried not to look, but I caught their impatient glares boring into me.

Hundreds of eyes were on us, and the reality of what today meant crushed me. This was it. The final test. After today, Willa and I would either be fast tracked to become leaders of the Dark Faction, or we'd simply go back to our lives as fledgling Wicked Born and suffer under the thumb of Nash Crane.

I dared a glance his way, and he caught it. I narrowed my eyes, but it only seemed to elicit a sly sneer from him.

I couldn't let Nash Crane win.

Mr. Blackwood took the stage and leaned into the mic on the podium. "Welcome, everyone!"

The room erupted in deafening cheer.

"I'm so pleased you could all be here to witness the final test of our decennial Courtship Program," he went on. "Our contenders this year have been more than worthy of our beloved and righteous event. Our three remaining teams have proven themselves commendable and have worked hard to be here on this stage today."

He paused to compose himself and then turned to us. "I'm so very proud of them all."

His eyes locked on me with that final statement, and my cheeks burned so hot they must have appeared crimson. I shook my head and let my scraggly black hair fall to the side, hoping it would hide my blushing face before anyone noticed.

"And with that," the dean added with enthusiasm, "I turn the stage over to our wonderful Game Designers to let us in on what they have in store. I'm just as eager as you are to learn what the final test will be."

That makes both of us.

Adrien and Adina Negrustea stood together at the podium as the dean took his seat in the front row. Their matching black hair and plain black outfits added to their soulless and equally terrifying demeanors. To me, they were like robots. Or Russian assassins.

Adrien leaned into the mic and cleared his throat. "Good day and welcome. We truly hope you've enjoyed the preceding challenges. This year's contenders were formidable, and we wanted to make sure we designed a series of tests that would push each witch to their limits." He exchanged an odd glance with his sister. "That is why we've decided that the final test will be one of the most difficult we've seen in many years.

One that will place the remaining contenders on a level playing field, but allow for only two clear winning teams, as intended."

My mind reeled as everything caught up with me. *Two winning teams.* This wasn't news to me. I knew this from day one. I'd be fighting for myself and Willa to be one winning team and Anson to be the other. In all the madness of the last couple of days, I hadn't considered that was no longer an option.

The best we could hope for now was at least to beat Nash and Ferris. If I won one of those spots, I didn't want to do this without Anson, but if my choices were Nash or Carol, I'd take my chances with her.

Nash had to be stopped.

"Adina," Adrien added, "would you do the honors?"

Her brother took a step back, and she moved into place with a long, flat black briefcase. She placed it on the podium and clicked the locks open. Her mouth leaned into the mic.

"The final test of this year's Courtship Program shall be," she said, flipping open the lid on the briefcase to reveal six items, too far for me to make out, "wand dueling."

Gasps of shock and horror pushed through the crowd as Mr. Blackwood jumped to his feet, his face red with anger.

"Absolutely not!" he bellowed. "Wand dueling has been long forbidden for its barbarism."

Adrien regarded him politely. "Yes, forbidden to be used in the real world." He gave an awkward smile, as if he was out of practice showing such a basic expression. "But here, in the confines of Arcane Academy and the protection of wards, it *is* permitted to be used for the purpose of testing one's magical ability." He quirked a challenging eyebrow. "You can seek assurance from the Elders, but we've done our diligence in obtaining the proper clearance for this test."

The dean displayed a torn expression. He had no power here and must have realized Adrien was right. His body stiffened as he backed away toward his chair and threw me a concerned look.

My heart squeezed with adrenaline, and I whispered to Willa. "Wand Dueling?"

"Have you done it?" she replied quietly.

I gave her an incredulous look. "No. Jesus, has *anyone*?"

She pressed her lips together, her eyes lost with worry. "I... I think that's the point."

Adina addressed the crowd once more. "The idea of this test is to disarm your opponent by any means necessary. The first team to drop their wand will lose, and the two remaining will win by default. Adrien will now let the contenders select their wands."

Her brother held the open briefcase as he made his way down the line, and we each chose our weapons. Willa picked a slight wand with a feather tip. Mine was completely black with red engravings of symbols I'd never seen before. It felt heavy in my hands.

The six of us were ushered to the center while Elders worked to throw up wards around the perimeter of the stage, caging us in like a bunch of animals. I mindlessly played with the syphon ring that sat on my finger while thanking the universe I thought to wear the gift from my mother. The other gift, my father's athame, sat secure at my side in a hilt covered by my long jacket—a garment I wore to cover as much of my body as possible this time.

We were directed to spread out, each team backing away into a corner of the magically warded cage. I didn't take my eyes off Nash. I was striking the first chance I got.

"Stay behind me as best you can," I told Willa over my shoulder.

"No way," she spoke in my ear. "You jump, I jump, Jack."

Gods, I loved her.

The judges signaled us from the outside of the forcefield, and we readied ourselves. I tested the weight of the wand in my hand: heavy and warm. Almost as if it had a life of its own contained inside it.

I fretted about how my magic would react when being funneled through a device like this. Wicked Born long gave up the use of magical devices like wands and staffs. The outdated notions only painted targets on our backs in the mundane world as we all moved into the modern era.

I could only hope my syphon ring would be enough to keep me stable. With the level of exhaustion and sleep deprivation I was experiencing, I worried using a wand might tempt me to lose control. I'd never wielded one before, but I knew they were meant to heighten and channel power.

The air inside the forcefield tightened, and the judges counted down from ten before they told us to begin. Willa and I moved toward the middle, headed for Nash and Ferris. But they weren't even looking at us. Nash had his wand out, ready to strike....and made a beeline for Carol.

Why wasn't he bothering with us?

That's when it hit me.

Nash made no secret that he wanted to stand with me in the end. Of course he was going right for Carol and Addy. One simple move would ensure not only his win, but that *I* was standing by his side in the end.

Part of me wondered if that might be even worse than losing.

With his wand pointed at the other team, a dense red smoke billowed out from the tip, like a shot out of a gun, and bounded for Carol's head.

She ducked out of the way and slung a bolt of magic right for Ferris, forcing Nash to lower his weapon and push his supplement out of the way.

"Cheating, as usual, Crane?" Carol yelled. "You only need to go for the wand!"

He shrugged and feigned surprise. "Oopsie."

Behind him, Ferris still had yet to raise his weapon. He

hung in Nash's shadow, almost as if scared. I didn't blame him.

I called to my magic and let it bubble in my gut before channeling it through my arm and containing it in the new extension of my arm. It felt weird. Unnatural. But I could feel the weight of the power now residing in my wand, like static electricity.

I caught the slight flick of Nash's wrist, and the slow billow of red smoke seeped from inside his long jacket sleeve. He was getting ready to strike again. With Willa behind me, I bolted forward and sent an emerald charge of magic straight for his arm.

Nash grabbed hold of Ferris as they stumbled backward, and Nash landed on his ass. He threw me a look of sheer disbelief.

"What are you doing?" he squawked. "If we work together, we can beat Carol!"

I mimicked his sly shrug. "Maybe it's Carol I want to stand with in the end."

"It can only be a male and female to win," he hissed.

My grin never faltered. "No, it's always been a male and female who've won, but it's not actually written in the rules." I arched an eyebrow. "I checked."

In the blink of an eye, he was on his feet, fury in his eyes and bracing himself to summon another powerful blast. He wasn't used to losing, and I loved that I ignited that kind of rage in him. He swung his arm, flicking his wand, and a steady stream of magic shot at me and Willa. It whipped by my head, just missing my face as I pushed Willa out of the way.

I looked to the judges for help. Nash was blatantly aiming for kill shots. Was that...was that allowed? But the entire front row, with the exception of the dean who was tensed on the edge of his seat, all sat bemused. We're they that oblivious or were they purposely ignoring Nash's behaviour?

By any means necessary, Adina's words from earlier echoed in my head.

Shit. Surely she hadn't meant…

But then again, we all knew the dangers involved with the Courtship Program. I just never thought it would get this bad.

Suddenly, Willa stiffened at my back and slung her wand arm toward Carol, who was readying to strike us. The magic sliced through the air like lightning, slamming Carol into the forcefield and causing it to flicker as she crumbled to the floor.

I glanced over my shoulder and gave my best friend a look of pride and awe.

She quirked an eyebrow. "You can't be the only badass."

I chortled. "Clearly. Nice job. But don't forget we need her by our side at the end of this."

But before she could respond, Willa's face twisted in pain, and the air kicked from her lungs as she was jolted away from me. Her wand fell to the floor, and the crowd rose to their feet to get a closer look.

My supplement was down, hurt, and wandless.

I was on my own.

I spun around to find Carol and Addy standing proudly as the crowd cheered them on.

My gaze pinned on Willa. "Are you—"

"I'm fine. Go. Don't turn your back for a second!" Willa winced and scooted into the corner.

Anger festered inside me as I turned and faced my opponents, both teams ready and waiting to duel it out once more. Our wands shook in our nervous hands as we stared at one another. My heart beat wildly in my heaving chest.

Like the snake that he was, Nash was the first to strike. It was so fast I hardly caught it. He aimed for my wand, apparently giving up on helping me win alongside him, and I held it tightly as his magic struck my hand, singing the skin and shattering my syphon ring. Bits of metal fell to the floor as

I stifled a scream, the skin of my knuckles now charred and bleeding.

I let my rage build and paired it with my magic. I called to it, reached deep down. I gripped the wand and swung my arm back and forth as I closed in on him and Ferris.

A blast of energy shot from the tip of my weapon like loud, thunderous cannon fire as it destroyed the floor around him. Again, and again. I'd demolish this stage until there was nothing left for him to stand on, and then I would take this competition for myself.

Nash scrambled backward and pulled a defiant Ferris along with him. His supplement struggled against his hold, and when I saw his eyes widen at something over my shoulder, I turned and fired a blast of magic at Carol, sending her crashing into the forcefield once again.

But the distraction was all Nash needed. He struck me again, failing to knock the wand from my hand, but burning more of my flesh. The sleeve of my jacket melted away, and I hastily slapped at it to put out the fire.

I let out a guttural scream, but it only empowered me more. I hated this man with every ounce of my body. I could *not* let him win. But I didn't want to be responsible for his death, either. I continued to pursue him across the vast stage, my wand shooting bolts of green at them, as hundreds looked on.

Ferris' sudden look of frightful concern shot over my shoulder, and I cast a glance to catch Carol aiming right for my back.

What was this final test turning us into, that we would consider destroying one another to win?

But what choice did either of us have? By any means necessary. We either had to take our win, or risk the consequences of losing. Which were starting to look more dire by the moment.

Without another thought, I ripped my wand through the

air and fired a bolt of lightning right at her and Addy that sent them slamming into the forcefield. I didn't wait to see them fall to the floor before I turned my focus back to a cowering Nash and Ferris.

My breathing quickened with every step. I was anxious and eager to end this. Right here, right now.

Nash protected Ferris with his body, blocking me from getting anywhere near his supplement's wand. It didn't matter, though. I had them. The two cowardly men backed into the corner as my relentless magic shot holes in the stage and all around them.

Just as Nash raised his wand in an attempt to push me back, the dean's voice boomed across the space.

"Enough! It's done!" he cried hastily. "We have our winners by default of death."

Everyone stopped, and a startled hush fell over the Great Hall. I couldn't tear my eyes from Nash as I fought to calm my breathing, but Mr. Blackwood's words echoed in my ears.

Death?

Fear and anger held me prisoner, my body refusing to let go of the magic that now covered the entire surface of my skin.

The noise level of the hall suddenly rose, but it was nothing more than a muffled racket against my thrumming ears. Nash and Ferris stuck tight together in the corner I had them trapped in, their gazes flitting over my shoulder to the crowd and those who were working to bring down the forcefield.

The walls of energy fell and disappeared around us, and the deep barrel of noise beat against my head. But I couldn't hear it—only *feel* it. I couldn't make out the voices.

My body remained frozen; I was ready to end Nash Crane. Carol's unexpected attempt to attack was what saved him, but it still didn't negate the fact that I was seconds away from setting him ablaze to get that wand from his hand.

It was Willa's gentle touch that finally ripped me from my state of shock. Her fingers slid over my arm and calmly tugged me back toward her.

"Lydia." Her calm voice seeped into my hot ears, cooling the boiling blood that beat there. "It's okay. You can let go."

I didn't want to look, but I couldn't help myself as the medical team hoisted Carol and Addy off the stage on stretchers, their bodies covered with sheets.

I did that...

Tears filled my eyes as I forced myself to look at Willa. The moment I did, something clicked in my body, and I felt my magic reign itself back as if it had a mind of its own.

I let it go. All of it. All the fear and anxiety that had been building inside of me for weeks over this Program. It was over.

We'd won.

But I'd taken a life, one I hadn't meant to. I'd have to live with that burden. I'd have to live with it forever...with Nash at my side.

My stomach lurched.

"You had no choice. Carol was aiming for a lethal blow at your back," Willa whispered, but her words were weightless.

Did it matter what choice I'd had? The sting of what I'd done felt like poison in my veins. Willa's hand slid down my arm, avoiding the scorched skin, and pried the wand from my trembling grip. My lips quivered as I tried to speak.

"W-we...won."

She nodded. "We won."

"And so did we," Nash chimed in like a merry elf as he slung his arm over my shoulder. "Thanks to you." He beamed at the crowd and waved to the reporters that swarmed the front of the stage. "Smile for our people, princess. We'll be their leaders one day."

All I could think about was the fact it was over. All of it. Finally over and I'd never have to worry about it again; and at the same time, I'd be haunted by it for the rest of my life.

I fought against the urge to flee. To hold Carol's lifeless hand and tell her I was sorry. To go check on Anson and see if my spell worked. I had no further need to be here in the Great Hall, on some disgusting display like prize-winning cattle.

Mr. Blackwood stood with the Gamer Designers at the front of the stage and raised his arms in the air as he announced the results, a sadness in his voice that I hadn't imagined would be there in this moment. I could see the mask he wore over the worry he harbored at what I'd just done.

"We have our winners for this year's Courtship Program," he said evenly. The noise level increased as people flew into fits of excitement, as if they didn't care at all that two of our own had died. "Nash Crane and Lydia Laveau, along with their supplements Ferris Cooper and Willa Stonerose, will one day join the ranks of our great leaders. Let's give them a well-deserved round of applause."

He half turned with a mask of a smile plastered across his face, but as he peered at me, the expression quickly morphed into a look of concern. His gaze flitted to my scorched arm, and I gave him a reassuring nod that I was okay. At least physically.

Nash's arm still hung across my shoulders as he boastfully spoke with the media at our feet. Their exchange of words fell on my deaf ears. My mind wasn't here. The burns on my arm screamed to be treated, and I winced with even the tiniest of movements. I tried to slink away from Nash's embrace, but he grasped my bad arm.

The pain forced my distant mind to the surface, and the sudden rush of clarity filled my ears.

"I think our close friendship will be the foundation that we'll build our leadership plan upon," Nash told one reporter, and I peered down at doe-eyes staring back up at us.

I tried to wiggle free of his grasp and, when he refused, I kicked his shin and hauled back before laying a hefty blow to his jaw.

"Lydia!" the dean exclaimed.

Nash went reeling to the floor as onlookers showered us in gasps of shock and awe. Then the wave of camera flashes and questions bombarded me from the row of media down below.

My anxiety shot into overdrive, and I backed away. I needed to get out of there. I needed medical attention and, most of all, I desperately needed to go check on Anson and see if the cryo spell worked.

I looked to Willa. My rock in all this chaos. Our gazes locked through the noise, and I willed her to understand the concern that filled my mind. Anson. My heart warmed when she gave a slight nod and motioned to the door.

I turned on my heel and bolted for the back doors of the Great Hall, leaving behind the cacophony of Wicked Born who demanded my time, and the wonderful sound of Willa's voice carrying out over them.

"Lydia requires medical attention and will be stepping out," she told them sternly. "I'll stay and address any questions you may have."

What would I do without her?

I never would have survived these few months at Arcane Academy without Willa, and I would thank my lucky stars every single day until I died for her friendship. I couldn't live without her in my life.

But I also couldn't live without Anson.

I only hoped the cryo spell worked.

CHAPTER 32

I BURST through the door to Anson's room and locked it behind me. I needed a moment's peace from...everything. The fact that we'd won...alongside Nash, no less...still had yet to truly sink in, and my wounds kept me from really thinking about much else outside the pain and worry in my heart for the man I loved.

My back pressed against the closed door, and I tipped my head back, just for a moment. Just enough to let the silence chase away the noise in my head and calm my rampant heart. My eyes flew open and fixed on the figure that lay in the bed across the room. I stared at him, unblinking, thinking of how proud he'd be of me and Willa.

Then I noticed something.

He wasn't moving.

Not a single breath. Fear froze me in place, and I continued to stare, my heart begging for a sign of life. But there was nothing.

"No…" The word died on my lips.

My fists clenched at my sides and sent a jolt of pain up through my wounded arm, reminding me of my extensive burns. The pain pushed away the fear, and my heart banged against the inside of my chest, crying for him. Aching to go to him.

My feet shuffled like bricks across the floor, and I fell to his side, the crushing defeat of reality just too much to bear. I took his lifeless hand in my trembling fingers, still unable to bring myself to actually look at his face. Hot tears streamed down my cheeks. I put my ear to his chest, waiting and hoping for a sliver of a heartbeat. But he was cold.

Slowly, I turned my head to finally look at him, and my stomach dropped. Emotions burst to the surface. Tears and cries erupted from my chest, and I fought to control the wave of nausea that crashed over me.

His pale face was completely covered with blackened veins, his mouth open and slack, his eyes—now open—staring up at the ceiling with an unnerving blankness.

The spell didn't work.

I clutched his hand tightly as a heart-breaking cry squeezed from my throat. My tears soaked into the thin sheet that came just above his waist.

"Anson…" I babbled. "You can't leave me. I *need* you. We did it. Willa and I won. But so did Nash, and I don't know where to go from here." I needed him to move. To take a breath. To prove my fears wrong. "Anson…*please.*"

I couldn't just lay down and accept this. I pushed myself to my feet and wiped at the tears under my stressed eyes, the skin there soft and sore. I paced the floor next to his bed, wringing my shaking fingers through my hair. Deep down, I knew what I could do. I had the solution in my head this whole time, but it came at a cost. It came with risks…

Talia's resurrection spell.

I knew it by heart after Willa and I read it a million times while replicating the fake. The ingredients were simple, except one. The blood of the willing. But I had that. *My* blood. I was willing to cut myself if it meant saving the man I loved.

I flew into a mode of determination, pulling things from

shelves. I needed a couple of things back in our quarters and closed my eyes as I snapped my fingers, manifesting the items before me. I dragged a wheeled table over to Anson's side and pooled together my ingredients.

I needed an urn.

I fetched a clay flower pot from the window and dumped out the contents before giving it a wipe to get rid of any remaining soil. I stood before my gatherings and let my lungs fill with air.

Calm down, Lydia. Focus.

I shook my hands and paced the floor again. It was too much for one person to take. I could hear rustling in the hallway outside, and another rush of adrenaline coursed through me.

I didn't have much time.

I hastily measured and added my ingredients to the clay pot while stealing panicked glances at the door.

Everything was ready. Just one final step.

I heaved a nervous sigh as I reached for my athame, sliding it from the hilt on my side. I closed my eyes and bit back the pain as I dragged the blade across one palm and then the other.

Blood immediately pooled to the surface, and I held my clenched fists over the make-shift urn. With a finger, I quickly stirred the contents inside the pot and then poured them over Anson's exposed chest.

More shuffling in the hall. Were they looking for me?

I held my bleeding hands out over my boyfriend's dead body as I called to my magic. Past the dark, past the light. I dug deep for the dormant red magic that I'd been so scared of and let it awaken, let it swim to the surface and fill my limbs.

The air in the room tightened.

At the same time, the door handle jiggled.

I'd locked it, so hopefully I had some time before they found someone to unlock it. I began to chant as the potion

276

seeped into Anson's skin and more blood dripped profusely from my hands onto him.

"*Vita est vita tua,*" I called out.

The windows in the room blew open, and a violent breeze filled the room, whipping my hair around my face and tossing items from shelves. A chair screeched across the floor. The doorknob jiggled again.

"*Vita est vita tua!*" I chanted once more and clenched my fists.

I could see it working. My own life force sunk into Anson's skin and began filling the blackened veins with life. Pumping him full of my blood.

His body convulsed on the bed, as if struck with a defibrillator. The door suddenly flew open, and I struggled to turn my head amidst the chaos that filled the room.

Mr. Blackwood stood there and quickly assessed what I was doing. He slammed the door and locked it behind him.

"Lydia!" he yelled. "What on earth are you *doing?*"

"I have to save him!" I cried. My feet lifted from the floor, and my magic suspended me in the air. "*Vita est vita tua!*" I forced the words from my throat, and Anson's body jolted once again.

Mr. Blackwood fought through the mess of debris and wind as he made his way toward me. "You have to stop! You don't know what you're doing!"

"Yes, I do!" I screamed down at him. "I'm saving Anson! He can't die! I *need* him!"

The truth was, I couldn't stop even if I wanted to. My red magic had completely taken over, and I was nothing but a mere tool in its grip.

Out of the corner of my eye, I could see the dean reaching for me. I flicked my wrist and sent him flying into the wall.

The look of betrayal on his face pained me in ways I never knew I could hurt.

CANDACE OSMOND & REBECCA HAMILTON

"I'm sorry!" I yelled through streams of tears.

A massive force channeled through me, and my head fell backward as I felt the life drain from my own body and funnel into Anson.

The pain tore through me like thick claws. But I held on with everything I had left. A ruffling at my side caught my attention, and I struggled to turn my head and peer down, only to find Mr. Blackwood reaching for my athame.

Before I could muster a response, he swiftly brought the blade down on the urn and shattered it, immediately breaking the bond that the spell held over me and Anson.

The air loosened around me, and I fell to the floor where he caught me in his arms. His hands smoothed over my face, pushing the mess of hair away.

My head spun with the loss of blood, but I managed to shove at him.

"What did you do?" I cried and made a poor attempt to stand.

When my legs buckled, the dean was right there, holding me upright. I fussed over Anson's body and noted the way the black veins pulsed with life, the darkness draining and the brambles receding. His chest rose and fell with a healthy, steady flow of breath. But he remained in some strange state of sleep.

The cryo spell. He must have died before it took hold. But now I allowed it to take effect. By bringing him back to life, the Mors Velox potion worked its magic; Anson was alive but held in some sort of suspended animation. Not totally living, but not dead, either.

"I...I did it," I whispered and cupped my hands over my face, filling my bleeding palms with tears of relief. "I did it."

The dean's comforting embrace kept me on my feet. But then...a thought occurred to me.

I pried my hands from my face and looked at him in

disbelief before glancing down to see the broken urn and the athame he used to smash it.

He wielded my knife.

The one enchanted to only work for those who had the blood than ran in my veins.

"How…how did you use that?" I asked him.

He followed my gaze and saw the knife, *really* saw it now for what it was, and I could see the shock enter his expression.

"Only one other person could wield that knife," I said slowly.

"Lydia, listen," he begged. "I can explain——"

"You're…my *father*?" My eyebrows pinched together as I let his grasp fall, and I backed away, shaking my head. "How could you not tell me? How could my mother…"

His steely eyes stared at me, almost willing me to understand. He gently reached for me and I jumped back.

"Please, Lydia," he said calmly. "I had my reasons, as did your mother. And I *will* share them with you." He glanced at the door. "But, right now, we have bigger problems to face."

"You both lied to me!" I said. "You said, in no uncertain terms, my father was dead! You let me think——"

I couldn't even finish the thought. Couldn't be thankful my father was actually alive after all. Not knowing even my own mother had lied to me about it when he'd been alive this whole time.

He held my shoulders and kept me in place as he looked me square in the face with a mix of concern and pride. "Lydia, you won the Courtship Program. But you've also broken a mighty law by using that magic in here today. They'll be coming for you."

"W-who?"

"Everyone," he replied. "We need to hide the evidence of what happened here."

"You mean…"

"Yes," he said curtly. "We need to dispose of the evidence.

I can do that for you. I can clean this up and spin the story that I put Mr. Abernathy in Mors Velox."

My lips trembled. "But won't you get in trouble?"

"For using Mors Velox without permission?" he chortled. "A mere slap on the wrist compared to the repercussions for Resurrection. But I'll take that. For you."

My mind threatened to check out. I couldn't form a single coherent thought or word.

"Lydia, please," the dean—my...*father*—said with urgency. "Let me help you protect everything you've just been given before it's taken away from you."

My breathing turned to hyperventilating as he held me. The burns on my arm pulsed with pain. Yet, I couldn't move. My life was a disaster. It was too much. I'd finally reached my breaking point.

But I had help now. The missing piece I'd felt this whole time, the reason why I couldn't bring myself to fully trust the dean. He wasn't hiding some horrible secret from me. He was hiding who he really was from me.

My dad.

"Lydia!" He gave me a gentle shake.

I blinked away the film that covered my eyes, and the room came into focus. I looked at him, this man, this person who shared my blood, and I saw it. The relation. I saw myself in him.

Suddenly, that initial sense of betrayal took its first step in fading, and my heart filled with a new sense of hope.

"Tell me what to do."

The End

~

Continue the Touch of Darkness Series with Book 3, Wicked Bones.

ABOUT THE AUTHORS

CANDACE OSMOND

Born in North York, Ontario, USA TODAY bestselling and AVN Award nominated author Candace Osmond now resides in a small town in Newfoundland with her husband and two kids. A full time writer, she enjoys writing all the novels, and a hoard of short stories, too. You can request a signed and personalized copy of any of Candace's books by contacting her through her website authorcandaceosmond.com

REBECCA HAMILTON

New York Times bestselling author Rebecca Hamilton writes urban fantasy and paranormal romance for Harlequin, Baste Lübbe, and Evershade. A book addict, registered bone marrow donor, and Indian food enthusiast, she often takes to fictional worlds to see what perilous situations her characters will find themselves in next. Get a FREE book when you subscribe to Rebecca's newsletter via rebeccahamilton.com

Made in the USA
Monee, IL
23 June 2022

98520874R10166